# The Secret
### in the
# Persimmon
# Wood Box

# The Secret
## in the
# Persimmon
# Wood Box

*A.B. Kreglow*

# DEDICATION

To Mary Murray Shelton for her love,
encouragement and feedback.
I could not have done it without her.

In Memoriam: Karlene Powell, a friend indeed

And to Karyl Huntley-Sadler for her constant
and unbounded generosity of spirit.

# ACKNOWLEDGMENTS

For friendship and feedback:
Amanda Cate, Spencer Gay, Linda Meyers Geyer,
Julie Haber, Kay Henderson, Tricia Johnson,
Lee Lewis, Victoria Light, Lida Matheson Stifel,
Jennifer Taylor, Vicky White

And to my editors:
P. Bryan Mauldin, Atlanta, Georgia
Melody Moore, El Dorado County, CA
Jennifer D. Munro, Writer, Editor, Seattle, WA
Waverly Fitzgerald, Writer, Teacher, Author, Seattle, WA
Lorraine McConaghy, Public Historian, Seattle, WA
Professor Emily West, Department of History,
University of Reading, Whiteknights, Reading, England

*My heart knows the way*
*Though I've never seen this path until today,*
*Still my heart insists that I go forward through this mist...*

# PROLOGUE

## 1868, *The Bradley Hotel,*
## *a high class brothel in Auburn, California*

A bigail Wilcox quickly gathered satchels and threw them into a pile on the floor. All morning she had sorted through her belongings to choose what to take and what to leave behind. Powder, lip rouge, and perfumes from her dresser she shoved into a sack, along with underthings and stockings. Shoes, she threw into another carryall.

Franklin Clayborn, her longtime lover, was due back in town in the late afternoon, and she had wanted to be gone before his arrival. Each time Franklin returned from selling his cattle, this time in Marysville, he came to see Abigail before going home to his ranch several miles northwest of town at Bear River. But when his telegram was delivered, she knew she'd stayed too long. Now she would have to find a way to make him leave before he went up to her rooms and found them emptied of her belongings. And because his temper at times was a lit firecracker, she feared once he found out, he might even try to kill her, something he had threatened many times in their long relationship.

Suddenly she thought she heard Franklin's horse with the familiar jingle of his spurs. She quickly pulled apart the lace curtains to look out at Main Street below, but it was only one of her girls, Susie Two Spirits, walking past the hotel.

Abigail stepped up her pace.

She pulled out a few of her favorite silk, organdy, and taffeta dresses and quickly folded each one before stuffing them into an oversized bag. Hatboxes were already piled against the wall next to the door. Tied together with twine were her charcoal drawings and art supplies. She took her journal pages and carefully placed them in the large persimmon wood box with an inscription burned into its lid, *Con Un Corazón Lleno*, with a full heart.

A knock on the door nearly sent her sprawling, but it was only Sam, who since the opening of the hotel almost twenty years ago had been the piano player and bouncer in her saloon.

"Shall I get the buggy?" he asked in a deep voice with a gentle accent, which was a mix of several languages common to Louisiana.

"No, not yet. Thank you, Sam. I'm almost ready though." She scooped up the gold jewelry–bracelets, necklaces, earrings and rings–left on her dressing table, put them into their case, and threw it into a bag.

Behind Sam stood Marguerite, the Canadian entertainer and saloon manager with her halo of untamable, flaming red hair. "You need help, Abby?" she asked in a French accent that had softened only slightly over the years since the hotel's opening.

Abigail answered without stopping, "The clothes I left in the wardrobe are for you and the ladies. Be sure to give some to Two Spirits. They'll be too small, but he–she can make them over to fit her."

She put the luggage by the door and quickly checked her two rooms once more. Then despite the sweltering midsummer temperature, she wrapped a lace shawl around her shoulders, pushed past Sam, Marguerite, and one of the girls with a customer, and rushed down the stairs to the parlor to await Franklin's arrival. She was terrified not only of Franklin but also at the prospect of stepping away from all she had known to go to God knows where. It left her feeling hollowed, but at the same time excited about making a new start.

The room was noisy with male customers of all ages and ladies-of-the-evening dressed in chemises, wearing too much makeup, hair a tangle, draping themselves alluringly on the arms of chairs and laps of the men. Conversation was spirited and the air thick with sexual tension.

Green velvet curtains hung heavily at the windows and soaked up the thick smell of cigar smoke, whiskey, old sweat, and cheap perfume. Lavender lamps hung on the walls and flickered black smoke onto the small mirrors behind them. The gilded couch, once her pride and joy, now sagged with constant use. As hard as she had tried to keep it clean, it was permanently soiled with the dust and grime from men who dug gold and silver in the mines or panned along the riverbeds. After nearly twenty years, the appearance of the parlor was that of a well-worn saddle.

Franklin was animated and happy having made plenty of money on his sale, but when Abigail saw him approach, her stomach tightened, her breath caught in her chest, and a stifling heat flashed through her body. In the past, she would have been pleased with his arrival, but instead she was like a horse ready to run out of the gate.

The summer temperature brought out stinging horseflies, which buzzed noisily around their heads.

"Dang pests!" He shooed them with his hat, his dark silhouette blocking the light as they stood outside the hotel's front door.

"I saw Doc Kinsey after you left," she said, changing his mood immediately. She fiddled with her diamond ring as she did when she was nervous or annoyed. He noticed and stiffly shifted his stance.

"Why'd you do that?"

Holding her temper, she said, "You know perfectly well why."

Franklin lit a cigar and blew the smoke. "What'd he say?"

"Nothing good." She stared at him.

"He don't know a fucking thing. Besides, you believe anything you hear." Even though the heat of the day baked the road, the plank-board walkway, and the horses tied at the saloon, she pulled her wrap more tightly around her shoulders, if only to keep her fear and anger in check. "Let's go upstairs, Abby, honey," Franklin said, squeezing her arm a little too hard. She pulled away.

"Not right now, darling. I have some things I want to do. Come back for supper. I'll have Cheng make us something good." But she knew he would be too tired after the long ride and more than likely would not return for a few days, which this time suited her just fine. His manly walk no longer mesmerized, nor did his ruggedly handsome face prove alluring to her. The attraction that had bound them together for all those years had finally released its hold. She was ready to be free of him forever.

Franklin looked intently into her striking blue eyes. "Abby, you're in one of your crap-assed moods! I'm going home. You'd better be more hospitable when I come back!" Once more her stomach knotted, and she felt she couldn't breathe. He grabbed her by the arm and gave her a rough kiss, then climbed back on his horse and rode off, the grit and dust flying back into her face.

She ran upstairs to change her clothes and look around her rooms for the last time. Sam brought the wagon around to the front and carried down her things.

She no longer owned the Bradley Hotel, an expensive and

classy brothel she had named after her husband, Bradley Wilcox. Twenty-one years ago, he was shot dead during a poker dispute in San Francisco. She had been eighteen years old. The two had talked of starting a business like the one her mother had owned, a cathouse in Marysville called The Quarter Moon Saloon. With Bradley's winnings and their shared savings, Abigail had been able to acquire the hotel at the beginning of what became The Gold Rush, the stampede of prospectors from all over North America, Europe, even as far away as China, that descended upon northern California to strike it rich. There were so many men and so few women that to own a brothel seemed a logical way for a lone woman, particularly a widow, to make a living. But now she had released that ownership, and Franklin didn't know it.

Though wealthy with gold, at this moment she felt she had no friends. Her whores, the staff of the hotel, and perhaps the bank manager, were, she told herself, merely acquaintances. Even so, she couldn't bring herself to say goodbye.

Her ladies watched in silence as she stepped out of the door of the Bradley Hotel for the last time. The cook, Cheng, with tears in his eyes, set a basket filled with bread, sausage, cheese, and a jar of water on the front seat of the buggy. Sam finished putting in her luggage, then remarked for anyone in earshot, "You have a safe trip. We'll see you in a few days." But she saw the sadness on his face and with it the realization they might never see each other again. The horse, restless at having to wait, danced as she stepped into the carriage. Marguerite clenched the curtains of the parlor window but turned away before she had to see the buggy disappear down the road.

The silver and gold hotel sign swayed in the slight breeze. Abigail looked up at it for the last time and snapped her whip. Only later would Franklin find that she was leaving him for good, and since she had not told anyone where she would go, and truly she didn't know herself, no one in town would be able to tell him where she was.

On the hill down Main Street was the usual hustle and bustle of the crowd. Horses clomped up and down the road, their tails swishing away flies. Children played games on the wooden sidewalks, and vendors sang about their wares— "New Castle mugs! Two penny a mug!" "Fresh fish! Caught today! Get your fre-sh fish," and, of course, the occasional blast of a gun from an overly excited miner. All this part of the lively music of Auburn, but for Abigail it soon jumbled together and faded into a background murmur. She snapped the reins and her horse trotted faster.

She rode north to make it look like she was headed to Nevada City and hopefully send Franklin in a wrong direction if he came looking for her, but then she circled around on back streets to the road leading southeast toward Placerville.

The horse began the pull up the long incline along the river gulch upstream. The heat and the arduous climb left him winded and snorting. Only a few valley oaks gave shade to livestock from the hot summer sun. Soon in the distance behind them, Auburn, surrounded by the round hills that resembled heaving breasts, looked like a cancer on the skin. Abigail glanced behind her relieved to see Franklin had not followed.

"Well, Bradley, where the hell am I going?" She spoke to her dead husband often since deciding to sell the hotel and found even after all these years she missed the sound of his voice terribly.

# The
# Bradley Hotel

# PART ONE

## 1849, Opening The Bradley Hotel

## ONE

A bigail wrote in her diary pages: *According to the bank president, Harold Brockweiller, this hotel has just come on the market. Lucky for me I was the first person to ask about it. It certainly does need a lot of work, but with Bradley's winnings and what we set aside for a family I should have enough for renovations.*

Throughout the hotel was pervasive smell of fresh paint from the walls, linseed oil and wax scrubbed onto the wood plank floors, and vinegar used to scrub the windows.

"Which room?" a man shouted to be heard over the sound of hammers pounding and wood being sawed as he carried a small table up the steps.

"Five," Abigail yelled. A drummer came in with his whiskey bill. She counted out the money, gave it to him, then added her expenses to date. Shocked at the total, she couldn't imagine that so much of Bradley's gambling money had already been spent though she still had no piano or dance hall girls for the saloon. "When the music plays, the men buy more drinks," her mother had said–she thought, *Christ, I need an entertainer.* With that the door opened and three women with faces leather tan, hair in knots, and clothing filthy and torn, walked into the newly furnished hotel parlor. Abigail had a hard time understanding them with their thick French Canadian accents. The leader was a tall, buxom, and attractive woman of imposing stature. Around her head was a crown of curly red hair, the color not her own, which she constantly rearranged with a comb. Nothing about Marguerite Atalier was small. With her satchel in hand and her two friends by her side, she studied the surroundings. Her torn and mended brown and black dress could not have been dirtier if she had dragged it through the street on a wet day.

"Hmph. This place could use a little life," Marguerite whispered in French to her friends. Then to Abigail, in broken English, "You have *chanteuse?*"

Abigail shook her head.

"I am *chanteuse,*" Marguerite said, then looked for the English words. "I am sing-ger et dahn-cer in Hotel Edward Deux in Quebec, nice enough place, but too small and customers, they did not tip well." While she spoke she inspected every inch of the parlor, then walked into the saloon. She pulled her hair up away from her face, and then inserted a comb in an attempt to hold one side of the red tangles in place.

"You've traveled a long way," Abigail responded.

"Hmm," Marguerite agreed, still examining the saloon. "California, *c'est magnifique,*" she said and searched for the word in English. "*Très jolie.* Hmm–beautiful." She pulled a crumpled postcard from her breast and shoved it at Abigail. On the back it promised, *Alta California: The weather is sunny and warm even in winter.* "Montreal *trop froid,*" she said mimicking the temperature. "*Aussi,* hot and wet. She threw her bag down on a table and tried to brush some of the dirt off her dress. "We come many miles with wagon train," she said. "I drive *le* wagon," she said mimicking snapping a whip.

"I see." Abigail wondered if Marguerite would be disappointed when winter came, and Auburn got snow.

"You hire us," Marguerite stated and nodded to the two bedraggled girls at her side. "My friends, Françoise Sault *et* Adrienne Villeneuve. They work upstairs. I entertain the bar." Her two girls nodded in agreement and looked hopefully at Abigail.

"How old are you?" Abigail asked.

"*Mon Dieu!* You ask a girl her age?" Marguerite laughed robustly and looked into the mirror behind the bar to see if her rouge was red enough, then pinched her cheeks. "*J'ai* eh, *vingt ans*, hmmm, twenty years, *et vous?*"

"The same," Abigail told her.

Marguerite rummaged through her bag, pulled out another comb, ran the prongs along the other side of her scalp, and proceeded to relate their adventures of the year before. She began dramatically, mostly in French. "Snow fell continuously, and the moist air was bitterly cold for a late March afternoon in Quebec. I decide then my friends and me will go to California." She hocked a ring of her grandmother's to buy tickets for a stagecoach from Montreal to Kingston, then finagled their way onto the steamship *Nodaway* to entertain while it sailed to "*Zan-Joseph-Misery.*" They froze in deep mountain snows, baked in heat that could cook food without a fire, and were nearly drowned crossing swollen rivers.

While Marguerite chronicled the story of her travels, all work stopped as the men and women gathered to listen. Abigail was reminded of how frightened she had been leaving Marysville at sixteen years of age. At eighteen, she'd become a widow living alone in San Francisco. To push those feelings away she set four glasses on the bar and poured cognac.

Marguerite's picture postcard, which she kept stuffed in her bodice along with the bag of her grandmother's jewelry, had been pulled out many times when she needed a reminder of why she had taken the trip. "Thank God we make it to California and are not sitting in those wagons anymore," she said as she finished her story with a dramatically feigned exhaustion pushing her empty glass toward the bottle of cognac.

Abigail poured the liquor, then shouted, "All right, gentlemen, back to work. Girls! Go on." Then she turned to Marguerite. "Why did you come to Auburn?"

"The men have gold! Why else?" She dug into her bag for a puff, patted her cheeks, powder flying everywhere, then threw it back into her satchel and dusted off the front of her dress.

"When you will open?" Adrienne inquired.

"Damn soon, I hope." Abigail thought again of how much money she'd spent.

Marguerite dug into her bag and pulled out some coins. "Françoise, go across," she said in French, "get me a sweet. *Merci.* Adrienne, you go, too." She turned to Abigail. "I run bar. I sing. I dance. You pay one price for all three. A bargain. The girls, they work upstairs." She flapped her hand in that general direction.

"I'll think about it," Abigail said, amused at her gumption but not wanting to be railroaded. "Have you taken men as clients?"

"*Non, non, non,*" Marguerite answered quickly. "I sing and dance for money."

"Are you married?"

"*Non.*" She looked at Abigail squarely, then turned and gazed out the window. "*Et vous?*"

"I was. I'm a widow." Abigail pretended to look over her accounts to give herself a chance to think through the offer.

"All right then, when can you begin?"

"And my friends?" Marguerite asked.

"Your friends, too."

Marguerite waited a beat, then added, "We need dresses. Flood washed all the clothes down river. Lucky to be alive."

"I'm to pay?"

"Unless you want me to entertain in this." The ragged appearance of her dress was emphasized by the amount of makeup she wore to cover the roughness of her skin from the harsh journey.

"Upstairs I have some extras. You and your girls try them on," Abigail said. "You can start tomorrow. Morton, our bartender, will work with you, and your girls can help me get set up. You can live here. Take the room at the end of the hall. It's large and has a nice view. The girls can take any other that is available, but not the suite, which is mine."

Marguerite looked around the saloon once again. "No piano," she said flatly. "I am to sing with no piano?"

"I have yet to find one," Abigail sighed, relieved to know the saloon would be covered at least and that she had two more girls for upstairs.

Later that afternoon, exhausted from the day, Abigail sat down in the parlor on the newly acquired gilded couch, and she saw a blond man ride by. "Anyone know who that is?"

Marguerite looked out the window and snuffed; three of the men stopped their work to look.

"*Si, Señora.* Franklin Clayborn," one said.

"Frank Clayborn," Abigail repeated.

"No miss," said another. "Won't answer if you call him Frank, only Franklin. He's a rattler, that one. If you want my opinion, *Señora*, keep away. You never know when that snake gonna bite."

Then the third piped in, "Ever since his papa die he been a wolf on the prowl for meat. Buying up properties, then makin' the tenant pay larger rent. And if you is late payin'? The son of a gun will dump your belongings out on the road. A hard man, that one."

The next day into the evening she instructed workers, unpacked items she had bought, and talked with merchants, who in the morning were to deliver serviceable dinnerware as well as food for the kitchen. In her suite, she had the men hang lace curtains at her windows and place a flowered carpet on the floor. For her living room they brought up a table, an overstuffed chair, and a couch covered in green velvet she had bought from a business that had gone under. Her bedroom had a bed and an armoire. She threw a shawl over the table in the living room, calling it done for the moment. Later she would add mirrors, lamps, more furniture and something for the walls.

From her desk by the saloon door, Abigail could see the whole parlor in the big mirror above the couch. In the evening, to keep out the cold, she closed the heavy green velvet curtains and lit the delicate lavender glass lamps placed throughout the parlor. "Now Bradley, look at that," she whispered. "The flames of the oil lamps," she pointed as if he was right by her side. "Hell on fire! They've already darkened my newly painted walls. Damn it! I'd better hang some mirrors behind them if I want to keep my walls clean. Besides, Bradley, it will brighten their glow, won't it?" All the while, she wondered if that wealthy Clayborn fella would come into her saloon to spend his money.

A few days later she hired Cheng Sung Lau, a small, square, stocky man, who had cooked in one of the many tent saloons in Auburn. There weren't many buildings constructed in town as yet, so he was overjoyed to have a fully stocked, indoor kitchen with a hard roof over his head. "Make good food," he told Abigail and waved his cleaver with enthusiasm. "Big pot mutton stew, chicken stew, beef. Taste good!" He landed the cleaver right through a large piece of meat, then diced it into bite-size bits. He threw the meat into the pot of sautéing onions, added water, seasonings, chopped vegetables, and a bit of flour. "Eat, missy. You like," he laughed, his eyes crinkling to slits as he continued to wave the cleaver while he spoke. "We sell lots! You see."

A few weeks later, above the bar, the workmen hung a large painting of Marguerite rendered as a mermaid by a local artist. How do you like that, Bradley? Abigail laughed to herself. The artist had perfectly captured the devilish twinkle in Marguerite's eyes, her curly brilliant red hair, and the bright green dress, which revealed a seductively naked shoulder.

"What happen when I not look so youthful *et merveilleuse?*" Marguerite sighed.

"Then we'll tell them it's your sister." They both laughed.

A month later the renovations were complete. To celebrate, Abigail invited everyone to drink beer, eat stew, and congratulate each other on a job well done. Cheng, Marguerite, Adrienne, Françoise, the three new girls (Ruby, Ruthie, and Elizabeth), plus all the workers raised a glass in honor of their success.

"Do you know a guy named Clayborn, Cheng?" Abigail asked.

"*Flanklin Claybon?* Gotta lotta money." He waited a beat then said, "No like him. Bad temper. Drink too much."

Everyone finished their meal and agreed, "Good stew, Cheng."

"It'll be perfect for the men. Thank you, Cheng. "Abigail headed for the stairs then turned back and said, "Goodnight, all." Because it made her feel less alone to think he watched over her, she said, "Bradley, I sure wish you were here. I want you to do the rest for me." She knew her husband would have kissed her, picked her up in his arms, and said, "Honey, take a load off your feet. Let me handle this." She sighed and continued up the steps to her rooms, pulled off her headscarf, unbuttoned the bodice of her dress, and let both slip to the floor, too tired to even think of putting them away. Her bed, unmade from the night before, was a tangle of sheets and blankets. She pulled them free enough to roll onto the mattress and fall asleep still in her bloomers.

The next day Abigail looked through the building for a final check. With a heavy heart she whispered aloud, "Honey, I hope you don't mind I named the business after you. It only seemed right since it had been your idea in the first place, and besides, it's your money that's paying for it. Wish me luck." Her footsteps reverberated against the walls in the empty parlor, and she quickly noticed the only sound of life came from the kitchen where Cheng and Marguerite were having a row. The cost of the chandeliers, rugs, paintings, and furniture was more than she had wanted to spend. The blood drained from her face and her throat tightened. *Customers. Where are the bloody customers? No one has even come to the door to ask if we're open.* "Everybody! Come here!" she yelled. Cheng came from the kitchen, followed by an annoyed Marguerite, and the girls came down from their rooms. "Cheng make a big pot of your stew. Girls put on your nicest chemise. Marguerite, sing. We'll celebrate tonight with the biggest dang party this town has ever seen!"

"With no accompaniment? I am to entertain without a piano!" Marguerite sighed to Adrienne.

Hung on either side of the front door, red lamps twinkled their invitation. The ladies, stuffed into the open doorway, shouted, "Free dinners! Have a drink! Come on in, handsome. You want a good time? I'll take you upstairs." They winked and lasciviously wagged their tongues. First one, then another, and eventually a constant stream of miners came into the saloon. The girls mingled, flirted, and invited them up to their rooms. Morton poured the drinks while Cheng served the dinners. Marguerite, who was bold, gregarious, and liked to have a good time, sang her spicy French songs, and danced on the bar, banging on a tambourine kicking up her heels to show her trim ankles. Though most customers, except for a few Canadians, couldn't understand a word of her saucy songs, Marguerite acted out the lyrics, winking at appropriate moments, and the men got the joke. Once the miners got some of the words, they even helped to sing the choruses. They hooted, whistled, and howled with laughter, but more importantly, they bought drinks. By the end of the evening, Marguerite was hoarse, the whiskey was gone, Cheng's stew was eaten, and the girls were exhausted from the number of men who came through. Now what Abigail counted on was that those men would come back often to her establishment to spend their hard-found gold.

Men who spent their days shaft mining in dark caves or panning in ice-cold streams came to town to get dry, buy supplies, and have a rest. For them the Bradley Hotel was a luxurious experience, a much-needed pleasure. Surrounded by velvet curtains, gilded furniture, beautiful rugs and sensuous paintings, the men felt wealthy and spent accordingly. The girls gave them the release they needed, and Marguerite made their time in the saloon fun. Word got around quickly, and the hotel was busy from the moment the doors opened.

When the last customer left, Abigail went up to her suite, sat on the edge of her bed and stared at the only image of Bradley she had, a quick sketch she had made one morning before he took the stagecoach to one of his poker games. For all she had to do to get the hotel ready, she had pushed down the unfathomable sadness of his death, but now she wept. Marguerite heard her and knocked.

"I'm all right," Abigail told her through the door. "It has just been a long day, and I'm tired."

"A successful party, no?" Marguerite hesitated, unsure whether to go in or return to her room.

"Yes. Yes, it was. The men liked your songs," she said wearily, then heard Marguerite walk away.

She sat on her bed hugging the persimmon wood box that had *With A Full Heart* burned into its lid in Spanish. Her father's ranch manager, Pedro Marsalis, had given it to her the day his family left Marysville. He had fashioned the finely made container, with its shiny brass lock and hinges, out of the variegated wood from the old persimmon tree that grew outside the ranch's kitchen door. Abigail had held the parting gift tightly to her chest when the cook Marisita, Pedro, and their three children climbed into their wagon and out of her life. She had been only sixteen when her parents died, and because her father had gambled away most of her mother's money, Abigail could no longer afford to pay the couple who had lived on the ranch since she was born. Once they were out of sight, she fell to pieces.

A breeze made the design of the lace curtains dance across the floor as the morning sun shone through her newly cleaned windows. Abigail looked at herself in the mirror and quickly dabbed her face with powder, particularly around the eyes, puffy from so many tears, then she went down to check with Morton the bartender about the drummer's liquor delivery and paying the bill.

Outside the front door was the cowboy who often peered in the windows. "You coming in, Mister?" Morton called. But when there was no response, he popped his head in the parlor door to tell Abigail the piano had arrived. It had come from San Francisco from a Sydney Town dance hall tent that thanks to a gang called the Sydney Ducks had gone up in smoke. The only thing standing after the fire was the piano.

Marguerite squealed with delight till she saw its condition.

"*Merde*. Does it play any good notes?" Amazingly, it still held reasonable tune except for the lowest keys where the fire had licked it.

*Piano player!* Abigail thought. *Oh, Christ! Where will I get a bloody piano player?* Marguerite and her friends put out the word.

A few days later, a tall man with dark curly hair whose persona seemed to fill a good portion of the room sauntered into the saloon. His leather shirt smelled as if he had not changed it since spring of last year, and its buttons barely stayed closed over the bulge of his muscular chest. But he didn't carry the dust of a miner. His hands were well oiled and his fingernails clean. Abigail reached for the pocket gun under the end of the bar.

"What can I do for you, mister trapper?" Abigail guessed.

"Joshua Samuel James, ma'am," he said with a slow southern drawl. "Most call me Sam. Yes, I was a trapper." He moved over to the piano and fingered the blackened edge and pushed down a couple of keys.

"Not trapping now?" She glanced at Morton, who moved closer to the rifle stashed under the till.

"In N'Orleans I heard stories 'bout money you could make fur trappin'. Sounded pretty exciting. Thought I'd give it a try, but I found the woods were trapped out and I was alone too much so came into town to find a regular job."

Morton relaxed, picked up the towel, and continued to dry glasses, and Abigail let go of the pistol.

"This piano, ma'am, you got somebody to play it? A fella at the livery says you're looking." She motioned for him to go to the piano to show her what he could do. As he sat, the chair creaked under his weight. He cracked his knuckles and proceeded to run his big fingers all over the keyboard like water over rocks. When Marguerite heard the music she came into the saloon immediately.

"This is Mr. James," Abigail told her. "See if he can follow one of your songs."

Marguerite began to sing and Sam, as easy as eating, accompanied her—and with feeling. Marguerite threw back her red curls and smiled.

"*Vous etes un*–big guy," Marguerite said, gesturing. "You handle ill-tempered miner?"

"I suppose I can, ma'am," he smiled.

"You're hired." Marguerite quickly glanced at Abigail, who agreed.

"Along with your weekly wage," Abigail said, "the contents of the money jar on the piano is yours, but if Marguerite sings you split the take with her." Marguerite turned sharply to see his reaction.

"Fine. But one thing before you take me on," he said with a slight challenge in his voice.

Abigail rested her hand on the Colt once more, and Morton stopped drying a glass. Sam told her he would not work from sundown on Friday till sundown on Saturday.

"Jewish," Marguerite snorted. "*Mon Dieu*. No piano player Friday nights. Friday is big money!" She turned away. Then he began to play again. "*Eh. Merde,*" Marguerite huffed. "All right."

But before they opened in the mornings, Sam was to teach Abigail to play.

Her decision to hire Sam turned out to be a good one. Tall and strong, he could handle a drunk easily. He played the piano well, but was also loyal and decisive, traits Abigail admired. When rowdies begin to nip at each other, he lifted them out of their chairs by the shirt collar, flung them out onto the street, and said politely, "Come back when you can calm yourself."

"*Mon Dieu,*" Marguerite told Abigail, "he run from piano mid-song, grab the fool, toss him out the door, and put hands back on the keys without missing a beat."

Because Sam was a gentle soul in a gigantic body, to the girls he became a big brother. Miners with too much liquor in their bellies could mean a bruised face or worse for her girls so Sam did his best to protect them.

In exchange for a mug of beer and some stew, the sheriff made it a point to come to the saloon on Friday nights when Abigail was at the piano or when Marguerite sang without Sam. The sheriff was a man heavily rooted in his boots, and with him standing at the bar the men were more likely to behave themselves.

To free her, Abigail needed someone to handle the men in the parlor. A tall, slim, and sultry woman named Hanna Brinson came in for the job. Hanna had worked in clubs in St. Louis. Practical, strong, and though she did not read easily, she was good with numbers and knew how to keep a financial ledger.

With the cornerstones of Sam, Marguerite, Hanna, and Cheng, Abigail felt the hotel would run smoothly.

# TWO

As the morning sun brightened, shining through her bedroom window, Abigail moaned, tossed, and turned, reliving through a dream a nightmare from her past:

Abigail left her Marysville home for San Francisco when she was sixteen. At the end of a long day, three brothers surrounded her wagon. Drunk, rough, and callous, they forced themselves on her, leaving her beaten on the ground next to her rig.

*In the dream she was fully grown, standing at the desk in the hotel parlor when the three brothers walked in. Two went into the bar, the third headed for the girls. When the man saw Abigail, a hint of recognition was quickly replaced by a moment of panic, but he pretended it was nothing and asked for a girl.*

*"Just a moment," Abigail said, and quietly whispered to Sam, "Get them out!" Sam grabbed the third brother and dragged him through the door to the street, and then with clenched fists punched the man in the stomach and kicked him over and over, the man groaning with each blow. When the brothers ran out of the saloon to help their kin, Sam seized them both and knocked their heads together, then picked up the three by their collars and hauled them away from the hotel.*

Abigail awoke with a sick feeling in her stomach. She had never told anyone about the incident, and till then, she had not been aware of feeling fragile or exposed. It had been a terrifying experience, one she thought she would never get over, but now with Sam in the building she felt safe and was relieved to know that nothing like that would ever happen to her again, or so she thought.

# THREE

About a week after the opening the tall, slim man with the bushy mustache and curly blond hair, the one who walked by so often that everyone at the Bradley knew the sound of his spurs jingling with his every step, finally came into the hotel. His shirt and boots were freshly cleaned and the saddlebag, slung over his shoulder, newly oiled. On anyone else his twenty-five years would look like a young man, but the heaviness in his soul made him look older. The low evening sun shining at his back sent his long shadow into the room.

"*Ce* cow-boy *est* Franklin Clayborn?" Adrienne asked.

"Looks like it," Abigail whispered.

Marguerite gave him the once over and snorted, "Hmph!"

Hanna said. "Nice clothes. Well, would be without the dust. Handsome in a rough sort of way. Needs a shave and a haircut, and you can have that mustache."

"*Mais très riche.*" Adrienne commented.

"Tell him to send in his rich friends then," Hanna quipped.

"Quiet now, girls. He'll hear you!" Abigail whispered.

By now Franklin not only owned many businesses in town, but he also bragged of having the largest herd in Grass Valley. Even before gold was dug, when the settlement was filled with trappers, he got wealthy by selling them supplies. And though Abigail owned her building outright, and so was safe from any takeover, one of his men had already come to find out if she wanted to sell. Marguerite told where to ask. But Abigail did not expect what happened next.

"Excuse me, ma'am," the man said and took off his hat, revealing a heavy tan across his cheeks and a white forehead. "My name is Franklin Clayborn. Welcome to Auburn, Miss...?" He replaced his hat, then extended his hand, giving her a smile that made her feel like she was swept into a stream. Her body warmed and she blushed, blind-struck with what she would later call a schoolgirl crush.

"Mrs.," she answered. "Mrs. Abigail Wilcox." When she took back her hand, her mind went blank.

Franklin found her perfume, with its hint of lavender, tantalizing, but it was the blue of her eyes that were so alive that made him wonder if they shone brightly in the night as well. "You are married then?" he asked, though he knew she wasn't.

"Wi–widowed."

"So sad for you," he said kindly. "May I buy you a drink?" Abigail felt as if her feet barely touched the ground.

"Oh boy," Hanna said as she and Marguerite watched Franklin usher Abigail into the bar.

"I do not like him. *Je ne sais pas pourquoi*," Marguerite scowled. "Something in his face. Too sure of himself, is he not?" she said a little too loudly.

Franklin asked for two glasses of whiskey. Morton poured one as instructed, then poured a glass for Abigail from a bottle of tea he kept for her under the bar.

"Where are you from, good looking?" Franklin, unable to keep his eyes off Abigail's blond curls and the mouth rouge that made her look prettier than a rose, felt a pull that was both intoxicating and frightening.

"Marysville, then San Francisco," she answered, flustered with no sense of what to say next.

"I've watched the men work on your hotel," Mr. Clayborn

went on. "The greasers have done a good job for you." He said, downing his drink and ordering another.

She started to chastise him for his derogatory comment about the Mexican workers who had labored hard and long to help her open the hotel, but she let it go. "I've seen you pass by, Mr. Clayborn."

"I was not aware," he smiled. "Forgive me then for not introducing myself sooner. With all the work, I didn't want to be in your way." Then he stared at her face. "Have we met?"

"I don't think so, though you do seem familiar, but I can't say where I might have seen you."

"San Francisco, you said. Perhaps there?"

Abigail and Franklin couldn't help it; as they talked the sound of his voice wove into her heart, and hers into his.

"You will have to excuse me, Mr. Clayborn," she said to break the spell. "I must attend to my duties. May I ask Hanna to select a girl for you?"

He looked into her eyes as if to say, *If that's the way you want to play this.* "Sure," he said, He paid the bar bill with a handsome tip for Morton and followed Abigail into the parlor.

"Adrienne, take Mr. Clayborn upstairs for some relaxation," Hanna called. Clayborn halted, but Adrienne took him firmly by the arm while they ascended the stairs. Each girl was assigned a room. Adrienne's was number three.

Abigail watched all evening to see when the door to number three opened. Several hours went by before Clayborn came down. He paid, touched the brim of his hat in Abigail's direction, and left the hotel with a smile on his face.

"Adrienne!" Abigail called up the steps, and to not appear interested asked, "Did he tip you well?"

"*Oui, Madame Wilcox! Un gentilhomme,*" Adrienne said with a slight swoon in her voice.

*Good heavens,* Abigail thought. *I'm jealous, and I barely know the man.*

It was another week before Franklin came back from a roundup. He offered Abigail a drink, which she accepted, this time taking a whiskey, but when she suggested he enjoy the company of one of her girls he told her it was not what he had in mind. He finished his drink then asked, "What time do you get off?"

"Usually around two, but I can be free by midnight," she said involuntarily.

"How about dinner?"

"Certainly," she said without hesitation. "Oh, but there's no place open for dinner after midnight," she added, disappointed.

"Don't concern yourself. I'll see to it." With a grand gesture he said, "I can move the world for you, Mrs. Wilcox."

Marguerite stared in disapproval as she handed Morton dishes to take into the kitchen. Hanna looked over at Marguerite and raised her eyebrows.

Franklin arranged for Cheng to make the meal, which he served in Abigail's suite. A pale sherry started the evening, then a pan-fried trout with lemon garlic butter and a baked squash glazed with honey. Franklin uncorked a bottle of Chilean wine from Valparaiso, which had been brought north on the *Ann McKim*, offloaded to another ship, then steamed upriver to Sacramento. They finished the dinner with a dessert of soft cheese and brandied peaches dusted with chocolate. After the dishes were removed, they sat on the couch and had a port.

"You are one fine looking woman, Mrs. Wilcox," Clayborn said, his eyes never leaving hers.

"Thank you, Mr. Clayborn," she smiled. "I admire your appearance as well." The truth was she could hardly breathe. She longed for the tenderness she'd experienced with

Bradley, but at the same time she became overwhelmed by the swirling rush in her body. Bradley, what should I do? she thought. Franklin took the glass from her hand and set it on the table, and suddenly she remembered where she had met him, at the mercantile the day she met Bradley.

*That man, I think the shopkeeper called him Franklin, offered me a sweet. He was attractive with his copious blond hair and mustache, but he was also crass with his intimate insinuations. I don't trust that sort of man.*

But at this moment she didn't remember how she had felt that day. "Do you mind if I kiss you, Mrs. Wilcox?" he said, taking her shoulders, bringing his face close to hers, and she responded, "I hoped you would, Mr. Clayborn." And they fell into each other's arms in a long luxurious embrace. Then she loosened his shirt and slipped it off his muscular shoulders. Franklin removed her shoes, undid the tie of her bodice, pulled off her skirts and stockings, and gently dove for her naked navel. He fondled every part of her body, stroked and kissed everything his lips could touch. The fire in Abigail rose faster than she had ever experienced, and she felt overwhelmed with carnal desire so intense that she thought she might perish from it. After her release, she undid his belt and helped him take off his boots and pants. Franklin rolled over onto her, entering her for the first of many times that night. By the time they fell asleep, it was almost sunrise.

The saloon was already abustle when Franklin and Abigail came down the steps at nearly noon. Franklin called to the prostitutes in the parlor, "Good morning, all, and how are you ladies today? It's a damn fine day, is it not?" He couldn't remember when he last felt this good, if ever. "Have you eaten, ladies? Where is that chink?" He looked toward the kitchen. "Cheng!" he called.

Cheng brought in coffee. *"Mista. Claybon, you want food?"*

"Good morning, Cheng. Wonderful dinner," he said. Then to the women who followed him into the saloon, "It's on me, girls. Eggs, grits, sausages, and coffee–all right with you, ladies?"

"Thank you, Mr. Clayborn," Ruby and Elizabeth said in chorus, and *"Merci, Monsieur Clayborn,"* said Adrienne and Françoise, who were just sitting at the table.

"Come here, beautiful," he said to Abigail. He moved his chair to the side and pulled one in for her. It was as if he enfolded the whole hotel in his arms the way he had done with Abigail the night before. "This is a day to celebrate! Morton, bring us your best champagne." The bartender brought the bottle to the table and glasses for all. "A toast to the Bradley Hotel and its new owner." He winked at Abigail, then downed his glass.

Marguerite continued to eye him suspiciously. She had dealt with men like him and knew that under all that celebratory glory was a darker side that would eventually reveal itself. Franklin paid the bill from a large fold of cash stashed in his saddlebag. "At least for now he is generous," she told Morton.

"You know, Franklin," Abigail whispered in his ear, "if you are going to be with me, you may not have the girls as well. I don't wish to compete with them. You understand."

His breath blew into her ear, "Abigail, no one can compete with you." She blushed uncontrollably, titillated from head to toe. And he felt the same.

From then on, Franklin Clayborn came in several times a week. Sometimes he spent the night, but mostly he stopped in on his way home to his ranch.

Abigail found him fun, charming, and having a playful sense of humor, all of which she enjoyed, and the lovemaking was passionate beyond anything she had experienced, even with Bradley.

Franklin was sitting in the saloon having a drink and playing cards with some of the regulars. "Hey, darlin'!" he called and opened his arms wide for Abigail. She sat on his lap, loving the embrace as he showed her his cards: a three of spades, a seven of clubs, two twos and a queen. *Two twos, not much to bet on,* she thought.

"Abby honey, shall I go with this one or fold?" He took a self-satisfied puff on his cigar and blew the smoke to the side. Abigail smiled to herself; because her father was a gambler, she knew more about poker than most dealers, but Franklin didn't know that. She pointed to one of the cards. "One," he said, and slapped down the rejected seven of clubs. "Show me the new one, Abby honey. Let me see what luck you have brought me." She lifted the corner. An ace. "Thank you, darling." He smiled and pushed all his money into the center of the table. Two of the gentlemen across from him threw down their cards immediately. The third wiped the sweat from his brow before he also dropped his. "You see, darlin', you're my lucky piece." Without showing his hand, he pulled in all the cash. "Here, darling," he said and gave her a handful. With his cigar clenched in his teeth, he slid back his chair. "Gentlemen, that is how the game is played, and now I bid you all good day." He took Abigail's arm and walked with her up to her suite. One of the men turned over Franklin's cards, swore, and banged the table with his fist.

Franklin and Abigail liked to drive into the hills for picnics, where they ate roasted meat, cheese, fruit, bread, drank wine and talked for hours. He asked about her upbringing, her parents, and life in Marysville. She told him of the cook and housekeeper, Marisita, who had helped to raise her, and having to sell the family ranch after the death of her mother from consumption and not long after her father from pneumonia when he fell asleep drunk in a cold night rain. They also discussed the news of the day and found that for the most part they agreed on who should run for mayor or whether city ordinances were fair. But when she tried to ask about his life, he avoided answering by asking her more questions. Afterward, in the open fields, they made passionate love.

"Here, Abby," he said one day and slipped onto her wrist a gold bangle set with three amethysts.

"Oh, honey. It is beautiful."

He kissed her hand.

"See what Franklin gave me?" she said when she returned to the hotel, lifting her arm to show off the latest bauble to the women in the parlor. "Damn! Is it not the most beautiful thing you have ever seen?"

Hanna and Marguerite looked at each other because as time went on, and as they expected, they could see the change in Franklin. If they were in conversation with Abigail, he found a way to interrupt it and take over, or he would ask her a question about something that was only between the two of them, causing the ladies to walk away. If Abigail had asked anyone in town, she would have known that Franklin drank too much, and that his good manners were lost with the excess of alcohol. He found whiskey was the only thing that kept the pain of his upbringing at bay, but it brought forth a bullish nature. He gave orders for everything he wanted, and harassed anyone he thought was in his way, and that included Abigail. Marguerite tried several times to tell her she didn't deserve to be treated this way, but Abigail thought it was jealousy speaking because she knew Marguerite was interested in her. Though Franklin continued to give Abigail expensive gifts, they began to feel like payment for services rendered. By then, though, they were a couple, and she had become used to how he was. "He's just in a fuckin' mood," was a phrase Marguerite and Hanna heard many times. But

Abigail did miss the funny, affectionate, and gregarious man who had come to the hotel when it first opened.

Abigail didn't have time to further her education, as she would have liked, with all that needed attention at the Bradley. But she did find reading gave her a way to escape the daily concerns and at times Franklin's moods. Novelettes sold at the mercantile, stories of hard drinking, hard-hitting mountain men fighting vicious Indians, were entertaining or perhaps just distracting, but it was books brought from the east, traded by miners for supplies, that brought her the most pleasure. She ate up romantic novels, particularly those of the Bronte sisters, but found stories by Edgar Allen Poe too dark and frightening.

Sam, as promised, taught her to play the piano, and after many lessons she was able to play a couple of songs. Her rendition of Stephen Foster's *Camptown Races* became quite good and soon became a saloon favorite, as did his *Oh, Susanna*.

Eventually she even learned a couple of Marguerite's songs so she could accompany her on Friday nights. But Abigail was not the performer that Sam and Marguerite were, and she knew her playing exhibited more enthusiasm than talent. There were not many complaints, except from Franklin. "Why do you waste your God damned time when you could hire someone who could play the whole week? Sam's a nice man and a good bouncer, but surely there's someone else available," he told her more than once.

Tired from playing all evening and hoping to avoid an argument, Abigail asked, "Shall I have Cheng send up some supper?"

"Not yet," he said and carried her up the stairs. His lovemaking was tender and gentle, and when it was over Abigail melted into his arms. "I couldn't think of anything but seeing you," he said and again kissed her tenderly. Swooning, she could barely remember what had happened since the last time she saw him.

# FOUR

## 1850

About a year later on a cold January morning, Abigail hung her head over the washbowl and released what was left in her stomach from the night before. This continued morning after morning.

Marguerite gave her a couple of tasteless crackers. "Eat first thing. *Grand-mère* always say they help with the morning nausea." She pointed to Abigail's stomach. "In case you not realize, you have Franklin's child." Abigail went outside for fresh air.

When she returned through the hotel's front door, Franklin shouted down to her from the top of the staircase, "Where've you been?"

"You know I was sick this morning, Franklin. The room was getting too close. For Christ's sake, I'm pregnant," she yelled up to him.

Franklin had let her know from the start he didn't want to have children. He was afraid he would turn out just like his difficult old man, and so he wanted none of it.

"Pregnant? Oh, horseshit! You're all balled up. You've just got the croup," he said as if this were the first time he had heard of this. "And if you are pregnant, which I don't believe, that child ain't mine. What louse made you pregnant?"

"Oh, God damn it, Franklin. Don't be ridiculous. You know as well as I do, it's yours." Weary of his ill temper, she ran up the stairs past him and into her suite, and he followed.

"You-you should think about what to do now," he stammered and fumed. "Certainly there is some potion, something you can take to get rid of that-that child," he yelled. "I told you I don't want children. For Christ's sake, think of me for a change."

"You bastard," she bit back. "I am not going to take anything, and mister, you'd better get used to that idea! Go home to your damn ranch and don't come back till you can be civil."

"For fuck's sake, what will you do with a-with a-baby? he barked, barely able to say the word. "You don't have time to take care of a child. Where will it sleep? Who will it play with when it gets older? You want it to live here at this-whorehouse? Remember what your life is like? You reside here, not in a home somewhere else. There's no Marisita to take care of it!"

These had been her concerns as well.

"You've been happy enough to come and go at your pleasure and stay here for free. A whorehouse! You don't like it? Go somewhere else! Besides, I could hire someone! Or maybe one of the girls-"

"Over my dead body," Franklin shouted. "You're not going to have those strumpets care for..." But he couldn't finish the sentence without admitting it was his child.

As time went on she became tired and hungry all the time, and she wanted less intimacy with Franklin. He made such a stink about it that Abigail became tense every time he came into the room. She was anything but happy about having this man's child. But even with Franklin's complaints, she was certain she wanted the baby.

Early in the pregnancy Abigail began to have abdominal

cramps and found blood spotting her sheets. The memory of the unbearable loss of her son reared its head. The labor had been intense and painful. Sweat and tears poured out as she pushed and screamed. "Bradley! You should be here!" she had thought. But when the baby was born, a bad silence had settled on the room.

"A boy," the doctor told her wearily. "I am sorry, Mrs. Wilcox. He was already gone. The cord wrapped around his little neck and strangled him."

First she lost Bradley and then her son.

When Abigail placed flowers on top of her baby's mound, a part of her heart closed from the intense despair. A tough exterior began to cover the wounded softness within.

"I don't want to impose on you anymore," she told the Ledlers, the owners of the establishment where she had been living and where Bradley had been killed. At their invitation, she had stayed until the baby was born, and then she returned to the boarding house in the center of the city where she had lived before she met Bradley. She was barely able to see out of her confusion, and felt like a drowning woman who thrashed about, unable to find something to keep her afloat. The Ledlers understood her distress and picked her up each Sunday to go on a ride into the countryside or for a meal at one of the many restaurants in town. Their outings had given her something to look forward to and helped her get through the long days and nights.

So frightened she would lose this baby as well, it was nearly impossible for her to settle down. Abigail began to feel as if the walls of her rooms were closing in on her. When Dr. Winslow told her not to worry, that she merely needed bed rest, she took a few days to be quiet. On the third day, Franklin went to the kitchen to get her something to drink to ease her discomfort and came back with tea.

He fluffed her pillow and then handed her the cup. "Abby,

honey, drink this. You'll feel better." He set a piece of corn bread on her bedside table. "Cheng thought it might settle your stomach." To be accommodating was not like Franklin, and his tidying the bedside table and folding the clothes that lay across the chair did not put her at ease either. He often complained there was too much clutter in her rooms, and when he felt ornery threatened to throw her belongings out of the window. "Drink your tea, Abby, honey," he repeated in an unctuous tone.

"Let me rest, Franklin. Doc said I just need sleep." She pulled the covers to her chin and closed her eyes.

"Come on now, darlin', drink. Have a bite of corn bread. It's warm. Made this morning."

"You eat it," she said with one eye open. "I feel nauseous."

He popped a bite into his mouth, then set the teacup in front of her.

"I don't want your tea," she said weary of his pushing. "Leave me alone. I'll be better in a couple of hours."

But he wouldn't let it go. He forced the cup into her hand. "Abby, honey, drink your tea."

"All right, then, just one sip." While she brought the liquid to her lips, she watched Franklin's face, for what she was not sure, but when she smelled the brew, she knew what it was, having made it for Elizabeth and then Ruby. "Pennyroyal!" She heaved the cup at him, he ducked, and it crashed against her vanity mirror, leaving a crack.

"Abigail, you don't want this God damn child," Franklin said. "Don't be so fucking bull-headed. Just drink the tea; it'll be over in no time."

"First of all, Frank, I do want this child, and second of all, it is too late to use pennyroyal. You son of a–Get out! Get out!" Because his father had called him Frank or Frankie just before lashing him with his belt, she knew calling him Frank instead of Franklin would piss him off, especially when he'd been drinking, Abigail picked up her hairbrush from the side table and heaved it at him, then searched for something else to chuck. When her hand mirror hit him in the shoulder, he escaped out the door.

But really, she didn't know what to think. How would she raise a child at the Bradley? Several of her girls had babies, and she saw how much work it was to care for them.

Later Franklin came back to apologize for his harsh words. "I'm so sorry, honey. I don't know what got into me." Abigail wanted to believe him, so she gave in to his pleading.

*More and more as the months went on, and to my surprise, I began to look forward to our baby's birth. Even after all the unforgivable things Franklin said and his attempt to abort my child, I thought once he saw the baby, and if I just loved him enough, he would become the doting father I knew Bradley would have been.*

# FIVE

O ut in the street, cheers rose, guns blasted into the air, and jubilant mayhem exploded all down Main Street. Men, women, and children hugged each other and rejoiced that California had just become the thirty-first state of the Union.

In the haberdashery, Abigail stood on the raised platform while the seamstress pinned the bodice on the dress she was having let out. Suddenly Abigail felt a pop and water trickling down her legs. "Oh dear," she said. "Damn it. Now I've ruined this lovely material."

With the help of the seamstress, a great deal of determination, and steadied breathing, she walked through the joyful crowd back to the hotel and up to her suite.

Marguerite went to the kitchen to get a pail of hot water and some clean cloths. Sam sent someone to fetch Doc Winslow, who came quickly, which was a good thing as the baby was in a hurry to come out.

"Mista Craybon," Cheng called, "you gonna be father." Franklin dropped his cards and bounded up the steps past the doctor.

"This your baby, Clayborn?" the doctor asked.

"So she says," Franklin sniped. He burst open the door to Abigail's apartment.

"Poor child," Winslow said under his breath and followed him in.

"Abby, honey, you hold Marguerite's hand while I speak

to one of my men. I'll be right back. I promise." Franklin returned almost immediately and took Abigail's hand back from Marguerite. "You can go now," he said to her.

"I would like her to stay," Winslow said, "as my nurse."

"Stay, please," Abigail said just as another contraction hit. Marguerite took hold of her hand tightly and Abigail breathed and pushed and breathed and pushed until finally she screamed at Franklin, "This is all your fault, you son of a bitch!" Then with a final push, the baby was born. It was a girl.

"Strong and healthy with a good set of lungs," Winslow laughed as the baby in his arms screamed its first cry. Like her parents, she had a head full of curly blond hair. The doctor cut the cord, wiped her tiny face, and wrapped her in a soft cloth. "She's beautiful." He carefully handed the mother the newborn. Soon Abigail drifted into sleep with her baby in her arms.

In the night the baby developed a cough. The next morning, the doctor came by to discover the child had gotten a temperature. To help her breathe, he swaddled her with peppermint oil rubbed onto her chest. But by noon the slight cough had become a hacking one, and her little ribcage heaved with the effort. Franklin came in and took the child out of the room to get a clean napkin from the laundry. Abigail, who had not slept during the night, finally fell asleep.

Three days later when Abigail awoke from a nap the baby she had carried for nine months, her baby girl, was gone. Franklin told her the little girl had died while Abigail slept. He told her he didn't want to upset her more by letting her see the child's dead body. Abigail didn't know how to continue to live. To lose another baby was too much for her to bear.

Marguerite stroked her head and pulled her in close. "If you want to talk, I am your friend. I can listen."

"Don't look at me like that. I'm the owner of this hotel, and you work for me," Abigail snarled and pushed her away. "I'm all right–besides, what the hell is to be done?" She shoved Marguerite aside and ran down the steps.

What Abigail couldn't say was that the loss brought with it an overwhelming, gut wrenching pain. Some days she had to drag herself out of a suffocating despair that was as deep and dark as a well. Abigail's savior came in the form of a hotel client, a doctor from Nevada City who gave her something to ease her distress.

"It's a good payment for my bill," he said. "You never know when somebody at the hotel might need it. Let me give you a taste, and then you'll know what you have."

He poured her a small amount of the clear substance and she drank it. In a few minutes the tension drained out of her body. Behind that warm, velvet, opioid curtain, she no longer cared about the sadness she felt from losing her daughter.

She knew Franklin would be furious if he found out, so she promised herself she would keep it just for others, but soon she began to crave the sensation of that release. The siren call of that peace-inducing substance became too strong to resist. Several times a day she went to her apartment and drank the morphine that brought with it a despair-free calm. For the next month, she walked around the hotel in a happy, if sleepy, temperate fog, barely able to notice she felt a little nauseous, that her bowels moved slowly, and she didn't want to eat.

A few weeks into her ecstasy, she descended the stairs. "Hello, ladies," she said and scratched her neck. In Abigail's ear, her voice sounded like it was someone else's, far off and blissful. Her ladies noted it with suspicion but said nothing, and the men wondered why she was so blandly congenial, not like herself at all.

Marguerite came into the parlor holding the drummer's whiskey bill. "Abby, what you want to do about this? Jacobs say you not pay him."

"He'll get his money," Abigail countered, not able to remember she owed him for last month.

"I pay from bar receipts," Marguerite said and followed her up the stairs.

"Don't get your dander up. I'm the bloody boss here, and I'll take care of it."

"The bar receipts will cover–"

"I'll take care of it, damn it. Go do your job."

Marguerite followed Abigail into her rooms. "What are you doing?"

"What do you mean?" Abigail pretended she didn't understand.

"*Merde! Merde! Merde!* You know what I say!" Marguerite took off her shoe and threw it against the wall. "You're on something. What is it?" She leaned in and smelled Abigail's breath.

"Leave me alone. I'm just in a good mood." But truly Abigail could not keep track of what she said or did.

"Good mood–Fuck, Imbecile!" Marguerite threw up her hands. "You give away the money!"

"I don't know what the hell you are talking about." Abigail turned to leave.

Marguerite marched around the room, hobbled by the one shoe. "You give the client more money in change than he give you for his time with Françoise. Now how you pay Françoise, heh? *Merde!*" And threw her other shoe which nearly went out the window.

"Leave me be, Frenchie." For Marguerite that was it. She grabbed her shoes and left the room.

When Franklin returned from his cattle drive, Marguerite and some of the girls took him aside to tell him what they suspected, and from then on he watched Abigail suspiciously.

"I was thinking it would be nice," Franklin began his test,

"if we got away for a couple of days." His eyes never left her face. "What do you think about going to Sacramento or even San Francisco?"

"Sure, honey, whatever you like," Abigail replied. "We could leave right now," she said in a rapturous haze.

"How about if we take the train to Los Angeles?"

"That would be exciting," she answered, her eyes only half open. "I've never been there."

Abigail never said yes to any of his suggestions easily, and because they had spoken of it only a few weeks ago, they both knew there was only talk of a train from Sacramento to Los Angeles. He watched her for a long time, then began to rummage through her nightstand.

"What's this?" he barked, pulling out a bottle of morphine. "You dang fool idiot! That stuff can kill you! You come with me." He took her by the wrist and dragged her off the bed and down the stairs.

"Franklin, stop. Franklin! You're hurting me, you bully!"

"Quit your whining." He shoved her out the front door.

"Outside? I'm not dressed, damn it. Where the fuck are you taking me?"

"Somewhere where you can't get any of that horseshit."

"How is my morphine any different from the booze you drown in? You're a mean, harsh son of a bitch. That's it. I am done with you."

"I should be the one done with you, then what would you do? Who would take care for you if I don't?" Franklin pulled her down the road to the jail. "Sheriff, this lady here needs to spend a few nights with you." He threw her into the cell, slammed the door shut, and bolted the lock. "Get Doc Winslow." He handed the sheriff a wad of cash. "And she's going to start puking, so you had better give that cussed fool a bucket."

"I'll kill you, you bastard," Abigail shrieked, both hands

gripping the cold bars of the cell.

Franklin returned to the hotel to find Marguerite. They both scoured Abigail's belongings until they found the rest of the vials hidden in the dresser, the armoire, and under her bed in the persimmon wood box.

"Jethro," Abigail wailed, "if you like my free beers, you'd better let me out of here. And I mean right now, you son of a bitch!"

"Abby," Jethro said. "You know I can't do that. Franklin would have my hide." He added with sympathy, "I'm afraid you'll just have to wait till it's all over." He gave her blankets and a wet cloth to clean her face. Later Marguerite brought clothes, then sat on the edge of the cot and gently wiped Abigail's forehead.

For almost a week, Abigail sweated, cried, screamed, regurgitated, and shivered with chills. Her head ached, her stomach cramped, and she slept very little. She became irritable, and at times was not able to understand where she was. She heard voices that chastised her for losing her children and she was sure she heard Bradley talking to the sheriff. As the week wore on, she became extremely depressed and lay on the bed in a fetal position, unable to move at all. When she woke she was anxious and fearful, but once her head cleared and her body was free of the drug, she slept better and began to have more of an appetite. It was a rough ride, but she made it through and was ready to return to the hotel.

When Franklin came to walk her home, she felt exposed and hid her face all the way up the stairs to her rooms. After she bathed and put on clean clothes, she sat alone, wondering how she was going to make it through the next day. Without morphine she was unable to contain her distress.

A crack of thunder and a jagged flash of lightning tore through the rain that fell heavily all day. Unable to settle her thoughts, she cried copious tears, neither the first nor the last she would shed for the loss of her children.

"Abigail, are you addled?" Franklin said. "The cough got so bad–there was nothing to be done. Doc tried his best. What the bloody hell am I supposed to do, produce her out of the air? She's dead and that is the end of it. Getting yourself all balled up is not going to bring her back. Really, Abby, it's insufferable. You are so bull-headed. Will you cry about that child every time I come to see you? I should just stay at my ranch till you get over this." Franklin turned his back and stared out at the storm. "It's for the best," he said quietly. He took another whiskey and fell sullenly onto the couch, then after a few more he blacked out and slept like a dead man.

But Abigail could not let it be. Distraught and angry, she paced the room like a caged cat. Finally, she ran out into the night rain, which poured so heavily she could barely see the path in front of her. She walked up one street and down another, then trudged for miles away from town. Finally, exhausted and in despair, she fell onto the road, but to where she did not know or care. In the dark, alone and soaked by the constant downpour, her arms wound tightly around her empty womb. She had neither the energy nor the will to live.

When Franklin awoke he was unaware Abigail had not returned. Marguerite banged on the door to ask where she'd gone, and even Sam came in unannounced to find out what had happened to her. Groggy from the night's drinking, Franklin couldn't fathom that no one knew where Abigail was. "What do you mean she's missing? She was here last night."

"Sober up, you damned fool," Marguerite chastised in French and gave him coffee.

But then he remembered their argument. "I'll find her," he said. The anguish of being without her was not something he wanted to entertain. He would find her and that was that but panic just under the surface reared its head before he could shove it away.

He rode down Main Street asking everyone he saw, but the storm had kept most at home, and those who had ventured out had not seen her. He went up and down the local neighborhood streets, then he went through farm roads and finally into the countryside.

When Abigail awoke, she was several miles from town, on the road to Nevada City. Stiff and cold, her chest felt tight and it was hard to get a breath. She pushed herself to sitting, but, too ill to move, she lay back down on the wet ground. "Lord, let me die here," she said aloud.

Then she heard a horse come up from behind. Franklin lifted her into his arms and took her home.

When they arrived, Sam felt her forehead and sent Adrienne for the doctor. Franklin carried her up to her suite, undressed her, and put her to bed. Doc Winslow examined her, then told Marguerite to bring in some camphor in hot water and put the bowl near Abigail's face.

A fever, a heavily congested chest, and a cough that racked her to her toes left her bedridden for many days. She slept like the dead, lost track of whether it was Monday or Friday, and couldn't remember what happened during the days she lay there.

When she finally opened her eyes, she saw Hanna close the door behind her, and heard her say to the girls who stood in the hallway, "I'll let you know when she wakes. Someone get Marguerite some clean clothes. The rest of you, back to work. I promise I'll let you know if anything changes. And for Christ's sake, your sniffling is not going to help. Go on now. Get busy. You know Abigail will have much to say if any of the men are wanting."

Marguerite, weary and disheveled, went with a heavy step to the window to pull the curtains closed on the sun that now streamed into the bedroom. She gathered the cups and plates stacked on the table and set them on the floor in the hall. When she bent down to pick up dropped clothing, she heard a moan. Even Abigail was surprised to discover the sound had come from her own throat. Marguerite took a cool wet cloth and laid it across Abigail's forehead. "You'll be just fine. You rest," she said, not sure that was the full truth.

Franklin opened the door. His face was drawn, he'd not slept, and his breath smelled of fresh whiskey. "Is she any better?" Marguerite shook her head. Franklin wiped his forehead with his kerchief, then took a cloth, dipped it into the bowl of cool water, and tenderly dabbed Abigail's face. "It was all my fault," he whispered to Marguerite. "We fought and she ran out into the storm. I was too damn drunk to go after her." He leaned into Abigail and said, "Honey, Abby, please forgive me."

She did feel like hell, but only pretended to be asleep for she was not ready to forgive him for the fight they'd had.

Franklin pulled Marguerite away from the bed. "I can't bear it," he whispered, his voice shaky. "She has had this fever too long. What if she dies? What would I do without her?" He waited a long moment and then admitted, "She always blames me. What can I do?"

"Better you step away from those thoughts. Abby's a strong woman. She needs time to accept the loss, heal her heart," Marguerite said, her own exhaustion limiting her patience. "Go on now. She needs rest."

Abigail turned over, which brought them to her side. "I'm not going anywhere, you lunkhead, now get the hell out of here and let me sleep. And Marguerite, who runs the hotel and the saloon while you stand over me?"

"Hanna and Sam."

"Be sure they do a damn good job," she snorted, as she turned away and pulled the sheet over her face.

As the day wore on and the sun turned the sky a bright orange, Marguerite sang quietly till the light was gone, but Abigail only heard a portion of one song as she fell asleep to the soothing sound.

Either Franklin or Marguerite was with her all the next day. Cheng brought them food, and each of the ladies came by when they were free. Abigail opened her eyes occasionally but didn't speak.

In a few more days she began to eat again, and by the next week, more often than not she felt like her old self-at least that is what she pretended. It was some time before she pushed through the sadness and went on with her life because always in the back of her mind was the loss of Bradley, her son, and now her daughter.

# SIX

## 1856

*The success of the Bradley was something I was proud of and could lean on when other parts of my life were rough or unsettling. But work has taken its toll on me and now I'm feeling worn, and as I look in my mirror, damn it, my broken mirror, it seems to have hardened my looks.*

On Abigail's twenty-seventh birthday, Franklin threw her a surprise party. Sam and the ladies hid behind the bar, and the whole saloon cheered when she walked in. Franklin served expensive champagne and cheeses, all shipped from France to New York, then around the treacherous Cape Horn to San Francisco, and finally offloaded onto a boat to Sacramento. Cheng baked her favorite vanilla honey cake with its distinctive aroma of fresh vanilla beans. All drank and ate and had a fine time singing the choruses to Marguerite's songs.

Abigail could see Franklin was happy with his surprise, and he knew she liked the attention. It was rare for him to regard her with love rather than lust, but this night he did, and she was touched.

"Happy Birthday, Abby," Franklin said as he clinked her glass. "This is for you." He presented her with a gilded box, which she eagerly opened. Inside was a delicate gold locket on a long gold chain. On one side was a picture of Franklin. "Do you like it?" he asked.

"Honey, it's lovely," she gushed and kissed him hard.

"You can put your picture on the other side, then when it's closed we will always be together," he chuckled. In those times, when she could see the best of Franklin, she loved him deeply.

After the party broke up and the saloon closed, Sam, Morton, and the girls left the bar, and Franklin went up to Abigail's room while Marguerite and Abigail stayed to have one more glass of champagne.

"*C'est très jolie*," Marguerite said, taking the locket in her hand. "Full of surprises, your Franklin. Though he should give you diamonds." She pointed to the ring Bradley had given her, which reignited in Abigail the ache for Bradley's tenderness.

Soon Marguerite stood to say goodnight, and she squeezed Abigail's shoulder, letting her hand linger.

"Good night," Abigail said and patted it in a friendly manner.

She took the glasses from the table and put them on the counter for Morton to wash in the morning; the dishes she left for the busboy. She climbed the stairs slowly; the steps seemed steeper than usual her legs heavy from too much champagne.

Franklin had fallen across the bed. He was drunk and feeling sentimental, his eyes half shut against the brightness of the lamp. "How long have we known each other, Abby?" He didn't wait for the answer and blurted, "What do you say we get married?"

"What?" Abigail said in disbelief. He was the only man she spent time with, and it had been that way since they had gotten together. Though she'd thought about marrying him over the years, now she couldn't say yes. It was enough for her that he slept at the hotel only a few days a week.

"Aw, come on, darlin'," he slurred. "You and me, we're good together. We can go right now to the Justice of the Peace and get hitched." When he started to pull on his pants, Abigail pushed him back onto the bed, and his head dropped heavily into the satin pillowcase.

"Honey, you crazy fool, it's past two in the morning. The Justice of the Peace has gone home for the day. And besides, Franklin, you're drunk. Ask me when you're sober."

She didn't think he was serious because she assumed Franklin liked his freedom. He could come and go from the Bradley with no one to tell him when to be home or complain when he was late. And because he was at his ranch or out on roundup for a good portion of the month, Abigail had breathing room. She knew that if they were married, she would not have time to recover from his outbursts. But when she removed his vest, she was surprised to find a little gilded box containing an engagement ring–gold with a large ruby in the center surrounded by diamonds and citrines. She put the box back in his pocket, covered him over with her soft satin quilt, and slid in for the night, hoping for a good night's sleep before the doctor came in the morning to check her girls.

But Franklin tossed and turned through most of the night, unable to sleep because of an idea that had been cranking through his restless mind. He could barely wait for Abigail to wake in the morning. When she finally opened her eyes he launched full steam into his scheme.

"You could take out a mortgage on the hotel," he said, "and use that money to buy another property. I know just the one. Needs renovating, but you could make a fine store out of it. It's not far from here, in Gold Hill. After that you could mortgage that place and buy another. See, Abby, honey? You'd make a fortune." Franklin knew Abigail had bought her hotel with cash and owned it outright, but he'd been trying to find a way to get his hands on it. Franklin knew if she mortgaged the hotel he could buy the loan, and then she would be paying him and be at his mercy.

"Sounds reasonable, honey, but I don't want to owe anyone."

"It's just good business, Abby."

"I'll think about it. Why don't you go get us some coffee?"

As he did every couple of weeks, the doctor came to check the girls for disease. It was the least Abigail could do to take care of her investment. Adrienne had been complaining, so she would be first.

Adrienne lay on her bed with her chemise held up over her breasts and her legs spread so the doctor could see her privates.

"Be sure to bathe, then put this salve on the area."

"Can she work?" Hanna asked.

"Better if not," Doc said, but he knew she would be back at it before his foot left the hotel door. Venereal disease was so common with whores and the men who frequented the bordellos that it was almost useless to give out instructions. And the doctor had seen many times that the men took it home to their wives

# SEVEN

A bigail sat at her desk, about to count out the cash receipts from the night before, thinking about how to get a replacement for Françoise now that she had married and moved to Sacramento. A girl walked in; her clothes and skin nearly the same color as her long, wispy blond hair. She seemed illuminated as if she had just stepped out of a dream.

"What can I do for you, miss?" Abigail asked.

"My name is Lily Sarrell. I understand from the men at the mines you are ready to hire another girl. I would like the job." The girl stood at the side of the desk, swayed slightly, and caught her balance by grabbing the bannister.

"Have you ever done this work before?"

"No, but I'm sure I can," Lily said and wobbled like a top winding down.

"Sit down, miss, before you fall."

Marguerite came in with the liquor bills from the drummers. "Hugo sold us five barrels of whiskey and fifteen of beer," she said, reviewing the receipts.

"This young woman is to take Françoise's place," Abigail told her.

A look of surprise filled Marguerite's face. It was clear to both that Lily was not a lady of the night and might not be able to handle the men's tempers.

Marguerite looked hard at Abigail, then asked Lily, "You married?"

"Widowed," Lily said. "My husband was killed at North

Fork Dry Diggings. When the men went to see why the dynamite didn't detonate, it blew up in their faces."

"I am sorry for your loss," Abigail said.

"Don't be. He was not-kind," Lily said.

"Do you have children?" Abigail asked.

Lily's eyes filled. "No, ma'am. Lost my boy last year." She took a breath, and added, "Ma'am, I really need this job. Please give me a chance. You'll not be disappointed."

"Mrs. Sarrell go tell Cheng in the kitchen to give you a bowl of his stew while I speak with Marguerite. When you have eaten, come back."

"Thank you, ma'am." Lily disappeared into the bar.

Abigail counted out the money to allow herself a chance to think. "She seems fragile," Abigail worried. "What about those thugs who come in with Franklin? Could she handle them?"

"She's hungry," Marguerite said flatly. "There are no jobs for someone like her. How will she care for herself? If you don't give her this work, she'll starve." Marguerite said out loud what Abigail had been thinking. Lily returned heartier for the meal.

"You will have room number five," Abigail said. "Lily Sarrell, this is Hanna Brinson. Hanna, take Lily to five and tell her what she needs to know. We'll get you started this evening."

Hanna peered at Abigail oddly as if to say, "This one?"

"Wait," Abigail said. "Lily, do you know how to dance?"

"Only a little," Lily answered.

"Think you could handle a couple of drunkards who want to lean on you while the music plays?"

"I could try."

"Marguerite, welcome another dance hall girl. Lily, that's a dollar a dance. You get half. Or would you prefer working the rooms upstairs?"

"I'll practice my dancing, ma'am," Lily smiled.

"Do you read and write or add up numbers?" Abigail asked.

"A little," Lily said. "Bible mostly."

"I teach some of the girls. Hanna is one of my best students." Hanna smiled, embarrassed.

"Thank you ma'am," Lily said. "You'll not regret this."

*Franklin always told me not to make friends with the girls I hire, so to keep the peace between us I haven't tried to get to know them until Lily Sarrell came in. Lily is different. I have to admit I am curious about who she is. She seems kind and generous if not naïve. Not much gumption perhaps. I did warn her that even those men can get rough. Lily, I fear you're too soft, too delicate, but we need a dance hall girl and I know you need the money. Lord, I hope I don't regret this.*

# EIGHT

"Listen, you doggery strumpet. How many times do I have to tell you, I don't want you to talk with those creeps?" Franklin glowered, and pulled back his fist, ready to strike Abigail. Instead he took his anger out on the washbowl. Ceramic chunks flew in every direction.

"Are you calling me a whore? I may own the business, but I don't *do* the business, bastard. Now, don't be a horse's ass, *Frank*," she countered and dabbed the blood from his knuckles. "Oh, Mother of God! How can I run this business if I don't speak to the clientele?"

"Do as I tell you and don't talk to them!" he commanded and pulled his hand away.

*Damn fool would tell me how to breathe if he could*, she thought, and picked up bits of the washbowl. "I loved this," she said as she put the pile on the tray with her breakfast dishes.

The men who now frequented the hotel were a different bunch from the ruffian trappers who inhabited the makeshift tent town in the years before gold was discovered. Many of the men were rambunctious, high-spirited, wanted extravagance in all things, and often paid for their fun with everything they had. Gold fever had brought men from all walks of life, all stratum of society-bankers, salesmen, farmers, and thieves. Abigail enjoyed them all. Many of her patrons were well educated, talkative, and fun, so she was not about to turn away from their conversation no matter what

Franklin said. Customers sometimes gave her expensive gifts in hopes of spending time with her. When she was annoyed with Franklin, she accepted their finery gracefully, which, of course, made him furious.

The one thing the men did have in common was loneliness. A desperate desire to find instant wealth made them leave behind all they held dear–parents, wives, children, homes, property, and jobs. They had spent a fortune and half a year to get to California, and the reality was that most could barely find enough gold or silver to pay for provisions let alone a roof over their heads. Many never had to take care of themselves without help from their spouses or servants, so living the miner's life was hard on them, but after they toiled in the mines or leaned over a creek for fourteen hours a day, the men became hardened.

Abigail found that, yes, the majority wanted intimacy with the girls, but not all. Those men wanted easy company with an unprejudiced ear, just someone to hold a hand. For some, merely to be seen with the ladies made them feel virile, and the more a man felt accepted and admired, the more he frequented the hotel, the better he treated his girl, and the more money she made. But it was a tightrope even in the best of times. The mine sites were rife with thievery and murder. Even the streets of Auburn could be unsafe with guns, knives, or a hangman's noose ready weapons to be used at the least provocation.

Eventually, when most of the gold had been panned out, the men became desperate to stay alive and would do anything to do so. But there were also the young innocents who ended up without funds or hope.

"The one sitting by the window," Sam indicated as Abigail followed him into the bar. "More a calf than a cow. Tall for his age. No bunko artist, but you can be sure there's not much jingling in those pockets. Been sitting there for the better part of an hour just staring out the window. What do you want me to do?"

The boy's clothes were several sizes larger than his slight frame should carry, his fingernails were broken and blackened from digging, his skin taut and dry, and his hair thickened by dust. Like so many who came into the saloon, he had the vacant stare of someone with nowhere to go. To Abigail, he looked to be twelve or thirteen, just a few years older than the age her son would have been if he had lived.

"How much is his bill?" she asked.

"Fourteen and a quarter."

"Damn! What did that cowchip eat?"

"A large plate of stew, buttered bread, a piece of pie and coffee and–a fresh pear."

"A pear! Jesus Christ." In her saloon, fresh pears went for ten dollars apiece.

When Morton leaned over the bar to tell the boy what he owed, he didn't move. But when he saw Abigail and Sam, he jumped up and ran for the door. Not fast enough, though, because Sam caught him by the collar.

"You planning on paying your bill, son?" Sam asked. The young man struggled, but Sam held him tight.

"I ain't got no money," he said through gritted teeth.

"You got a big appetite for somebody who ain't got no money," Sam said.

Abigail looked at him squarely. "You know, mister, there is one thing I cannot tolerate in my saloon, and that is someone who steals from me. You do recognize, young man, that's what you are doing? Do you not?"

"Now that you put it that way, ma'am, I..." He squirmed. "I guess I do." Sam let go of his grip and waited to see if the boy would try to run again.

"What the devil do you suppose I should do with you?" Abigail said.

"Ma'am, I reckon I don't know, but I hope you won't send me to jail."

"I should. After all, you did steal from me. Maybe a good whuppin' is what you need."

"Yes, ma'am." He stared at the floor.

"Look at me when I talk to you." To her, he didn't seem like a thief, but was someone who had not eaten much for a very long time. "All right, mister, you go into the kitchen and tell Mr. Cheng you are there to work. Whatever he tells you to do, you damn well do. You hear me?"

"Yes, ma'am," he said, his eyes once again glued to the floor.

"When you've worked off your bill we'll be square, but after that, I don't want to see your sorry ass in here again. You got that?"

"Yes, ma'am."

"How old are you, son?" Sam asked.

"Just shy of thirteen, sir. I'm big for my age."

Sam shook his head. "Boy, you be sure this is the last thing you steal unless you want to end up at the undertaker's. Someone else may shoot first and find out what kind of man you are after." Then Sam took the boy into the kitchen.

Every once in a while, a fellow came to the Bradley and attempted to pay with counterfeit money, fool's gold, or, as in this case, nothing at all. It was Sam's job to grab the hustler by the collar and take him over to the jail two doors down. Of course, Abigail would have a few choice words to say to him first. The next morning the sheriff would bring him back to work off the bill. Marguerite or Cheng made them wash dishes, carry in supplies, or mop the floor. But word got around fast they couldn't get anything for free more than once or they would be put in jail on a more permanent basis. As for the men who had given all they had in the mines and had come up short, as long as they asked for work, Abigail would find something for them to do to pay for their meal. When the mines ran dry, she had steady help.

But Franklin felt differently. "What does one broke idiot matter? You just threw your money into the fire." And he had no tolerance for the Washoe Indian families who came to the kitchen door asking for food. They were also starving, but for different reasons. With the influx of white settlers, game retreated up into the mountains, and the Indians, living on reservations below, had no animals to hunt. Nor could they forage for nuts or berries, mainstays of their diet, without buckshot being sent their way from the gun of an irate landowner. The government supplies offered to the tribe were of poor quality, let alone enough to feed the starving families. So to any Indian who asked, Cheng gave them the remainder of the evening's stew.

On the other hand, nothing was more critical to Abigail than the money that came in. So she could keep track of how much was made, the cash went through her hands first. The men paid the house for every girl they wanted, and Abigail in turn paid the girls. If the men gave the girls a little extra, well, they could keep it.

*Being loyal by nature, my attentions are never given to anyone else, but Franklin refuses to believe it. And besides, no matter what I say, he's always right and I'm always wrong. It sure can be tiresome. And Franklin doesn't like it when I stand my ground so I must give him lots of praise and affection. Besides, if I love him enough I'm sure he'll relax, though I have yet to find what enough is.*

Over time she had learned how to handle her customers' jealousies, but Franklin's mistrust was impossible to manage. Like water tossed onto an oil fire, he could billow up steam and spit grease, so she knew better than to make a joke while he was in a mood. However this night she was tired and didn't have the patience for his outbursts. "Pull in your horns there, Frankie. You are not making any sense. For Christ's sake, calm down," she pleaded. "I just stepped out of the hotel to run an errand. You're going to wake all of Auburn and maybe a few folks in Sacramento with all your bellowing."

When Franklin didn't see Abigail right away, he felt like a child who was abandoned and alone. It frightened him, but he could never acknowledge that, so it came out as suspicion and then rage.

"That man's mind rouses to a fever pitch faster than a cornered bull," Marguerite told Abigail. "You never know which way he is going to take something. *Imbécile.*"

Abigail knew he did not tolerate any concerns about his past even if they were sympathetic. But one day he couldn't help himself and revealed the abuse he had suffered as a child. "When Pa arrived home stoked on liquor, he'd be looking to pound something, usually me or my younger brother Joe. It seemed like Ma was too busy raising my two sisters, working the ranch books, or fixing meals to notice where Pa let off steam. Most nights, he came for us with his belt already in his hand because, in his jackass mind, Joe and I were always up to no good." Franklin's chin jutted out like a prizefighter with fists raised. "A tough old bird, that son of a bitch. A real bastard!" Franklin poured himself another drink. "My sisters, they're much older than me so I didn't see them except at supper. Besides, Ma kept herself and them away from that fucker." Franklin looked out the window. "Best times were on the range when Joe, the men, and me herded cows. No one to bother or blame me for something I didn't do," he said and downed his glass.

"That's horrible," Abigail said.

"Just the way it was back then," he glowered.

"And where is your brother now?" she asked innocently.

"Dead," Franklin stated flatly. "Kicked in the chest by a calf." What he couldn't say was after they had been branding calves for a full day his brother was too tired to finish the remainder, but his father forced him to continue. Franklin blamed his father for the death of his brother.

"Your sisters?"

"Don't know. Don't care either."

Franklin did not want anyone to think him weak. In his mind, concern for him made him feel so. The man had few friends, except for his hardheaded crew who were always trouble when they came to the hotel.

"Those sons of bitches!" Abigail yelled at Franklin. "Yesterday Lilah's lip was bleeding, and she had a shiner that closed her eye. I don't care if they are your men, you bastard; they're not allowed to use my girls! They can eat and drink in the saloon, but that's it!"

Franklin grabbed Abigail's shoulder and shook her hard, then pushed her against the wall, his acrid breath biting at her nose. "My men have just as much right to use your 'ladies' as those idiotic miners who grace your door." His hand flew up so fast she didn't have time to brace herself for the sting. Her eye smarted, and she knew it would be black in no time.

"Get out of my room! Get out of my hotel!"

"Shut your big bazoo," he slurred and lunged at her.

"You drunken, bull-headed, asshole!" Frightened, she pushed him hard and he fell. She ran to the kitchen before he could get up. Cheng gave her a cool steak to help with the swelling, but the eye turned dark within the hour. "Damn fool idiot. I should kick his sorry ass out for good. Have Morton water his drinks from now on," she told Cheng.

"Can, but then Morton have black eye," Cheng said.

A heavy rain mixed with snow began in the middle of the night, making the road the next day thick with mud and slush. Abigail and Franklin ran back into the hotel from an apology lunch of oysters and clams at the Gold Stone Cafe. All through the meal Franklin had been attentive and affectionate, the way she remembered him from many years ago and the way he tended to be after an argument. She was giddy from his amorous affections.

Franklin used the boot scraper at the door and went on into the smoky saloon. Abigail stood in the entryway and shook off clumps of slushy mud from the hem of her dress.

"The men have only their fricking boots to clean," she huffed. "Elizabeth, get this crap up."

Abigail heard a deep hack come from within her parlor. Fast as lightning she turned to see who had made it. She knew the sound of that cough all too well because her mother had died from it. Consumption. Because it was contagious, she never let anyone who had it stay in the hotel.

"Sam!" she called into the saloon. "The older gentleman there in the parlor, the one with the dark bandana." The man hacked again. "Get that fucking fool out of here quick!"

Sam approached the customer and guided the man to the door, speaking softly, "When you feel better, mister, Mrs. Wilcox would like you to come back for some time with the ladies. She says she hopes you feel healthy real soon. And when you do return, it'll be on the house–long as you are hearty," he added.

"Lilah open the windows," Abigail barked, holding a kerchief over her mouth.

"But it's cold and the rain will come in," Lilah said, her brown skin shiny from the exertion with the fifth client of the day.

Abigail waved her hand in every direction. "Yes, yes. Trust me, you don't want what that idiot spewed into this room."

"He was older than the stones of St. Peter." Hanna joked.

Everyone in the parlor joined in the laughter.

"He may have had a few years on him, but it's that cough that will kill him, and believe me, no amount of gold is enough to take that on," Abigail said.

She went into the saloon to find Franklin at a poker game, which was in full swing. With only two players left in this hand, Franklin pushed in a large stack of chips.

"Call you," the cowboy said and took a satisfied puff on a foul smelling stogie, then pushed the rest of his chips into the center of the table. Franklin thought a minute and shoved in his. "Can you beat this one, Clayborn?" The man fanned out four aces. Franklin threw down his cards and threw back his drink. The man smiled, pulled in the large pile of chips, and began to sort them by denomination. Franklin pushed back his chair, knocking it over, and stormed up the steps. Abigail waited before she followed to give him time to defuse, but rather than calming down, Franklin's anger built and exploded when she came in.

"Why can't you keep your big bazoo shut?" he growled and slammed the door. "You and your incessant questions!"

"What? What questions?"

"You threw me off my game," Franklin yelled. "You damn piece of a cow chip. You know you did."

"How? What did I do? And don't call me a cow chip, you horse's ass."

"You couldn't keep your damn mouth shut." He glowered at her before pouring another whiskey from the decanter on the table.

"I didn't say a word."

"Keep your God damn fucking mouth shut when I play," he yelled.

"It's not my fault you lost, you dumb lunkhead!"

"It is your fault!"

To change the subject, she mentioned that she had seen

him speaking to a family in front of the dry goods.

"Oh, shut your trap." Franklin surveyed the room, then gathered Abigail's stockings and dainties from the floor, dresses from the couch, and several pairs of shoes left haphazardly in front of the armoire. "Do you ever put anything away? I should toss all of this crap out the window."

"Stop it, Franklin. Those are mine and this is my room. Why do you make everything such a big deal? I just wondered who the family was."

"Shut up!" The first crack of his fist sent her across the room. Blinded for a moment, she couldn't get her bearings. She crawled toward the door, but before she could get out Franklin grabbed her by the back of her dress and dove at her with all his fury, hitting her again and again.

"Stop it, Franklin, stop!" she cried, but his rage had no ears.

Marguerite heard the row and opened the door. "Enough, Clayborn!" She pulled Franklin away. He yanked his arm free and she stepped back, afraid he would hit her as well.

"Stay out of this, Frenchie."

Sam sent for Jethro, but by the time the sheriff arrived, Franklin's rage was spent. He sat on the couch and threw back another whiskey. Abigail lay on the floor in pain, her face bloodied.

"You'd better come with me, Clayborn," Jethro told him.

"What for?" he slurred.

"You need some air."

The sheriff lifted Franklin to his feet and ushered him down the steps. Even though it was battery, there was nothing he could do because Abigail would not bring charges.

Meanwhile Cheng ran up the steps two at a time, his meat cleaver held high above his head.

"He's gone, Cheng," Marguerite said flatly. "Put the knife down before you hurt somebody."

Cheng poured some water from the pitcher into a bowl as

Marguerite got a clean kerchief and gently cleansed the blood from Abigail's face.

"Missy," Cheng said, "Eye need Doc." Sam went to get him, and thankfully he came within minutes.

Her neck hurt and her eye was so swollen she couldn't see out of it. "Don't move till I have a chance to examine you, Abby," the doctor said and slowly turned her over. "All right, now, try to hold still. Marguerite, hold her head while I stitch this." The doctor put a chloroformed rag to Abigail's mouth. She inhaled and was out cold while he put in five stitches to mend the tear above her eye.

"What lit his tinder?" Marguerite asked her later.

"He said I distracted him with my questions. Blamed me for his loss at cards. What questions? I don't remember asking any. I don't even remember saying anything at all. Damn fucking fool. He's lost at cards before, but without this kind of tirade. It's as if a goddamned ghost crept up on him."

That afternoon, Franklin rode into the countryside to clear his head and come to terms with his outburst at Abigail. But the thunderous echoes from his past - his father's cruelty and his mother's indifference - shouted louder than any rational thought about the incident, so when he returned to his ranch at sunset, he still blamed Abigail for the unrest between them.

That evening Lily stopped by. She didn't say anything but put her arm around Abigail's shoulder and sat her down at her dressing table. The swelling had gone down some, but the eye was definitely black. Lily took a brush to Abigail's hair, then gently dabbed powder on the bruise to hide the color before she put a scarf over her forehead to cover the stiches.

As expected the next day when Franklin was sober, he looked at her eye and mumbled shamefaced, "I am so sorry, darling. I promise it will never happen again. I love you. Please, darling, forgive me. I don't know what got into me." He cajoled and pleaded for over an hour, and once again she chose to believe him.

Sam never said anything, but Abigail knew he didn't like Franklin and would have risked his life to take him on in her defense. "Let it go, Sam," she told him more than once. "The bastard is just in one of his fool-headed moods."

But Abigail went over and over the incident, trying to understand what could have caused the outburst. In her journal she wrote: *It must be something I did or said, but I don't know what. Marguerite told me it was not my fault, but–it must be or why would he erupt like that? Really, I have thought it through and can't find an answer. It leaves me depleted. Now it's all I can do to shake off the feeling of dread at seeing him again.*

*Sometimes when I'm with Franklin, and feel the tightness of his grip too closely, it feels like I've been bought and can't get away. But to get along, she pushed those feelings far, far down. Besides, we are so passionate in the night, surely Franklin can feel my love for him.*

# NINE

## 1857

Getting enough rest was difficult for Abigail. She went to sleep easily enough but woke with the least sound and found she stared for hours at the flicker from the starry sky she could see through her window. When she did fall asleep, she was often troubled by the same dream: *She was running over a hill and through a pasture calling out for her daughter. Men and women resembling Franklin, Marguerite, and the girls, hidden in the shadows of the trees, watched as she flailed this way and that.*

*Sitting at the base of a huge stand of oaks was a woman who held a baby wrapped in a shawl.* "My baby," *Abigail choked and ran toward the apparition.*

*The woman smiled and asked,* "Is this your girl?"

But this night, shouting in the street woke her. The orange glow that filled the night sky was beautiful, but anyone who saw it knew it could only mean loss, injury, sadness, and pain.

"Oh, Christ! Franklin!" Abigail called. He went to the window, pulled on his pants, then bolted down the stairs just as the bell clanged at the Auburn Volunteer Fire Department.

"Fire at the Marsh's!" Hanna yelled. "Fire! Fire at the Marsh's!"

The Marsh family's small farm had only a handful of dairy

cows just outside of town. They sold milk, buttermilk, and cheese, were decent people, and well liked in town. The youngest Marsh child had dropped her lantern as she went to the outhouse. Hay on the ground caught and spread to the barn faster than anyone could put out the flames.

Sam pulled out as many buckets as the hotel had and handed them off to each man as he ran through the door.

"Fill your water pitchers and take a mug with you," Hanna told the ladies before she and Abigail ran up the road.

"More buckets over here," the Fire Marshall shouted. Water splashed as each container was passed hand-to-hand in a snake of neighbors that formed from the pump to the barn. They labored to keep the fire away from the Marsh's house and also to keep it from spreading to the neighbors. It's surprising how fast a fire fueled by its own hot wind can travel across a dry field.

Bright red embers fell from the hot flames, and smoke filled the air. The fire had already consumed much of the barn and sadly some of the animals. More still locked in their stalls screamed in panic. Peter Marsh, his lanky frame silhouetted against the bright, hot glow, leapt again into the burning barn to free more animals. Franklin pulled on leather gloves, covered his face with a damp kerchief, and followed him into the blaze along with Peter Marsh's young neighbor, Jeff Landercum.

The men ran through the scorching heat, unlatched the gates, and slapped the animals on their rumps, shouting, "Geehaw! Geehaw!" Terrified horses and cows galloped past the crowd, toward the bank and down Pleasant Street to the river.

Just as the last horse ran free, part of the roof gave way. Peter ran out as timbers fell inward from the walls. Blazing planks crashed to the ground all around the men, some on Jeff. Franklin was knocked to his knees. He managed to throw the boards off with his arm, but more cascaded down in an avalanche of flames. He pulled those out of his path, but he was cut off from Jeff.

The line passed buckets as fast as they could, but the flames were so hot the liquid barely made steam. Franklin dug at the fallen timbers with a pitchfork and threw them off Jeff, but then burning hay bales from the loft above began to fall over the men. Franklin batted them away before they could land on Jeff, then dove for the man's leg, pulled him free, and hoisted him over his shoulder. More hay and boards fell from the hayloft. Franklin tripped on burning tack and fell to his knees, dropping Jeff. Stunned, he couldn't get his bearings. The smoke singed his lungs and his legs could barely move, but he knew he had to push through the pain or be consumed by the fire. With one final heave, he lifted Jeff and ran through the conflagration to safety.

"Over here, Doc," someone called as Franklin lowered Jeff to the ground.

"Get Caroline," said another.

Franklin ran to Abigail, sweat pouring from his whole body, his blue eyes showing brightly from within the black soot covering his face. He coughed hard to ease the pain in his lungs. She gave him a cup, and he took a swallow of water, pouring the rest over his head. He seemed not to notice that his wrist and arm were badly burned.

Abigail reached for his injured arm. "Not now," he said, breathing heavily. He took another gulp of water before he ran back to the barn to see what more he could do.

Caroline Marsh, a sturdy woman with thick arms and legs, had grown up on a cattle ranch. Her heavy work apron was covered with milk stains. She and her three little children huddled against a near tree. At this moment, with her eyes filled with fear, she seemed surprisingly delicate.

"I don't know what we will do if the house catches. All we

own is in there," she said as her mind rolled over her worries. "Got nothing in the bank to start over with."

"Lily," Abigail called, "escort Mrs. Marsh and the children to the hotel. Have Cheng give them food and then put them in my rooms." Lily held the hands of the two little children and walked them to the Bradley. Mrs. Marsh followed wearily carrying the baby, without judgment about the hotel or its owner.

It was a hard fight, and it was many hours before the men dragged themselves into the saloon, tired, hungry, and thirsty. Cheng's stew as well as beer was on the house to anyone who had helped with the fire.

"Anything left?" Morton asked.

"Just the barn is gone, thank the Lord," one man said.

Peter Marsh came into the saloon last. "I put all the cows I could find into the field behind the house. Two are still missing. If anyone finds them, please do the same." He sat heavily on a stool at the bar.

With the help of the dance hall girls, Doc tended to the men's wounds. Only when all who needed care had been helped did Franklin let Abigail bandage his injuries.

"That smarts." He clamped his teeth against the pain. "Couldn't feel it before," he said. Abigail wrapped his forearm and the back of his wrist. The burn was bad and would leave a scar, but he'd be able to use his hand. Some of the other men were not as lucky. Jeff Landercum was terribly burned. His wife was beside herself with worry. It would take many months for the singed skin on his cheek and back to heal.

Abigail went up to check on the Marshes. Caroline woke when she heard the door open. "Your home is safe, but the barn is gone," Abigail told her. "Some of the animals..." she started. Caroline wilted with that news. "Stay here tonight if you like," Abigail offered.

"Thank you, but I need to see for myself."

Caroline roused her children, lifting the baby into her arms. Lily pushed into the room past Abigail and picked up one of the sleepy boys. Peter met them on the landing and took the other, and they walked back to the house.

After the fire, even though his arm and hand were badly injured and painful, Franklin was particularly appreciative of Abigail and held her close with great tenderness. But the next morning he awoke from the recurring nightmare that had plagued him since he was a boy–the sight of his father's belt looming in front of his face. Covered with sweat, he lay in bed listening to his heart pound.

"What's the matter, honey? Your arm hurting you?" Abigail asked.

"Yeah." He turned his head away. "It smarts a bit, that's all. Nothing to worry about. Go on back to sleep." He continued to tremble with the memory.

In the coming weeks the townspeople gathered to help rebuild the barn. Peter was concerned about how they would be able to increase their herd again. He already had two bank loans, and they wouldn't give him another after the fire. A few days later Franklin rode to the Marsh's farm.

"I suppose you can find something to do with these," Franklin called out as he loosed seven milkers into the field. The next week he brought Peter one of his prize bulls. "You'll need to build your stock," he told him. "I'll come get him when he has had his way with your girls." Franklin rode off before Peter could thank him.

"Damn fortunate the whole town didn't go again," Franklin told Morton. Two years earlier the Bradley was almost lost in a fire that burnt nearly 300 wooden structures in town.

# TEN

For Abigail, the Bradley Hotel was merely a livelihood, a way to keep food on the table. That the men found the ladies alluring was all part of it, of course, but was of little interest to her. She had always thought that if she had enough money she would have chosen to live on a farm, raise chickens, and spend her days enjoying a garden and sewing clothes. The men at her mother's "House" had tried to lure her into the business, but her mother put a stop to that right away, sending her home to do homework or draw pictures, as she liked to do.

"Good evening, sir," Abigail said. "Come right this way. Which one of my good-looking girls makes a tickle in your pants tonight?" The man hesitated. "Perhaps you would like me to choose for you?"

"All right children, up we go," Elizabeth called from the kitchen where she and the young ones had eaten supper. The offspring of Gabriella and Lilah needed to be tended until their bedtime, which was in a few minutes. A girl and three boys, ages three to five, made their way to the room upstairs assigned to be the nursery.

"Jessica, let me hold your doll while we take the stairs." The little girl held tight to Elizabeth's hand. "Honey, keep your other hand on the spindles."

"Excuse me, miss," the gentleman whispered to Abigail. "I would like her."

"Which girl? Elizabeth?" Abigail asked, surprised because

Elizabeth was old enough now that the men no longer asked for her.

He whispered and pointed to the three-year-old who climbed the steps with difficulty.

"I see," Abigail said. "You want the little girl, the one on the steps? The three-year-old?"

All of a sudden to Abigail the room seemed huge: *"Papa, please don't," young Abigail pleaded.*

*"Don't tell your mama," he said as he pulled on his pants. "It is our little secret." She wondered what she had done to cause him to come to her bed. She felt so ashamed she didn't speak to anyone for some time.*

"Yes," the customer whispered. "That one." His excitement grew as he pointed to the child.

"Sam!" Abigail called. He popped his head into the doorway from the saloon. "This gentleman would like to hire little Jessica. Would you please take him where he needs to go?"

"You bet!" Sam grabbed the man by the collar and threw him out of the hotel.

Lily came in the front door just as Sam returned. When she saw Abigail's face, she gave her an understanding smile.

Abigail turned to the men in the parlor and yelled, "Any piece of horse shit that wants children will not be allowed in my establishment. Do you all hear me?"

Though this was not the first nor would it be the last time she would hear this request, whenever she did hear it she felt enraged. And Franklin was no help. He couldn't understand what she fussed about. "What do you expect? It's a fucking whorehouse," he said. "He's gonna pay you, isn't he?"

# ELEVEN

## 1862

F ranklin is a most delicious lover and companion when the door of love opens for him. My feelings for him then become profound and exhilarating. I begin to lean on him for comfort and fun, but unfortunately, the fucker turns it around and calls me needy and weak. That man is like a smoldering ember that bursts into flames without warning.

*As a boy he had to be strong to withstand his father's temper, so to him strength means distance. Marguerite thinks I should end it, but when I saw him ride into town this morning, once again my heart fluttered like a schoolgirl's. I raised my hand to wave, but he didn't see me. He and his men stopped in front of the hotel. They went on into the saloon while he ran across the street to speak to a family who were headed into the photographer's studio.*

Often over the years when she felt down or frustrated with Franklin, Abigail would muse on what life would have been like if she had lived with her husband in their home together. In the evenings the family would gather around supper, and later, once the children were put to bed, Bradley would embrace her tenderly. But Franklin hadn't wanted children, nor did she want him to live at the hotel.

Late in the afternoon when Abigail walked across the

street to buy some sweets at the mercantile she asked the owner about the couple and their child, but he didn't seem to know who they were. She didn't dare ask Franklin, because lately to ask him anything only inflamed his temper, and she didn't want another black eye, a broken rib, or worse.

The late July sun felt good on her shoulders as she walked to the bank to make the daily deposit. Though many of the mines had dried up, men still filled their rigs with ropes, hammers, and shovels, with staples of eggs, flour, beans, jerky, dried fish, and containers of honey, molasses, and coffee, all the supplies needed for hard work at the diggings. The sweaty scent of horses tied up and down the street filled the air. Tired from the trip to town, they whinnied, shook the flies from their manes, and munched on oats.

"Morning, Abigail," said a dapper man who stopped for a moment to tip his hat. "Mrs. Wilcox," called another.

"Good day to you, Eslyn," she called back. "Charlie, how's your family? Your mother feeling better?"

"Yes, just fine now. Thanks for asking."

"Will we see you boys in the saloon later?"

"You bet," they both smiled.

Lilah, a black woman, and Lily–or Chocolate 'n' Cream as the girls liked to call them–passed by with baskets of bread from the Star Bakery. Normally the dance hall girls didn't associate with soiled doves, but these two had become fast friends, and if Abigail was to admit it to herself, she was a bit jealous. She looked forward to those moments when Lily made a point of saying a word or shared a drink with her in her apartment.

Townswomen, in groups of three and four, walked along the boardwalk gossiping with each other before they entered the mercantile or the haberdashery, but when they saw Abigail, they turned their backs. Over time she had learned to ignore the razor wound of being ostracized.

Suddenly a familiar voice came from behind, its tone gritty and annoyed. "Abby, honey, where you going?" Franklin said.

Abigail turned slowly. "I have some errands to run."

"Do them later," he insisted and took her arm. His free hand flashed up and caught a fly midflight. He smiled and tipped his hat, "Ladies," then pulled Abigail back to the hotel. To avoid an argument, she didn't resist.

Luckily, he was in a hurry, so she didn't have to listen to his boasting or smell his strong hair tonic for too long. His mood was rough and belligerent, making her time with him uncomfortable. Though she did all she could to not inflame his temper, she couldn't always keep that fire out. His bullishness frightened her, and often she felt trapped in her own bed.

Marguerite and Abigail sat in Abigail's parlor at the end of the evening and shared a glass of champagne. The night had been busy, and both were tired from the work. As they relaxed, the alcohol untied the knots in Abigail's neck and loosened Marguerite's concerns. To Abigail, Marguerite was a comfort though she wouldn't admit it, and for Marguerite it was the same.

Marguerite poured each another glass. "One of my friends says she saw him in Sacramento with a woman on his arm. She says they looked very close. Abigail, that man is a brute and treats you badly. I know you don't want to hear this, but I say it for your own good. You deserve better." But Abigail couldn't hear what her friend was saying and dismissed the concern.

When Franklin returned to the hotel, he wanted to know every detail of what happened in his absence, and when she spoke of Marguerite with obvious affection, he did his best to negate those feelings and insert himself between them. But

Abigail had not forgotten what Marguerite had said.

"Now Abby, honey, really, it didn't mean a thing. You always want me to wait till I get back to you. But hell, I'm gone for weeks! What do you want from me anyway? A man has needs," he said, clenching his cigar between his teeth and rubbing his head where her shoe had landed. "Sacramento's far from here." Franklin jammed his smoke into the ashtray.

"You slithering varmint!" she said, ready to wring his neck. "People I know saw you with that harlot."

"What woman? I-I don't know what you are talking about," he tried to lie again, but she knew Franklin always stammered when he wasn't telling the truth.

"Roostered son of a bitch!"

"Honey, it-it didn't mean anything." He thought for a moment. "See! I don't even remember her name."

"Well, let me remind you. Florence," Abigail said through gritted teeth. "Florence Ritchfield."

"Abby, honey, please, settle down." He reached for her.

"Not going to happen, not today and I am not sure if it ever will again." And her other shoe hit him squarely in the head.

"Ow, honey! Jesus! That hurt!"

"Be glad it's not a hammer, you bastard!" she said.

With effort he softened his tone and kissed her neck. "Aw, Abby honey, you know I love only you."

"No!" she screamed at the top of her lungs and pulled away. He leaned in to kiss her again. "Didn't you hear me? God damn it, I said no!"

"Well, hang me from a tree! I have had it with your insinuations, you back end of a mule. You can go to hell! If I'm not here, who's going to want you? You're not young anymore, you know. You need me!"

"I'm not the only one whose hair is turning gray. I can take care of myself you ungrateful son of a...Get out. Get out!"

They had screamed at each other for nearly an hour. Finally he grabbed his hat and stormed out. When he slammed the door behind him, Abigail felt like she had been hit broadside by a wagon. Through the lace curtains of the bedroom window in the glare of the noonday sun, she watched him spur his horse to a gallop. *His complaints and criticism are endless. Mine, well, the same, I suppose,* she thought and turned back into the room. The quarreling had left her exhausted.

When Marguerite knocked on her door, Abigail couldn't hold back the tears any longer. Marguerite wrapped her arms around her slumped shoulders, whispered consoling words into her ear, and kissed her tear-stained cheek. With that came a heavy memory of Bradley's gentle embrace, and the touch of someone who truly loved her.

And for Franklin, dallying was not a welcomed two-sided affair. He was none too happy when he saw anyone's interest in Abigail. She was his, and he made sure everyone knew it, particularly Marguerite.

# TWELVE

A year after the Civil War started, a girl named Bertie Hetch began working at Sawyers's Haberdashery. Even as young as she was–seventeen-years-old–she was an expert seamstress and helped design and make many of Abigail's dresses. She was born in Pea Ridge, Arkansas, and though you would not say she was a pretty woman, she did have a stately bearing about her so you would notice her right away. Abigail could not know at the time, that she would later become a beloved part of her life.

*You might not be aware at first of the deformity in Bertie's face, a scar in her lip she's had since birth. Though not grave, hardly noticeable at all really, it does give her upper lip an off-centered fullness and her speech a slight nasal tone. She is a woman with an easy laugh and boundless, affectionate warmth, despite the teasing about her lip growing up and the horrid war atrocities she saw in Pea Ridge before she fled. I like her a great deal, but I certainly won't tell Franklin that.*

Tien Wah, the Bradley Hotel laundryman, handed Bertie a list of clothing items. Many of the men came in rags from all their hard work. If they wanted new clothes, Tien Wah bought hats, pants, shirts, long johns, socks, and boots in their size, all charged on the hotel account. The filthy clothes were tossed into the fire. If the men chose to spend the night, which cost much more than just an hour with the girls, they could have their clothes washed.

"Do you need more lavender soap?" Bertie asked, picking up the soap and putting it to her nose. He shook his head. She wrapped up the clothing and threw in a few pieces of mint candy they kept at the counter. "For you," she said, and handed him the package.

Later Tien Wah, his sleeves rolled up from doing laundry, came into the parlor looking worried. "Missy not know what do," he began but stopped when he saw the bruise on her face. "Missy, what happen to eye?" But when he noticed Franklin watching from the saloon door, he recoiled. "Um," he stammered, "Mr. Jackson take bath," he began hurriedly. "Thought man wanted new clothes so burnt old smelly! But no want new! Now he mad, like hornet. Please, missy-fix?" On cue from Abigail, the girls flirted with Jackson and then she sent him into the saloon for a free drink.

Abigail whispered in Tien Wah's ear, "Go to Sawyer's and ask Bertie for the name of the family Franklin talked with yesterday." He said he would, but he dared not ask for fear of Franklin's reprisal.

Franklin told her when she came upstairs, "I swear, Abby, you could sell a man a dead horse, and the fucking fool would be happy 'cause it had four new shoes on its lifeless hooves."

Like most miners, Jackson had come into the Bradley Hotel muddy, exhausted, and smelling from the long days of working and sleeping in his clothes. A hot bath served several purposes. The miners could be charged more for the service, and also checked for disease without their realizing it. Unfortunately, the baths did not always keep the girls healthy. It was a hazard of the trade, of course, but it did keep the doctor busy.

For some men, merely having a bath soothed their soul as much as having one of the girls, but most of the time a bath and a girl, with a glass of whisky and a bowl of Cheng's stew, lifted their spirits and made them feel new again.

Cigars clouded the saloon with a thick smoke, and laughter filled the air. Sam played lively tunes on the piano and Marguerite sang her ribald songs to the man paying the bill. The camaraderie was so infectious that some even became friends, but not near the diggings. They would shoot each other in a heartbeat if it guaranteed their stake was in the ground first.

But while the men partied, Abigail counted out their gold.

"What is that he/she Indian doing here?" The man looked at Susie Two Spirits with disdain. Two Spirits, embarrassed, turned away.

"No one's making you spend a minute with her. If she is not to your liking, choose someone else," Hanna said and turned to Abigail. "How can men be so damn ignorant?"

*That night Abigail tossed and turned in the throes of a nightmare. Her arm was in icy water up to her shoulder and she struggled to hold down a monster, afraid it would jump out and kill her. Terrified, she screamed for help, but there was no one to hear. Then she noticed the shriek was coming from beneath the churning water, the sound gurgling up through the darkness. Blond hair swirled wildly in the current of the struggle.*

"But I recognized the beast immediately," she told Franklin. "It was—me. It had my face. Isn't it odd, I held my own body under the water as if to drown myself? When I finally let go I felt a profound sense of relief."

"Hmmm," Franklin hummed and fell back into his own dream: *Ten-year-old Franklin was on his bed reading a book when he heard his inebriated father enter the home. His older sisters sat motionless staring at the fire while their mother knitted in silence, all fearing his inevitable rage would spew in their direction. Franklin had learned long ago not to run or he'd get a worse beating. He gritted his teeth and took the lashing without a sound, but his* younger brother, only eight, screamed at the top of his lungs with each strike. "You sissy boy," his father taunted. "Be a man. Joey, there are things that happen in this world you just got to accept, like it or not. Now quiet while I finish your whipping." But Joe screamed even louder.

# THIRTEEN

## 1865

At noon on April 15 Abigail had a bite to eat, then left the Bradley to find a large crowd gathered at the telegraph office. Only a few days before, the streets had been filled with revelers celebrating the end of the Civil War, but now the crowd had a heavy, somber tone. Across the wire had come news of how just the day before President Abraham Lincoln had been shot and killed while attending a play. When she heard, Abigail felt as if the floorboards on which she stood dropped away, and she couldn't keep her balance.

Instead of going to the haberdashery as she had planned, she rode her buggy into the countryside to clear her thoughts. Normally she had a sense of happy anticipation when the new green grass pushed its way through the prickly remains of last year's growth, but this news just matched the tone set by the argument she and Franklin had had the night before. The unrest and disappointment that colored her day had been mirrored in the somber faces at the telegraph station.

She shook her hair away from her face, stretched out under a favorite black oak, closed her eyes, and reached back for a soothing memory, the one with the waterfall on the land Bradley had promised to buy and build their home; they lay on the blanket under the tree with the view of cascading water and the pool below it; he played with her curls with gentle affection and they talked of starting a family. But soon the sound of heavy boots with spurs trudging up the hill broke her reverie.

"So this is where you come to get away," Franklin growled. He threw himself down onto the blanket and pressed his mouth to hers in a rough kiss as if nothing had happened the night before. "Big news in town," he said. "Lincoln assassinated. Some dang-fool actor shot him dead while he and his wife watched a play. Everyone has something to say about it."

"I heard," she said, annoyed.

"You know word of surrender hasn't gotten to all the generals so they're still fighting in some states. Fools. Men dying for no reason." Franklin lit a cigar.

"Careful with that," Abigail warned. "The grass is still very dry."

"Confederate warships in the Pacific are still fighting, too. It's been all over the papers," he said ignoring her warning.

"So I heard," she said flatly.

"Well, you are in a mood. What bit your butt this morning?" Franklin rolled onto his back with his arm behind his neck and began to boast about his business dealings.

"How did you know where to find me?" she said. He took her hand to stop her from fingering the diamond ring she always wore. She pulled her hand away.

"A songbird told me," he said mischievously. "You know I can always find you." He puffed his smoke. "The only way you'll ever get away from me is in a coffin," he laughed.

She was shocked at the implication and got up to leave. "Watch that cigar." She pulled the blanket from under Franklin, folded it, and got in her carriage.

Marguerite, whose arm was badly bruised, averted her eyes when Abigail asked her about it.

*Many times I have wondered if I should leave Franklin, or even how I could, pinned here in Auburn by the hotel. Marguerite encourages me, as she tends to do, saying the door could be locked to him if I wanted it to be so. I even packed a bag once, but lost courage.*

# FOURTEEN

It was a dark, cold, and wet night. By the time the young mulatto boy snuck in to sleep on the dry bales of cotton cloth in the storage area at the back of Sawyer's Haberdashery, everyone had gone home. Like a feral cat the boy bedded in alleyways, under rigs or, on a good night, in someone's barn. It was still raining the next morning when Sawyer discovered him.

"What do we have here?" He grabbed the boy by the ear and dragged him to the front of the store. The eight-year-old looked like a rabbit caught between two dogs. His crimped pale yellow hair and blue eyes, which sparkled brightly against his soft brown skin, made him stand out from other children, whether they were black or white.

"Mr. Sawyer," Bertie said. "We could use someone to sweep the shop. The boy could work for his supper." Bertie pushed until Sawyer agreed. The bell over the door rang when Abigail came in to pick up her finished cape. "Good morning Mrs. Wilcox," Bertie said and went to the back to retrieve the clothing.

Abigail told her she had seen the boy a number of times at the hotel doing chores for Marguerite. She had insisted the boy take a bath. Because his master's wife had liked to watch him bathe, he didn't like to take off his clothes in front of anyone. But Marguerite took him by the ear to the bathhouse and set him in the warm water, telling him, "Here's the soap. Scrub your body unless you want I should come in there and wash you myself." While he soaked, Marguerite went to the mercantile to pick out clothing that fit him. His old shirt and pants, worn about a year too long, smelled so much she tossed them into the fire. The boy swept the shop, loaded and unloaded rigs, and helped Bertie put away the merchandise. He was little but was a hard worker. From his accent they could tell he was from Texas, but he would never say where because he was afraid they would send him back to the plantation. Since he would not tell them his name either, they began to call him New Boy.

"I have a pallet you can sleep on," Bertie told New Boy. "The window will be open so you can climb in and leave when you want."

In the morning the bed was empty but slept in. Sawyer warned Bertie the boy might steal from her, but the only thing that was missing was the milk and bread or the occasional piece of pie or cookies she left out for his breakfast.

Bertie had a kind heart and New Boy knew it. Once he began to come in through the front door, he told her his name was Reginald, or Reggie, whichever she chose. Bertie in her fashion adopted the boy, and he appreciated having a warm, dry home.

# FIFTEEN

## 1868

S ome days the light shines brightly on the world, but sometimes darkness comes at daybreak. If I thought the killing of our President was upsetting, it was nothing like this.

Marguerite, now breathless, had searched the whole hotel. "Lily's missing," she said. "I saw her last night after the bar closed when she left to go home, but no one has seen her since."

The sheriff found Lily in the back alley-her clothes torn off, a belt wrapped tightly around her neck, her body bruised all over. Her skin, which had always been the color of porcelain, now was almost blue.

Sam grabbed hold of Lilah to keep her from seeing her friend's body. "Sorry, honey," he said, and she melted with tears.

Gripped with anger and blanketed with guilt, Abigail felt the murder was her fault. Sam, Hanna, and Marguerite all told her it wasn't, but for her those who worked at the Bradley, and particularly Lily, were the only kind of family she had, and now one of them had been raped and killed. She felt as responsible as the man who actually did it.

After Lily's murder, everyone at the Bradley was shaken

and there was a pall of sadness over the hotel. Lily had been at the Bradley for at least ten years and now with her gone, Abigail felt she had no one to turn to when things got rough. But then Hanna and Marguerite walked into her room.

Hanna poured three glasses of port and raised her glass, "To Lily. A friend to us all."

"A great loss for us, but particularly for you, Abby?" Marguerite said. "She was a friend. Yes?"

Abigail had not thought of it one way or another, but now she realized that, yes, Lily had been her friend, and she burst into tears. This realization changed something in Abigail, a small shift: but if you were on a ship it would mean the difference between landing on the coast of California or the coast of Mexico. So despite Franklin's constant objections and with effort on both sides, her friendship with Hanna and Marguerite grew, though it was more like a stunted plant than a hearty crop.

"Abby!" Franklin called out several times. "Come here, honey. I have something for you!" When he came into the Bradley bellowing for her she was not sure which Franklin she would be seeing, but this time he was in a good mood. The sale of his herd in Sacramento had gone well, and he had also made a good deal of money at the gambling tables. He bounded up the steps two at a time and took her hand affectionately.

"I brought you a birthday present. Guess what it is?" Franklin teased.

"Jewelry? A dress? Oh, the lamp in the window at the mercantile, the one with the rose-colored glass base?"

"No, no, no. You wanted that? Oh, you'll never guess," he said, slightly nettled. He led her to the street, where in front of the hotel was parked a shiny and new four-seated buggy. It was black with gold trim, a black bonnet, and gold fringe that danced as the horse pulled the cart. The seats were covered in soft black leather, and across the back of the front bench lay a raccoon throw. The buggy and spirited quarter horse, Franklin had brought from Sacramento. They were beautiful. She loved them and told him so.

"What do you want to do with your old one?" he asked. "Shall I sell it for you?"

"No. Marguerite needs one," she said. "Since hers broke down, she's always borrowing mine. I'll give it to her."

"Give it to her? You want to give that strumpet your buggy? You don't want me to sell it? If I park it outside the livery, bet I could get more than a good price for it."

"I am sure you could, honey, but I would like our entertainer and manager of the saloon to have it. You know she couldn't buy one this good." Abigail was annoyed at his insistence and that he called Marguerite a whore.

He stepped back, irritated. "If that's what you want, but I could get a damn good price for it." Then he changed his demeanor and boasted, "Will you not look fine in this? My girl rides in style," he said and puffed on a smoke.

Over time Franklin had convinced Abigail she could not live without him, and during their intimate times, which were hotly passionate, she felt fulfilled and loved. He pretended that she was not the strong businesswoman who owned a very popular and expensive brothel, just a woman who needed looking after, and she knew he would be less moody if she loved him enough.

But all this changed the next morning. The joy she had experienced the night before disappeared in an instant. It felt as if her insides dropped away. "Oh, my God! Franklin what have you done?"

"What?" he said as he picked up his long johns.

"What the Sam Hill is that?" She pointed to the welt on his privates. "Never mind, I know what it is, you son of a bitch! It's the pox. What have you done! What have you done!" She repeated it over and over till she nearly fainted. If she'd had a gun she would have shot him dead right then.

"Don't go losing your head. It's nothing." Franklin reached for her.

"Don't touch me, you bastard!"

He slammed the door when he left, and she was grateful he would be gone several weeks to gather a herd for market in San Francisco.

She knew all about this disease. Some of her ladies had gotten it, and she had let them go. Now she could barely hear what the doctor had to say, "fever and fatigue, joint pain–a systemic disease, affects all internal organs... No, no real cure."

She returned to the hotel and scrubbed every part of her body till her skin was raw. When she finished, as the doctor suggested, she filled a bucket with lye soap and scrubbed her rooms, top to bottom. The silk bedding as well as the clothes from her body she threw into the fire. In case she had missed something, she placed clean sheets over the furniture, which made her room resemble the mountains in snow. Then in a self-chosen exile, she would stay in her room until she knew if she was infected or found she was not.

The next morning there was a knock on her door.

"Go away," she yelled between tears.

"It's Sam, ma'am. I've come to empty your chamber pot and bring you a pitcher of water." Normally one of the girls or Tien Wah would have done the job, but Sam wanted to check on her and came every day. Though she opened the door, she hid behind it. "Is there anything I can do for you, Abby?"

"No," she whispered. Marguerite, Hanna, and Sam ran the business while she waited for a telltale sign of a rash or a sore.

*With so many hours spent alone I have had time to reflect on what has happened in my life, especially in my relationship with Franklin. I have come to realize that not only is he my lover, but that son of a bitch is also my keeper, and I feel trapped by his demanding affections. Any sense of lightness in the relationship has long been overshadowed by his requirements. And as hard as I've tried to keep things calm, his flashes of anger are impossible to avoid. More and more, no matter what I say or do, it always catches him sideways. In his mind, he is smarter and always right, or so he has told me so often I had begun to believe him. I realize now that only when he is away do I have time to get my bearings. I finally understand how unhappy and frightened I have been.*

Within a few weeks, the thing she feared the most was realized: a small red sore appeared on her labia. It had been an ongoing problem for the girls. They got the most hideous diseases from the men—gonorrhea, chlamydia, genital warts, and the like, but she never thought she would get it. And now she had to come to terms with the fact that she contracted syphilis and had put her ladies in this position every single day.

Generally, Abigail liked surprises, found them fun and exciting, but sadly not all surprises bring joy, and this one, to her mind, was nothing but a goddamn present from hell. She rode around town in a new rig from her generous lover, feeling as if the sun shone its light just for her, then he gives her another "gift," one not only unexpected, but grave. She could not return it or in fact be rid of it. It was a surprise she did not ever, ever want. She'd been faithful to Franklin for nearly two decades, but he'd not been with her, and that was the problem. Now she had syphilis, and there was no cure. Mercury treatments might cause insanity, and the illness would kill her anyway. If she didn't take them, as she chose, among the many nightmarish symptoms she could expect including sores, rashes, fevers, and cancroid ulcers–was that her heart would give out. The choices from any angle were not good, but what to do now?

She could hardly stay in her skin let alone look at herself in the mirror. Agitated and unable to be still, she was engulfed by an emotional, black whirlwind. She cried from the deepest part of her soul and felt a desperate desire to disappear, to not exist. Finally she ran out into the road to get away from the fury in her head. And even though she pulled her shawl across her face it didn't hide her from what she perceived as prying eyes. Everywhere she turned she felt people saw the disease–in her appearance, in her walk, in her very countenance. She ran from street to street to look for somewhere to hide. Finally, exhausted and unable to go further, she heard the choir rehearsing in the Baptist Church. The sublime harmonies of the Charles Westley hymn, *Millbrook*, pulled her in. In the back, in a shadowed corner, she stood and listened.

Sinners on ev'ry side, stepped in,
And washed away their pain and sin;
But I, a helpless sin sick soul,
Still lie expiring at the pool...

Thou seest me lying at the pool,
I would, thou know'st, I would be whole;
O let the troubled waters move,
And minister thy healing love.

The choirmaster sang *"love"* with them, then, closing his fist in the air, cut them off. "Hold that word as if it is a baby in your arms–tenderly. Again, the last line." The rehearsal ended and the choir members gathered their things and departed.

Abigail looked up at the arc of the ceiling, then down to the cross on the altar, but felt no God anywhere. *How could*

*He make such a hideous disease?* She sat for a long time in silence.

Soon the pastor came in to rearrange the altar. "May I help you?" he asked quietly.

Though she had often donated to the church for various charities, she didn't actually go to services or even know anyone who did, but when he asked, she could not stop herself. She told him all about the illness, Franklin, the Bradley Hotel, and the husband and two children she had lost. She worried he might chastise her, maybe she even wanted him to, but he never did. He simply listened. And when she was all talked out, she knew what she had to do.

The pastor took her hand as if he was going to say something, but then thought better of it. "Godspeed, Abigail."

Many times she had toyed with the idea of breaking it off with Franklin. Syphilis just forced her hand.

So she went to the bank and arranged to sell the hotel and leave Auburn. One thing she knew for sure, though, she would not pass this disease on to anyone else.

Marguerite was shaken by the news. "What will you do with the business?" she asked in private.

At that moment, all Abigail wanted to do was get in her buggy and ride away from it all, but she said, "I have asked the bank to put the hotel on the market. I want to leave before Franklin returns."

When the girls came into her suite, she told them the truth. Some understood without explanation, some burst into tears, but others were more than horrified. It was going to be rough on some of them to get along, especially the older women. In a brothel no matter how fancy it was, as youth fades so does your income, and though she had always found something for the older women to do to pay them a wage- clean the saloon, change bed linens, empty chamber pots, and the like–she could not know if the new owners would keep them on.

A few days later all the ladies plus Sam gathered in the parlor. Hanna asked Abigail to join them. She sat heavily at her desk.

"We are just waiting for Marguerite," Hanna said.

When a man opened the door and headed for his favorite girl. Hanna barked, "We're closed! Get out!" He retreated into the saloon.

Finally Marguerite came in holding some papers. "You know the hotel is worth much money. The girls, Sam and me, we pool our resources, and even with a loan from the bank, we know it's not what the business is worth, but we want you to take what we have, so we can buy it from you."

Marguerite handed her the piece of paper with the amount of their offer, and yes, it was far below what she thought she could get.

"Who will run the house?" Abigail asked wearily.

"Hanna, ma'am," Sam jumped in.

"And the saloon?"

"Sam and me," Marguerite answered.

"You will continue to dance and sing?"

"*Non,* too old now anyway," Marguerite admitted.

"We'll hire a young high-kicker to do it for us," Sam said. "One of the girls in town has been wanting to try."

So the girls and Sam bought the business. It had been a good exchange, nowhere near what she could have gotten, of course, but in Abigail's mind satisfactory. She had plenty of money anyway, and now they could keep their livelihood, and she could leave without worrying about their future.

Even though it felt to her that she was about to jump off a cliff with nothing under except a hard landing, it was done, and she had moved on.

# Hahl Ranch

# PART TWO

## SIXTEEN

The night air was brisk, and the horse's nostrils puffed out steam. Abigail, who hadn't eaten all day, finally noticed she was hungry, and took a bite of the bread and cheese Cheng had put in her basket.

She chose not to stay at an inn because she didn't want to leave an obvious trail for Franklin, but where to stop now that the sun had gone behind the trees? Under normal circumstances it was a long day's ride to Salmon Falls, where she had planned to rest, but she had left later than anticipated so she had only gotten as far as Coloma.

Asking for help from strangers had always unsettled her, and to approach anyone in this part of the county, she chanced rejection. Although the men would tip their hats, the women would turn away. It didn't matter how much money she had donated to local schools and churches she was not welcomed. It only softened the sting when she took their husbands' money to the bank.

When she saw a light in the window of a home on a cattle ranch, she decided to ask to stay in their barn. As she drove down the unmarked road to the entrance, which read Hahl Ranch, she said her kind of prayer, which went something like: "All right, God, I need a place to sleep!" She knocked on the door. A dog barked from within, and the door opened.

# SEVENTEEN

## *A cattle ranch in Coloma, El Dorado County near Placerville, twenty-seven miles southeast of Auburn*

A gentleman in his early sixties opened the door. He stood at eye level with Abigail, with brown eyes and dark hair grey at the temples. He wore a clean, tailored shirt under a vest that held a gold pocket watch. His wife, also finely dressed, sat by the fire in an intricately carved rocker. When they saw her at the door an alarmed expression came to both their faces. The black and brown dog barked again but wagged her tail.

Over the years, Abigail had spoken whatever came to her mind, including language peppered with obscenities, but these were genteel folk so she knew she would have to watch her tongue.

"Thank you, Nanny. Go lay down," the man said in a kindly manner.

The woman closed her book and nervously pulled back strands of her graying dark hair. "Come here, girl." The dog, her back-end hunched slightly, limped slowly over to her chair.

Abigail thought they must know her from town, the way

the couple looked at her, so she explained she had sold the Bradley Hotel and was not sure where she was heading exactly, except away from Auburn, and to please forgive the late hour, but could she sleep in their barn.

Abigail fussed with her gloves until the woman said, "Dear, get some blankets from the wardrobe."

The man spoke slowly, hesitantly, but with determination. "I am Preston Hahl and this is my wife, Helen. Let me fetch you a pillow from our daughter's room. I'll be just a moment." He returned with some bedding and a soft, fluffy pillow whose case was embroidered in pink with the initial "J". He took Abigail to the barn and hung his lantern from a nail on one of the posts. She set her satchel on the floor and looked around. Though her bed this night would be made of straw, she was grateful for it. Oddly, she became filled with a sense of lightness, as if she could float up to the ceiling, the way it feels when someone takes a heavy load out of your arms, one you have carried for too long.

"We would put you in the bunkhouse, but I'm afraid it's been overrun with mice. The privy's 'round back." Mr. Hahl hesitated, then said, "Is there anything else you need, Miss Wilcox?"

"Missus," she corrected him automatically and again scanned the barn. "No, this will be just fine. Thank you."

Mr. Hahl un-hitched her horse, cooled it down, put it in the stall and gave it oats and water. "Goodnight, then," he said. "Mrs. Wilcox," he started, "hmm, sleep well," then he pulled the barn door closed behind him.

Once she set her clothing, comb, and brush atop a hay bale for the next morning, she settled down for the night. Though the smell of the stable was strong, the air coming in was fresh and cool. Used to the constant noise from the hotel's bar as well as street traffic, she was amazed that the stillness seemed loud, and feared she might remain awake. And though concerns of Franklin did tumble through her mind like churning water of a swollen river, once she doused the lantern and pulled the soft green quilt to her chin, she fell right to sleep. The last thing she remembered was the sound of heavy droplets pounding on the roof from an unusual summer rain.

Generally a fitful sleeper and never an early riser, to her surprise she woke with the sun and found she had slept soundly. Except for a bit of stiffness in her back from sleeping on the barn floor, she not only felt energized but also had a profound sense of relief, an elation filled with joyful anticipation.

The sun streamed through the slats of the barn walls, and when her horse stomped his foot he kicked up dust, which sparkled like gold in the light. In the eaves, several birds chirped their morning song, and outside Helen Hahl sang to her chickens while she cast grain. "Come on, ba-bies. Here chick, chick, chickies. Henri-et-ta! There you are. Come on now. Get your breakfast. Have you girls left me some wonderful fresh eggs? Oh, hello, my handsome rooster. Good morning to you, sir. Here you go."

Mr. Hahl knocked on the barn door. "Mrs. Wilcox, will—will you join us for breakfast before you go?"

Unprepared for this generosity and used to every exchange with men having rough edges, she was taken aback. But this offer was as if a light shone through an open door to a grand ballroom, and she was being invited to walk in.

"Thank you. I'll be right along."

The Hahls' home was large, with many good-sized rooms: a drawing room, dining room, main bedroom, separate kitchen, an office for Mr. Hahl, a library where Mrs. Hahl planned classes as well as their daughter's old bedroom, which they kept for her when she visited with her husband and their two-year-old twins. Most of the furniture had belonged to Mrs. Hahl's parents, but some she had brought from San Francisco where she had gone to school. All of it was graceful and expertly made. The drawing room felt inviting with its rocker, sofa, and two comfortable chairs placed on oriental rugs at the large fireplace. Delicate lace curtains hung at all the windows. Paintings hung on every wall. Her favorite one was of a vase of yellow tulips in a shiny silver mug, within which you could see the reflection of the window. On the dining room table was a sparkling cut-glass vase holding fresh flowers. Mrs. Hahl's bone white china with blue edging and delicate glasses for wine and aperitifs were housed in a stately maple sideboard. It was a warm, comfortable, and cultured home, one with more subtle color than the Bradley Hotel, Abigail noted.

Mrs. Hahl had set the table for the three of them using English sterling silverware, the bone china, and exquisite glassware. She served a breakfast of shirred eggs, sausages, and biscuits with jam and coffee–much more than Abigail normally ate first thing, but this morning it all seemed perfect.

"Did you sleep well, Mrs. Wilcox?" Helen Hahl asked sweetly, a gentle kindness being a part of her nature.

"Yes, thank you." Under the table, the dog rubbing Abigail's legs lay down at her feet. "Good morning, Nanny," she said and patted her head.

"Help yourself, Mrs. Wilcox." Mrs. Hahl passed the plate of biscuits. "There are plenty, and the jam I made myself."

"Thank you." Abigail placed one on her plate. "I see you have many books, Mrs. Hahl. Do you have them sent?"

"Oh, yes. Through Mr. Maude at the mercantile. I also have a standing order with A. Roman & Company in San Francisco for the newest, most popular books. It's like a birthday gift when they arrive," Mrs. Hahl said cheerfully. "Do you like to read, Mrs. Wilcox?"

"I do. If there is writing on the page, I can't help myself."

"Reading is so important," Mrs. Hahl went on. "I have taught my students for many years at the Coloma School. The schoolhouse is on the road about a half a mile back. You may have noticed it when you came last night? I think education is so important. Don't you agree, Mrs. Wilcox? I just wish children could learn to read and write no matter what their color, if you don't mind my saying," she explained, practically without a breath.

"Yes, I agree." Abigail took the last bite of her biscuit with butter and jam dripping onto her fingers. "My, this biscuit is good, and your jam is delicious. Do you mind if I have another?" Mrs. Hahl passed the plate and lifted the napkin for her to take one.

Mr. Hahl took a sip of coffee and pulled open his copy of the *Sacramento Bee*. The headlines were about the Civil War that had raged in the southern states. It carried stories that made note of how many miners had gone back east to join the ranks of the Union army, while some slave-owners brought their slaves to do the hard work digging in the mines or panning the streams. But when the war started their slaves walked away to find work in towns throughout the state.

"It says peace has come in the east," Mr. Hahl said. "Well, this old paper was wrapped around some of Helen's books," he said, distracted. "I do realize the war has been over for several years."

"It could not have come too soon for my money," said Mrs. Hahl. "Slavery is no longer legal. What do you think, Mrs. Wilcox?"

"I have to admit, I didn't keep up with information on the war efforts, but I don't believe that one man should own another."

"You see, Preston," Mrs. Hahl clapped her hands together. "We all agree!"

"It says here ex-slaves have left the south to find homes in other parts of the country. Do you suppose any will come all this way, my dear?"

"Only the hardiest of souls would make such a long journey," Mrs. Hahl answered and finished her biscuit.

To make conversation, Abigail asked, "You have just the one child?"

"Just our Julia," Mrs. Hahl said carefully. "She and her husband, Bernard Brown, have two children, twin boys. They live south of Sacramento. Do you have any children, Mrs. Wilcox?" But she didn't wait for an answer and continued, "Where did you say you were headed-a long drive ahead for you today?"

"Jackson or Mokelumne Hill, but I'll probably stop in Placerville tonight." Abigail bit into her second biscuit and considered having a third.

"Jackson's far," Mrs. Hahl said. "What will you do there?"

"Since I've taught my ladies to read, write, and compute numbers, perhaps they will need a teacher, and no, I have no children." The walls of the house were filled with paintings of mountains and streams and still-life pictures of fruit and flowers in assorted glass vases and pitchers, giving the room a lively and exuberant sense of play. "Are you the artist who made these beautiful paintings?"

"No, no," Mrs. Hahl laughed. "That would be our daughter. She is the artist in the family. Neither Preston nor I have a lick of artistic talent."

"I like to draw a little, with charcoal." Abigail finished her coffee. "Not much good with color though." She wiped her mouth and put down her napkin, remembering to fold it rather than toss it onto the table as she usually did. "Thank you for this lovely meal. Now I'd best get my things together and get on the road if I'm to get to Placerville in good time." *And avoid that son of a bitch, Franklin*, she thought.

"Feels like it might be another scorcher. Air's warming up

fast," Mr. Hahl handed her Chen's basket, which his wife had filled with a small loaf of bread, chunks of pork, two pears, and a large jar of water.

"Thank you so very much," Abigail said. "Something to look forward to. You both have been very kind."

"There's a stream a few miles ahead, and also the South Fork beyond to let your horse drink," Mr. Hahl suggested.

Abigail, filled with joy from the unexpected kindness of the Hahls, and with an added sense of purpose, waved goodbye and headed on to see what, if anything, might keep her in Jackson, Mokelumne Hill, or somewhere in between.

She progressed at an easy pace. The clip-clop of the horse's hooves played like a lilting song. The sky was clear and a bright blue, and the rain overnight meant less dusty roads. Within the parched woodlands and grassy hills she saw black circles left from fires caused by neglect of a campfire or a smoke thrown from a rider. Because the heat from the flames makes its own wind along with the natural updraft in the canyons, fire can travel faster than a bullet. She kept an eye out, but more for signs of Franklin than for anything else.

On one side of the river, the boulder walls sloped upward, with the hills spreading out into the distance on the other. Cows hovered under scrub bushes while others stood in the cool mud and ate what was left of dried grass on the river's edge. Soon hot waves began to pulsate off the land. The heat became oppressive and baked her even through the canopy.

She tied off the buggy, gave the horse some oats, then washed her face in the refreshing river and watched as the powder and rouge she had put on in the morning floated down stream. As usual, she had dressed in a corset, but now she sweated beneath it, so she took it off and replaced her shirt. Unintentionally, she knocked the garment into the river, but rather than reach for it, she watched it bob downstream out of sight. Then in a capricious moment with no one near but her horse, the cows, and the turkey vultures circling high above on the currents of the wind, she threw off all her clothes and plunged into the river. She splashed and dove under the water and cleansed away the dust and grime with an ecstatic sense of freedom. She felt young again. It had been a long time since she had been this happy.

Dried off and dressed, she sat under the shade of a scrub oak and pulled out the lunch basket, while her horse took long sloppy draws of water. Before long, off in the distance, a dust cloud billowed from a horse and rider approaching at a fast gallop. Her stomach tightened and she was filled with a familiar sense of dread. She hid behind the trunk of the tree and watched as the man came closer, but it was not Franklin. It was Mr. Hahl. He waved his hat high above his head, not in a friendly greeting, but in a desperate, beseeching call.

Only minutes before while exercising a horse in the paddock, Mr. Hahl heard the thunderous crack of a tree limb falling. Mrs. Hahl, sitting on a blanket reading in front of the house, was hit by it squarely in the chest. By the time Mr. Hahl got to her, she lay motionless under its weight. He had tied a line to his horse and was able to drag the limb off her body but struggled to lift her into the house.

"Since there is no one else on the ranch, I came for you. I hope you don't mind. We must hurry," Mr. Hahl said without stopping, and they galloped back to his ranch. "We're here, darling," he said. "Mrs. Wilcox has come to help me."

But Helen Hahl was still, and Abigail could see there was no breath. The falling branch had cracked her skull and crushed her ribcage, deflating her lungs.

"Mr. Hahl," Abigail said. "I am afraid it is up to our Maker to take care of her now."

"No. It cannot be," he said definitively. "Helen, darling, look at me. Helen. Look at me!" He raised her head, but when she didn't respond, sorrow filled his face. "I guess she was already gone. I just didn't want to see it."

They carried her into the bedroom, then he dropped into his chair. Under the best of circumstances, a goodbye to a loved one is difficult, but the loss of his wife in this way had left Mr. Hahl inconsolable. He either stared into nothing or heaved with tears.

While Abigail brought in the dog, put away the chickens, and let the horses loose in the paddock, Mr. Hahl bathed his wife, brushed her hair, tied a ribbon around her neck, and wrapped her body in a sheet. Abigail noted that even in death her face held an intelligent, quiet strength. Though she had known her only a day, Mrs. Hahl had been so generous, that even to Abigail her passing seemed unusually sad.

"We only have an itinerant minister who won't be here again for another week. With the weather so warm, we'd best bury her right away. I'll get the shovel," he said.

With great difficulty, he dug a hole within the grove of madrones on the hill above the house where a white picket fence encircled a family gravesite.

Abigail took the family Bible and flipped through it till she found a passage she hoped would be comforting. *Don't let your hearts be troubled ... When everything is ready, I will come and get you, so that you will always be with me where I am...*

"Dear Heavenly Father, please take care of my Helen," was all Mr. Hahl could get out. After a long moment he shoveled the dirt into the hole, covered the grave with flowers from Helen's garden, and retreated into the house. Helen Hahl had only been fifty years old. Now she was buried alongside members of her family: her mother, father, and several young siblings who had passed before the age of ten.

As Abigail walked back to the barn, she considered what to do next. She wanted to go on her way, but to leave this man alone with this heavy sadness didn't seem right. So she put her things back into the barn for what she thought would be just one more night.

On the stove she found a fresh stew. "This smells wonderful," Abigail said with feigned lightness. "I'll fill a bowl for you, Mr. Hahl. Try to eat something. You'll feel better."

"Thank you," he said politely. She put it on the table, but he couldn't eat. After a few hours she tried again with bread and coffee, but he didn't stir from his chair then either.

The next morning she found him asleep by the cold fireplace. He had touched neither his supper nor the coffee and bread, and the blanket she had put over his lap had fallen into a pile on the rug. Nanny, on the floor next to him, whimpered to go out. Abigail found some meat scraps to put in her dish, lit the fire in the kitchen stove and in the fireplace in the drawing room where Mr. Hahl sat. He ate only a little of the eggs and bread she put in front of him, but he did drink most of the coffee.

She found some of Mrs. Hahl's jams in the pantry: cherry, apricot, and peach, even persimmon, made from the fruit from the trees outside the barn. Spreading some cherry preserves on the warm bread, she let herself have a small bite. "Mrs. Hahl made tasty jams," Abigail said in an effort to disperse the sadness that hung in the air as thick as tule fog. "Do you have family nearby?" she asked. "Is there someone I should notify?"

Mr. Hahl tried to smile. "Just our–Julia," he said thoughtfully. "I'll ride to town later and send her a telegram."

Abigail told him she planned to leave in the afternoon.

"But I can't see myself without help just yet. My wife was such a part of my life, I don't know how I'll get along without her." Then to Abigail's complete surprise he said, "Would you stay for a while?"

"Yes, of course," she answered too quickly, and then was

immediately concerned about being close enough to Auburn that Franklin might find her and blacken her eye.

"You must move your things into the house, Mrs. Wilcox," Mr. Hahl suggested. "It doesn't seem right for you to continue to sleep on the floor of the barn. Please, use our spare room."

The spare room was the library. It held a small bed, a writing table, a chair, and cases filled with a variety of books. Hung on the walls were several of the Hahl's daughter's paintings.

Helen Hahl's presence filled the house. With the books in the library, the furniture, and the general tone of the home, Abigail had a sense of the kind of woman Helen Hahl was- educated, refined, straightforward yet kind. She was everything Abigail had once hoped she would become.

*Perhaps I am more headstrong than straightforward,* she wrote that evening, *but refined? No, but I do appreciate refinement when I see it.* She slipped the pages into the persimmon wood box, shoved it under the bed and turned back the covers, and thought, "*I wonder how long he will expect me to stay.*"

# EIGHTEEN

*I have been here several weeks now and watched Mr. Hahl work through his grief. He seems to find comfort in everyday chores-feeding livestock, throwing grain to the chickens, affectionately petting Nanny. He seems to appreciate everything around him. The contrast between Mr. Hahl and Franklin is so stark I can't help but see it. Franklin wouldn't notice a chair even if he tripped over it, particularly when he is drinking.*

Abigail could not shake her confusion about whether to get farther away from Auburn or continue to stay and help Mr. Hahl, but then grunts coming from the drawing room interrupted her thoughts. Mr. Hahl was setting the fire and struggled under the weight of a large log.

"Mr. Hahl, Mr. Hahl!" she called. "Stop before you hurt yourself."

"I can do it," he said, breathing heavily, but he was clearly not able to lift it easily.

"I know you can, but since I'm here to help you, you might as well let me." She took one end and together they threw the big piece into the fireplace.

"Please, call me Preston," he said.

"Then you must call me Abigail or Abby if you like. Any word from your daughter?"

He had not heard from her directly, but from Maria, her hired woman. Julia and her children were in San Francisco to help care for one of her husband's oldest and dearest friends who was ailing. Maria didn't have an address but promised to let Julia know as soon as she could.

It was clear that Preston could use some help in running the ranch. The large property had only a few animals–some chickens, a couple of horses, and a herd of only about fifteen cattle. Although he had a bunkhouse, it was empty with no men working for him. The property was unkempt and needed repairs on the buildings and fences. Abigail noticed a sense of emptiness all over the ranch, and not just because of Mrs. Hahl's passing.

When she asked about the vacant bunkhouse he told her he had had a large herd–over four hundred head. A year ago he'd hired a man to take them to market. "He and his crew took them all right. Drove the herd to Sacramento and never came back. Took all my cattle and all my money." He stared out the window for a moment, then went out to feed the chickens.

Abigail had brought no clothes for this kind of work, but even so she cleaned the house, gathered eggs, and cleared out the mess in the chicken coop in her fine shoes and good day-dress, which now looked like Marguerite's after her long journey west. When she finished she went to find Preston, who mucked out the stalls in the barn. The pitchfork full of soiled straw was heavy and he labored to throw it into the wheelbarrow.

"Preston, you're going to wear yourself out," she admonished. "Here, stop, drink some water."

He took a long draw. "Just one more stall," he said.

Winded and fatigued, he finally stuck his pitchfork into a hay bale and rolled the wheelbarrow to the side of the barn. Abigail put the horses back into their stalls and they both walked to the house.

"Sit while I make us something to eat," she said.

Preston dropped into his chair at the fireplace and Abigail

dragged herself into the kitchen. She already wished she had watched Marisita or Cheng cook, because rice and beans, eggs, and toasted bread were about all she knew how to make. After the midday meal Abigail took a long walk on the property. She noticed Preston hadn't made the simplest of repairs on the ranch: fences needed mending, boards needed replacing at the front of the house and at the kitchen entrance as well; even the outhouse door swung open by just one hinge. He told her that though he often hired men to work on the ranch, most dreamt of instant wealth in the gold fields and didn't stick around. The ranch needed someone trustworthy who could do the handy work as well as oversee the care of the animals. *Now where in the bloody blazes is he going to find that angel?* she wondered. "Perhaps in Placerville there's someone to help you with the ranch," Abigail suggested. "I'll post it in the morning."

"Can't think about that now. You will stay a while longer, won't you?"

"I can't run a ranch, Preston. A hotel, yes, but a ranch?" She knew little about the care of animals, let alone having the stamina needed to do so, and she told him as much.

"You know Julia has wanted us to move in with them, but now with Helen buried here... Please stay till I can decide what I need to do," he sighed.

"Well, all right for a while. I'd better have more appropriate clothes though if I'm going to be of any help with farm work."

To his relief, the next day she went into the Placerville Dry Goods. She pulled out several skirts and blouses and went to the back of the store to try them on. The skirts were sturdy if not plain, by her standards, but she knew they would be what she needed. The blouses were the same, but she did find one or two in less severe colors than black, brown, or navy blue.

Just as she started for the divider curtain, she heard his voice. Franklin. His tone was annoyed, and he was slurring his words. All she could do now was pray she would not be found out. Luckily, the store clerk was in no mood to deal with a drunken man no matter what he asked for and asked him to return when he was sober. Franklin practically fell out of the door on his way to his horse–or was it to another saloon? Abigail, with heart pounding, waited to come out till he was far away from the store.

# NINETEEN

While Preston harnessed the horse to the buckboard, Abigail wound her hair up into a bun and grabbed one of Helen's straw hats with a large brim before climbing into the rig. They were heading to town for farm supplies. To her amusement she noticed how plain she looked in her drab gray dress and serviceable boots, her brightly colored organdy, silk, and taffeta dresses having been packed away in the barn.

Preston climbed aboard. While the horse clip-clopped along, he talked through where they would go in Placerville. This was the first time he had left the ranch since the death of his wife over a month ago. He felt unsure like a man who just awoke from a dream and was not quite sure where he was.

"I'll pay you back," he said, embarrassed he couldn't afford even some of the ranch's most basic needs.

"That's not necessary, Preston." She was only slightly aware of how awkward it was for him, because her concern was about running into Franklin again. Even Preston who had met Clayborn many years ago was certain they wouldn't see him.

"Shall we dine in town? There's a delightful café where Helen and I used to eat." But Abigail thought it was not a good idea. Franklin could still be close by. "Yes, I understand," he said disappointed.

It was not very long before they heard a rider coming up

behind them, the horse's hooves pounding heavily against the dusty roadbed. Abigail took a furtive glance, raising her head just enough to see, but not enough to show her whole face. But the rider passed them by without a hello or a good day.

About a half-mile up the road, they saw another man trot along. Abigail stared wondering if she should be concerned, but when he stopped to say hello, Preston introduced her to Grant Edgewood, the father of one of his wife's students.

"So sad about Helen, Preston. Marge and I hardly know what to say. I know she'll want to bring you some food. I'll tell her I saw you."

Abigail relaxed and began to chastise herself for thinking that every person on the road was Franklin.

As they traveled, they chatted about Preston's life with Helen and raising their daughter. "Helen went to school in San Francisco to learn to be a teacher. After we were married we grew to like living with her parents on their ranch, so she taught at the Coloma School. Our daughter went there as well. Julia's a darling girl who we–I adore." Then Preston sank into the darkness of his sadness and both were quiet.

As they got closer to Placerville there were many riders and wagons that passed by, but it was the sound of one particular horse that had for many years brought her either joy or terror, depending on how their relationship was going, that set her on edge. The sound of his spurs was so ingrained in her psyche, her body automatically responded–for a moment her breathing stopped, and her heart ceased to beat. She seemed to float above herself, looking down from above, wondering how her body could remain upright with her somewhere else.

Preston wanted to take his horse into a canter but was afraid it might look suspicious. "I'll handle this," he told her.

Franklin's horse whinnied as he slowed to a walk. "Hello, Mr. Hahl, Mrs. Hahl."

Keeping her head down, Abigail nodded. Preston reached over and took her hand to cover the diamond ring she always wore, the one Franklin surly would recognize. "How is your lovely daughter?"

"She's fine. Thank you for asking," he said.

"I'm looking for a friend, might you have seen her?" Franklin described Abigail.

"No, I'm sorry, sir. I don't know the lady. Good luck. Now you'll have to forgive me for continuing in such a hurry. We're late for an appointment." When Preston clucked, the horse took off jerkily and brought Abigail back into her body. "Are you all right, Abigail?"

"I can't believe that son of a bitch is still looking for me. Excuse my language." She was rattled for a good portion of the day.

# TWENTY

Julia came to the ranch once the news of her mother's passing finally reached her. Preston introduced her to Abigail. She spoke with Julia briefly, then went for a long ride over the hills.

Later Abigail stood on the porch gazing at the setting sun and tried to gather her scattered thoughts before entering the parlor, but when she heard the conversation in the drawing room, she had to grab onto the railing to steady herself. Though Julia and Preston lovingly embraced each other in shared grief, Abigail could hear Julia's distress plainly through the door.

"Who is she, Papa?"

He explained that Abigail had been nothing but considerate and obliging. "I can understand your disquiet, but you must believe me I have been blessed that she knocked on our door." He did not tell her Abigail had owned the Bradley Hotel.

"Papa," Julia cried out. "How could you so soon after Mama died? You don't even know her, and she lives in our house!"

"No more now," Preston said. "She'll be in soon to make supper."

"Papa–" Julia started again.

Preston's tone became annoyed. "That's enough. It's nothing like what you think. Your mother meant the world to me, and I can hardly see ahead of me since she's gone. Mrs.

Wilcox came when I needed someone to help, and she has done only that. Give her a chance, Julia. I know you'll come to like her."

He didn't notice that Abigail stood on the porch as he went past her on his way to the barn.

The glow from the fireplace behind Julia's blond hair made a halo around her head. She stood tall, slim, with clear blue eyes and fair skin, and, as Preston had often commented, looking like an angel.

"Your father tells me you live on the other side of Sacramento," Abigail said, trying to ease into a conversation. "It's a long way. You–you came by yourself?" she said stumbling over her words.

"Yes, we have a ranch between Sacramento and Freeport." Julia, though curious about who this woman was and why she was here, was genteel like her parents, and spoke only kind words. "Bernard–my husband–is presently in San Francisco with an old friend who is ill. That's where I was when I heard about Mama." She crossed over to the window. "Thank you for your help here," she said graciously. "I suggested to my father he come to live with us, but he says he wants to stay here. As you may know, this was my grandfather's property, and because Mama is–he doesn't want to leave because she is buried here."

"I understand," Abigail answered, and moved about the room nervously to straighten curtains and dust off surfaces with her handkerchief. "I don't know how he'll get along here without help." Abigail felt awkward and couldn't make sense of her thoughts or what she wanted to say.

Julia reminisced that she was happy on the ranch and felt close to both parents. "I think the sound of her voice is what I'll miss the most. She loved to read to me, and I loved to hear her stories. And I will always remember her songs to the chickens," she smiled at the memory. Then she peered into

Abigail's face as if to take charge. "Her voice was strong, commanding, but in a gentle way, which made you want to do what she asked of you," Julia held her gaze on the guest's face.

"I know you'll miss her. Please accept my condolences." When Preston came in from the barn, Abigail felt relieved, but also wished she could have had more time to talk with Julia. Julia went for a ride, and when she returned Abigail knew she still wondered who this strange woman was living in her parents' home. Later, as they ate dinner, Preston told his daughter again of how Abigail had come to the ranch, and while they reminisced about Helen, Julia seemed to become more at ease.

Abigail might have been envious of the bond the family had, but instead she was intrigued about how they had lived. But then a deep sadness filled her. For Abigail saw what she had missed by not raising children of her own. Preston saw it and offered her an understanding but melancholic smile. Julia saw it, too, but took it as a moment of grief about her mother's passing.

Abigail excused herself and disappeared into her room for the night, her eyes wide-open as she thought about what her life might have been.

Julia stayed for just another day before she wanted to return to her children. When it was time for her to leave, Preston, crestfallen, looked deflated and sad.

"When will I see you again?" he asked.

"Papa, just a couple of weeks. Once Bernard gets home. Papa, are you all right? You seem tired. Are you able to sleep?"

"I'm resting well, but your mother's passing has taken it out of me." She hugged him tightly, then got into the buggy and left for home.

# TWENTY-ONE

One day led to the next and before Abigail knew it she had been living at Hahl Ranch for more than two months.

At night, with chores done and meals eaten, she and Preston sat in the stuffed chairs in front of the fireplace and talked about their lives. He didn't seem to mind that hers had been unusual, and she welcomed getting to know about his.

One evening, Preston told her, "I know what you're thinking. Helen said it to me many times—what is this dog doing in the drawing room? Nanny has retired from herding though she's only six. She was a wonderful companion for me while I gathered cows. Could herd them as well as any cowboy. But she had a bad fall, and now her back-end is creaky. If she spends the night outside, she can barely walk in the morning, so she lays here with me by the fire." He scratched the dog's ears and ran his hand along her back to the tip of her wagging tail. "Her bark is good and loud, so I know when people come to the door." Then out of the blue he answered the question Abigail had wanted to ask. "Doc says I have a growth in my male parts. I know you can see I'm in pain and get tired out quickly, but you're considerate so you haven't asked me why."

"My goodness, Preston, what a terrible thing. Is there anything they can do?"

"Just keep me comfortable is all," he stated. "Doc comes by periodically, and though nothing changes for the better it is a comfort to know he's there."

"Will your daughter be coming to help you?"

"No. I haven't told her," he said in his usual careful way. "And I don't want anyone else to tell her, either," he added quickly. "With her mother just gone that's enough for her right now." He shifted uncomfortably in his chair. "Tell me more about your life. You were married, you said?"

Abigail told him the story of how she and Bradley met in the mercantile in San Francisco and about their life together there, but when she saw he had become fatigued she stopped.

"All right, but you must continue tomorrow," he countered. "Promise?"

"I promise." When he stood to retire, he lurched. Abigail reached out to help him catch his balance.

The next night she told him of how Bradley was shot to death during a gambling dispute. Many of the tender memories of her time with her husband and their life in San Francisco floated through her mind and with it a terrible longing for him.

"What a shock it must have been to lose him in that way," Preston said with compassion.

"It turned my life on its side. With Bradley gone, my mind was in a fog for quite a while. Just to get through the day was hard. It even hurt to breathe from all my tears." She had not planned to divulge so much to this near stranger, but when he asked she couldn't help but be candid. "Preston, it's too soon after Helen."

"Please, your story takes my mind off my own troubles. Go on, Abigail."

Fortified with a sip of tea, she told him of the loss of her children.

"How...how difficult it must have been for you," Preston said with great sincerity. That night her heart ached with a tumultuous grief that talking about her family brought up

# TWENTY-TWO

Now with Helen's death, Preston's health took a bad turn, and he began to lose strength in his legs. At times his groin became so painful that even to sit was a challenge, and he could only do so for short stints. She didn't know what to do for his pain, but she could wash him, help him dress in the morning, give him food and drink, and support his getting from chair to chamber pot and back to bed, all very intimate activities, which to their surprise held no sexual tension for either of them. It was a strangely satisfying existence for Abigail because Preston needed her to be a friend and nothing more.

In Abigail's mind they were quite a useless pair. She, who had not lived on a ranch since she was sixteen - and by this time was thirty-nine - was not strong either, but even so, she cleaned the house, made meals, and helped with ranch chores. The cattle she had to let be, but she weeded the garden, threw grain for the chickens, milked the cows, put out hay for the horses, and mucked the soiled stalls. Her hands went from baby soft to leather hard in no time with broken fingernails and bloody blisters along the way even wearing gloves. But she felt so content with the work even concerns about her own illness fell away.

One evening, the bright new moon illuminated the path to the road outside Abigail's window. In the distance an owl called, and coyotes howled in the hills. Abigail lay awake thrashing in her sheets, titillated by the memory of intimate times with Franklin. It pulled her so hard she quietly slipped out of bed and dressed for travel. She tiptoed through the parlor to the front door and undid the lock. But Preston heard her. He was awake from the pain in his back and sitting in the kitchen sipping tea and eating a bit of cake.

"You couldn't sleep either?" he called. Abigail said nothing. "Why don't you come in and have something to eat? You'll feel better. I always do." But again Abigail didn't answer. When Preston heard the door open, he pushed his cup off of the counter and it crashed to the floor. Fearing he'd fainted, she ran to the kitchen only to find him sitting in his chair, taking a bite of a cake they had bought in town. "Have some," he said. Nanny nosed his hand, wanting some of his nighttime snack. He broke off a small piece and gave it to the dog. Abigail started to leave. "You sure you want to do that?" he asked.

"Do what?" Abigail said.

"Go back to the life that caused you such unhappiness." Preston took another bite, then gave some more to Nanny. "I won't stop you, but you might want to think about it a bit."

Abigail knew he was right and sat heavily in a chair. Tears filled her eyes as she remembered a time when Franklin had hit her so hard she fell to the ground.

# TWENTY-THREE

*U*nfortunately, most of the repairs needed on the ranch are beyond my capabilities, Abigail wrote. With Preston's health waning and mine being unpredictable, I am fairly certain the two of us can't do it alone. I decided it would be prudent to pray for a ranch manager, just in case there is a God who looks after us.

"Lord, I know I am not one of your best, but Preston is, and he needs help, and I mean now. Are you hearing me?"

One morning, Preston sat in the parlor drinking coffee when he noticed a wagon coming down the drive carrying a Negro family: a man, a woman, and three young children.

The man, tall and muscular, a mountain with legs, came toward the door to what he hoped was Hahl Ranch and a job. He took off his weathered straw hat, untied the red bandana around his massive neck and wiped the sweat from his brow and the back of his head. His pants were filthy and well worn, and his torn shirt barely covered the cross hatch of flogging scars across his back and arms.

As he approached the house, Nanny ran to the door and barked, but soon wagged her tail and lay down. Preston opened the door.

"Good afternoon, sir," the man said with a southern drawl and a voice as deep as the ocean. "Damien Adams, sir. Just wondering if you might need a extra hand here?" He reached into his shirt, pulled out folded pieces of paper, and handed them to Preston.

"Says here all of you are free," Preston smiled. "War's been over a long time now, Mr. Adams. No need for you to show these papers anymore."

"Yes, sir!" Damien said proudly.

"Where are you from?"

"Louisiana, near Shreveport."

When Abigail heard Nanny's bark she was afraid it might be one of Franklin's men-or worse, Franklin himself. She grabbed the shotgun from the kitchen and pushed through the door with the weapon at her shoulder.

"Put your gun down there, Abigail," Preston said. "The man just wants work."

Relieved, she set down the weapon. "What can you do, mister?"

He told them they had lived on the Clive Adams Cotton and Hemp Plantation in Natchitoches. "I a blacksmith, but also know 'bout cattle 'n' raising horses, chickens and the like. Slaughtered a pig in my time. Master had me learn all kinda things. Sure better than working in them fields where you break your back 'cause you gotta bend over all day." Damien took his kerchief and again wiped the sweat from his broad forehead. "I's a good carpenter." He pointed to the dilapidated privy. "Fix that outhouse door in a jiffy. Whatever you like."

"You've come a long way, Mr. Adams" Abigail said.

"Once we free, we set out to find a safe home. Too worrisome in the south." He looked off into the distance. "I be a hard worker." Years of swinging a hammer, shoeing horses, fixing iron fences, making tools and repairing buggy wheels, working from sunup to sunset and never taking a break or "Overseer take a stick to my back." He could go all day without resting. "My wife here cooks good and can clean your house, and the children be no trouble."

Preston introduced himself, and then introduced Abigail as his houseguest. "We sure could use some help in the barn, couldn't we, Abigail?"

Four frightened faces looked out from behind the wagon. "Mr. Hahl, Mrs. Wilcox, this my family." He gestured to the little group huddled by the rig. "My wife, Mildred, she called Millie." Millie, with her arms wound tightly around their children and head bowed, curtsied and took a furtive glance at Preston, Abigail, and the ranch. "My two boys, Daniel, and –"

"Timothy. I be Letty Ann," the little girl shouted, but then caught herself and hid behind her mother. Abigail thought Timothy looked to be about eleven, Daniel, who had lighter skin and blue eyes, maybe a couple of years older and Letty Ann was the youngest around ten..

"Welcome to all of you," Preston said. "Why don't you make yourselves at home in the barn for now. The bunkhouse needs some cleaning. Mr. Adams, if you don't mind, you can start with the stalls."

"Be glad to." Mr. Adams smiled a full toothy grin.

Abigail took a relieved breath. "Well, Preston, this is our lucky day."

"Angels must have heard you to send this man to our door," Preston whispered. "We're not on the road to anywhere special, you know, so I swear it must have been some heavenly being who answered your prayer."

"Thank goodness somebody was listening."

"You're a little late for panning gold, Mr. Adams, if that is what you're hoping for," Preston said.

"No, sir. Just a safe place for my family," Damien replied.

*Yes sir,* Abigail thought. *Our lucky day.*

It took Millie and the children the better part of a day to make the bunkhouse livable. Dust and mice flew out the door in a cloud, and she scrubbed the inside from top to bottom. Nanny helped the children choose their beds. Millie pushed two small ones together for her and Damien and found some wildflowers to put in a mug on the table.

Once they were settled, Preston called them into the house. "Mrs. Adams," Preston said, "Mr. Adams tells me you are a wonderful cook."

"We certainly could use one," Abigail laughed.

"Yes, sir, I cook good," she said, her eyes on the floor. "I be cooking and cleaning in Master Adams' house since I be small."

"I would like you to do the same in this house. Would that be agreeable to you?" Preston asked.

Millie, confused, didn't lift her gaze. "I guess I could be doing the same for you," she said suspiciously.

"I'll pay you, of course," Preston reassured her.

Millie's eyes lit up with excitement. "When you want me to start, Mr. Hahl?" Later Abigail heard her say to Damien. "He gonna pay me! Can you believe it?"

When Millie went to the house to find Abigail, all the children followed. She knocked on the door and stepped back. The door opened and Abigail held it for them to enter.

"Children," Millie said, "go out and see them chickens and horses and all, while I speaks with Mrs. Wilcox. Your Pa's in the barn." The boys ran to find their father, but Letty Ann clung to her mother's skirt. "Honey girl, go follow the boys."

"I stay with you," Letty Ann said, her face buried in her mother's back.

"It's all right, Millie," Abigail said. "The children are welcome anywhere on the ranch."

She showed Millie the house and went over her duties-cook the meals and clean. Millie listened with both curiosity and restraint as she tried to determine what was allowed in this house and what was not. Then they went to the garden to pick what was needed for the day.

"We all gonna eat these?" Millie asked.

"Are there some vegetables you dislike like, Millie? You

don't have to eat anything you don't like."

"I means is we allowed to eat anything here?"

"Of course. Whatever you like," Abigail said. "Oh, and Mr. Hahl is particularly fond of pie, any kind really. He even ate mine with a crust as hard as tack, so you know he must be partial to it."

"And you, Mrs. Wilcox?"

"Me?" she laughed. "I like anything I don't have to cook."

From then on each morning Millie came into the house to tidy the rooms and prepare the day's meals.

Before Millie came, Abigail and Preston ate a lot of eggs, or whatever Preston was able to shoot. Even though she had grown up on a ranch Abigail had a hard time killing anything, but Millie could wring the neck of a chicken and pluck it without a fuss.

Abigail found Millie to be a practical and organized woman, who right away put the kitchen to suit her cooking needs. But underneath the new brightness in her eyes was a familiar weary sadness she had seen on the faces of the women who worked for her. Since she had been old enough to fold a napkin Millie had been a house slave. She made beds, folded sheets, carried in wood, lit fires, polished silver, and shooed flies from the food on Master's table. When she was older she became cook's helper, and eventually the cook. She spent long arduous days preparing the meals, cleaning the kitchen, and readying the next morning's breakfast. She was thrilled with her freedom, but at the same time, she was aware of what was around her at all times. And though she had no physical scars like the ones on Damien's back, Abigail saw she had them on the inside.

A few days later Damien spoke with Preston. "Just thinking about where we gonna live. When I able to pay for it, we buy a place, but that be a long way off. So I's wondering if I might make use of the tool shed the other side of the barn.

Build it into a home for my family, if that be all right by you. Plenty of room in the barn for tools."

"It seems rather small for all of you, Mr. Adams," Preston said.

"Sir, I add onto the back. Enough wood in the barn for it. B'sides you need the bunkhouse for the men you hire once things be running as they should. Will you think about it, sir?"

"If it will accommodate you and your family, I don't see any reason why you couldn't build out the shed. What do you think, Abigail?"

"You'll be within shouting distance of the house," Abigail remarked. "I hope you don't mind, Mr. Adams."

"No, ma'am, that be just fine," Damien smiled.

"All right then, let's see what you can do with it," Preston agreed.

When Damien had finished building out the shed, Abigail brought out a table and chairs, a rocker, and mats for all to sleep on. Damien built a bed for himself and Millie that was twice the size of the one in the slave quarters on the plantation. Preston gave them dishes and extra bedding. Abigail found enough material from curtains Helen had made for the kitchen windows to make some for Damien's house. And she had read that slaves were not allowed to have mirrors, so she placed a large one on the wall next to their bed.

When Millie Adams entered her new home all she could say was a breathy, "Oh!" Her fingers covered her open mouth and tears rolled down her cheeks. She threw her arms around Damien's big neck, and a satisfied toothy grin spread across his face. She sat down in the rocker, closed her eyes, and sighed once more.

"Thank you, Mrs. Wilcox," Damien said, looking over the cabin. "It looks right homey."

The children bounded in like puppies and claimed their mats. Nanny ran in behind them, licked their faces, and swung her tail so hard she nearly knocked herself over. Damien brought in their few things and they made themselves at home.

"Grab your cup and let's go outside for a sit," Abigail said to Millie the next afternoon.

"Sit with you?" Millie asked.

"Just need to look out at this beautiful land. Admire it. Don't you think, Millie?" Abigail continued to walk out the door and onto the porch. Millie sat, not knowing what to expect. "I am so glad you and your family are here. It's good to have the company." Abigail took a sip of coffee. "Do you need anything for your house? More blankets, pillows, rugs?"

"No, ma'am," Millie said, uncomfortable with the familiarity. "I best get back to the kitchen, so I get dinner on the table." She curtsied and returned to the house. But Abigail persisted, so each afternoon she asked Millie to join her on the porch for some coffee and a sit. Sometimes Preston joined them, but most of the time it was just the two.

Abigail's life at Hahl Ranch could not be compared in any way to the one she'd lived at the Bradley. After a lifetime on the plantation, it was the same for Millie. Like horses after a roundup, it took both of them time to settle down and cool off. At first Millie sat stiffly on the porch chair next to Abigail, who would engage her in conversation, but because Millie wasn't used to being allowed to share her thoughts, especially with a white woman, it took time for her to trust she could do so without reprisal. But once Millie became comfortable with it, for an hour most afternoons she and Abigail sat in the kitchen or on the front porch, drank coffee, ate some of Millie's biscuits or a bite of her sweet bread, and talked. The two came to understand each other, and before long became fast friends.

In the past, Abigail was not able to recognize the loyalty given to her by Sam, Marguerite, and the ladies. And with Franklin there was little faithfulness and only occasional kindness, so she kept her feelings mostly to herself; but now Abigail was learning to share her life with others, something she didn't know she had longed to do.

What would make the Bradley run well had been Abigail's first and only concern: what to offer clients or what would help the ladies bring in more money; but she couldn't remember if she ever truly gave consideration to what would make Franklin happy, only how to get what she wanted out of him and keep his temper quiet. But now seeing the kindness Preston gave so freely, his love for his daughter, and how he treated his animals, along with Millie's partnership with Damien and the care she gave her family, Abigail began to have a new perspective.

## TWENTY-FOUR

B efore long Damien and his family felt settled. The boys followed their father wherever he went, and Letty Ann stayed at her mother's side. Nanny accompanied whoever she thought might have a bite of bread for her.

In the mornings Damien would catch Preston before he could try to lift a log to the fire. "Now, Mr. Hahl, you gonna let me do that for you, right?" Both Abigail and Preston had always struggled under the weight of the wood, but the big man could lift an armful of logs, take them into the house, and drop them into the bin with ease, then carry in another armload for the kitchen and all of the bedrooms without producing one drop of sweat. "Mr. Hahl, after feeding the animals, I ride the fence line and see what needs mending."

"All right, Damien. Listen for the dinner bell."

"I come back when I hear it, sir," he smiled and disappeared out the door.

"Damien is fine with the animals, cleaning out the barn, and digging fence posts, but we'll need to hire more men to help him with the herd, once I build some reserves, I mean." Preston turned the page of the Sacramento Bee he was reading. "Eventually he can well help us manage the ranch, and maybe even take the herd to market. He can't read, but he does the math in his head. I can follow how much we spend and keep the books on it."

Abigail agreed that Damien was trustworthy, and Millie was a dear, so the Adams family became a permanent part of

Hahl Ranch.

The first new man they hired was Jeffery Smathers. Smathers had heard Damien ask for recommendations at the blacksmiths. They talked and he went to the ranch to meet with Preston. He was dependable, worked hard, and got along well with the Adamses. But what Jeffery really wanted was his own store. Sometime later Abigail helped him open Smathers Emporium in Auburn.

"Now that you have people to care for the ranch maybe you don't need me to stay any longer," Abigail suggested to Preston. "You can hire someone from town to help you." She really didn't want to leave, but she felt she might have overstayed her welcome.

"Leave? Have I made you feel uneasy, Abigail? Have I, in any way, indicated you should go away? You know what I need, and I feel comfortable with you. I know I don't have the right to ask, but I wish you would stay."

"It's just that Franklin might still be sniffing about, and I suspect he has. Placerville is so close to Auburn."

"I've already asked the businesses in town not to tell anyone of your presence here. Besides the school needs a teacher," he pressed. "Classes start again in a few weeks, and with Helen gone we're in need of a schoolmarm."

"I'm sure the parents will be thrilled to have a former madam as their children's teacher."

"You let me handle that. You'll make a fine schoolmistress," he said flatly.

"I know I can teach. It's not that. I always made sure my ladies could read because some of the gentlemen liked to be read to: stories, and poems, often an outdated newspaper was enough. And I knew that if they could read, it would be a help to the girls when they no longer worked for me. It's just that surely word will get to Franklin if I am so close."

"My friends in town will honor my request not to give you

away. And I also know you'll make a fine teacher," Preston stated.

"I'll think about it," she said disquieted by the thought of Franklin finding her.

The next morning Abigail walked through the front pasture and considered his offer. The sun shone brightly with not a cloud in the sky and reminded her of those rare days she took away from the Bradley when she drove her buggy off into the hills to where a small herd of cattle pastured. Several cows would take a turn and corral the young bulls and heifers toward the greenest grass. The young ones ate and played under her watchful eye, while the rest grazed where they wanted. *Like a teacher caring for the children?* she wondered.

With some consideration, and a good amount of trepidation, she decided she would stay in Placerville even if it meant she was very close to Auburn and to Franklin.

"All right, I'll do it," she told Preston. "Maybe I'll teach them how to run a hotel," she laughed. The students would come after their chores in the morning and leave in the afternoon by the time Abigail needed to be home to help Preston.

She toyed with the idea of changing her name. Though not sure why, she decided against it. She thought maybe she wanted Franklin to find her just so she could leave him all over again. And the students were not her ladies who were paid to do as she asked. They would be children. *Children! Lord in heaven, what am I getting myself into?*

Abigail went to the dry goods to buy clothing for her role as schoolmarm. On the first day, she gathered pencils and paper and what little wits she had available and walked the half mile to the Coloma School. "Mrs. Hahl, if you are listening," she said aloud, "if you care to give me any tips, I'd be open to that." *Franklin would certainly get a good laugh out of this*, she thought unsettled by the idea.

Waiting outside the schoolhouse were twenty-one students—eleven girls and ten boys, sons and daughters of farmers and ranchers. The girls chatted, and the boys told each other jokes and threw a ball of twine. And of course, they had banded together to ignore the new teacher. Abigail opened the door and let them in, but now they stared at her and whispered in each other's ears. For the first time in a long time, she felt self-conscious. They would know where she came from and what she had been at the Bradley Hotel. It reminded her of the women in Auburn who had glanced at her furtively. But she also knew how to handle miners who were rowdier and ornerier than these young ones, and she caught her feelings before they could run away with her.

"Children, I am sorry you have lost Mrs. Hahl. You must miss her. And though I knew her only for a short while, she seemed like a fine person." Then Abigail took a deep breath and began. "I am Mrs. Wilcox," which she spelled out on the chalkboard. "Now—who can read?" All hands shot up except for the two youngest. "All right, you two will learn to listen while these hooligans read to you." They all laughed. She looked at her list and picked a name. "John Addington. Where are you?" He raised his hand slowly. "Please start on the top of page one."

# TWENTY-FIVE

"Really? Millie's never had any money of her own?" Preston said after he gave her the first wages. "Sure makes me proud to be the first one to pay her for her work."

A shift happened in Millie. Right before their eyes, she changed from enslaved to truly free.

"Why, I can get me some material for new clothes for the children, a hat for Damien, a bridle for the horse," Millie said and smiled. "Mrs. Wilcox, will you go with me to the mercantile?"

"Of course."

As they rode the buggy into town, Abigail and Millie talked about what life could be now that her family earned a living.

"Millie, money gives you freedom to do what you want when you want to do it. So, yes, you can even buy things for yourself. What would you like? Something just for you—a dress, a hat perhaps?"

"Have to think 'bout it some. Never thought 'bout me," Millie said with her fingers to her mouth and tears in her eyes. "I were just breathing in and breathing out getting through the day. But I free. Now can do what I want." She smiled her beautiful smile with her face lifted to the sun.

"Coloma is small but with Placerville close by you can find everything you'll need for your family and the house." Abigail tied off the horse and her heart nearly stopped. Though the road was crowded with women in buggies, men driving delivery wagons, and cowboys riding to the saloon, there might as well have been only two people on the street. Franklin stood down the way in front of a saloon talking with the sheriff. *Oh, Lord help me,* she thought. He showed the sheriff what she assumed was a picture of her. The sheriff saw her and started to call her name, but Abigail shook her head, and the lawman handed the picture back to Franklin.

"Come on, Millie," she said and ran into the mercantile.

"What's the matter, Miss Abigail?" Millie asked, feeling herself being pulled through the door.

"Someone from my past," Abigail said. The sheriff glanced her way again, but when Abigail ran toward the shop, he shifted positions so that Franklin couldn't see her.

"That be that Clayborn fella, the one you talks about, the one in your locket?" Millie asked. "He see you?"

"I don't think so," Abigail said and peered through the window, "and I certainly don't wish to see him."

Franklin drove a buggy up to the mercantile, and next to him sat an attractive, well-dressed woman. Someone of means from what Abigail could see through the store window. When Franklin headed for the door, she pulled away from the glass and ran through the curtain to the back storage area.

"I'll be right back, honey," Franklin called back and approached the counter. Millie turned away and pretended to look at a stack of honey jars.

"Give me a couple of cigars and a bag of sweets–the mints," Franklin said. The shopkeeper set the items on the counter. "Have you seen this woman, blond, good looking, blue eyes, about this tall?" Franklin showed him a photograph. "She ever come in here?"

Millie, out of Franklin's sight, turned to the shopkeeper and quickly shook her head.

"Not that I remember."

Franklin paid for his goods and left the store; his spurs jingled as he walked past Millie.

"He gone now!" Millie called into the curtain at the back of the store. Abigail pulled it aside slowly and looked around the room. "You all right? You shaking."

"Fine now," Abigail lied.

Millie went over to the window. "From what I see, that man is lightning–comes in fast and snaps you silly." She looked up and down the street. "Ain't there now. Went off with his lady." She went over to the bolts of material and fingered each one carefully.

"Morning, Mrs. Wilcox," the attendant said.

"Good morning, Eldon. Thank you for not saying anything. Eldon, this is Millie Adams. She and her family have joined us at Hahl Ranch. You've already met her husband Damien, I believe. Millie, this is Eldon Maude."

"Nice to meet you, sir," Millie said and curtsied.

"You as well," he responded. "Mrs. Wilcox, that cowboy came in here a few days ago. I didn't say anything then either because he was pretty inebriated."

"Thank you, Eldon. I'd just as soon he not know where I am."

"Yes, ma'am." Eldon lifted a wrapped package onto the counter. "Your books are in."

Millie, excited to make her first purchase, fingered the pink gingham, then leaned in to Abigail. "I make a dress for Letty Ann. She be pretty in this color!"

"Here's a beautiful satin ribbon to go with it. Let me buy it for you?" Abigail said.

"Thank you, Miss Abigail. That be mighty generous. Will look right pretty with the dress, but I buy it myself."

Along with thread, buttons, and the ribbon for Letty Ann's hair, Millie made a pile of the blue checked cloth she had chosen for her men and enough pink cloth for herself and

Letty Ann. "How much am all this, Mr. Maude?" she asked, the tips of her fingers covering her mouth, as she tended to do, then whispered to Abigail, "Hope I have enough."

"One dollar and fifty cents even," he told her.

Slowly she counted out the cost to the penny.

"That right, Mr. Maude?" Millie asked.

"Yes, you're correct, ma'am," he said and winked at Abigail. Millie beamed and held out her palm for Abigail to see there was still money left over.

"Gonna put this in a jar on the shelf above the kitchen counter," she whispered. "Keep it for something special. Maybe each week I put some money in that jar. Lord'll tell me what it be for."

As they walked out the door Abigail automatically looked up and down the street for Franklin.

# TWENTY-SIX

M illie often told me stories of her life on the plantation during our afternoon coffees on the porch. *Some left me giddy as a baby goat dancing in the sunshine, while others were more like standing in the middle of a black-gray storm cloud:* Word went around that Master Adams intended to let go of some of his slaves in order to buy others for his Natchitoches, Louisiana, cotton and hemp plantation. Everyone was afraid. They knew families would be torn apart, never to be reunited, but there was nothing they could do except pray. Even though Millie was a house slave and cook's helper and therefore less likely to be sold, it still set her on edge.

Millie had worked in the kitchen since she began to bleed four years before. Her sixth-month-old child, Daniel, had milky brown skin even lighter than hers and eyes the color of his father's, blue. Daniel never got to know his father because Millie made sure he was kept away from Master Adams, for fear the man would do him harm or sell him. Her master's wife promised Millie her husband wouldn't hurt the child, but since Master Adams had forced himself on her, making Daniel, she didn't share Mistress Adams' belief.

Damien, slave-born, tall and muscular, with hair just grown on his chin, waited with his family in their one-room shack. He and his mother, father, and younger siblings–a brother and two sisters–might be taken tonight from the Jenkins Sugar Cane Plantation in Biloxi, Mississippi and sold, never to see each other again.

Screams shattered the night quiet as on both plantations the overseers chose which chattel to keep and which to sell. There was no disturbance in the Big House where Millie slept, but the door flew open in Damien's house and overseer's men pushed in. They grabbed Damien's father, dragged him to a cart, and came back for his mother and brother. Damien threw himself at them with all his might, holding onto his family members as best he could, until the whip came across his back and he fell to the floor. Fifteen stood in the wagon pleading to remain with their families. Wives, husbands, children, mothers and fathers stood in shocked silence as the cart drove down the road. The wailing echoed for at least a mile. That was the last Damien saw of any of them.

And in a few weeks Damien was loaded onto the cart, leaving behind his young sisters to care for themselves while he headed to a slave auction in New Orleans.

Millie swallowed a big gulp of coffee. "The first time I see Damien, he just 'bout to be sold. It were dark and rainy on that Saturday." She and her mistress were to pick up material for a new dress. The town square was filled with an undercurrent of fear and pain. All the slaves to be sold, men and women, stood in the pouring rain in a line, with chains around their necks and clothes mostly removed. The crowd was a good size because there was promise of a lot of money changing hands. Damien was up last. Clive Adams had already checked him over to be sure he was of good value. The boy's teeth were good, his muscles were strong, and as far as Adams could tell, he was sound. And Millie couldn't keep her eyes off him.

"Saving the best for last, ladies and gentlemen," the slave auctioneer called, "Strong as an ox this young buck is. Make a good blacksmith with a little training. Do I hear four hundred dollars?" He looked over the crowd. "Four hundred to Mr. Adams."

"Five fifty," a man called out, and another yelled, "Six hundred." "Seven fifty," said another.

"Eight hundred," Adams called.

"Eight hundred," the auctioneer said. "Eight hundred going once, twice–sold to Clive Adams for eight hundred dollars. A bargain at any price." He rapped his hammer on the desk.

"You better be worth it," Adams hissed at Damien.

Just as Damien stepped off the auction block, he saw Millie walk by, carrying a basket over her arm and her little boy on her hip. He thought Millie was the prettiest woman he had ever seen, then a feeling of shame and anger came to his stomach, but Millie smiled at him in a kind and understanding way.

From then on Damien was trained to be a blacksmith on the Adams Plantation. Millie looked for him wherever she went, and when he could sneak away, Damien went for Millie.

A church marriage was not allowed for those who were not free, but it was not too long before Master Adams gave his permission for the two to jump the broom and live together, and within the next few years they had two children, Timothy and Letty Ann.

Clive Adams gave his slaves a measure of food once a week–salt pork, potatoes, and corn flour. Though the children didn't dare take apples and pears from the trees near the cabin where the family lived for fear they would get whipped, they did share chickens with an enslaved family who lived next to them, so they had eggs except when the chickens were molting.

While his wife finished up in the Master's kitchen, Damien with Daniel, Timothy, and Letty Ann worked the vegetable garden into the dark. He and the children brought home possum or coon and on a good night turkey-anything they could trap.

If Master wanted his slaves to work harder or if someone had tried to run away, he would stop giving them food for a time. Then Millie had to steal flour, sausages, bacon, or ham from the kitchen in the big house to feed her family. She didn't like stealing, but her babies had to eat. During those hard times, without Master's knowing, Master's wife, whom Millie called Mrs. A., put bread and meat into Millie's sack.

Millie got along well with her mistress. Delia Adams confided in Millie more than she should have to any slave. Once she told Millie she didn't like how her husband treated them. Millie knew he was cruel, but she did not find this was true of his wife. She always spoke to them in a kindly way, never yelling or beating them. She told Millie she didn't like feeling mean. And because Mrs. A. was so nice to her Millie did her best to do what her mistress wanted. "I think it get her in trouble with her friends, being so nice to us," Millie told Abigail.

Millie sighed and began again thoughtfully, "There was so much to cry over on that plantation, I be miserable all the time. Everywhere was sadness and hurt, easy to see: families torn apart, punishments you can't even imagine for the slightest thing, sickness, injury, or death with no help of a doctor. Be afraid night and day. Finally had to find things to be cheerful about 'cause I not like being unhappy all the time. Hunted for the good things. You understand? Looked for them rose flowers instead of thorns. Now, not to say I always see them pretty blossoms, but I learn to hold them thorns with a lighter touch, if you get my meaning. Besides, the more roses I look for, more I saw." Millie took a bite of her bun and washed it down with a gulp of coffee, then poured herself another cup and took a sip before she continued.

It was against the law for an enslaved person to read and

could mean a blinding of one eye for the mere possession of a book. Even so, Mrs. A. decided Millie would learn. Millie didn't know what to do. "I like having two eyes, Mrs. A."

"Never you mind. No one here is going to hurt you, Millie." Mrs. Adams came into the kitchen with a recipe she had received from her sister. "We're going to make a pork and apple pie, Millie. I know you know how to make a pie, and you make good ones, but I want you to use this recipe. Now, as I put my finger to the word you say it after me. I'll help you." She pointed to the page, "Two, written the number 2, that's two and one half cups of flour." Millie repeated it. "Are there any other ingredients with a two in it, Millie?" Millie pointed. "That's good. It says two tablespoons of sage." Then she touched each sound with her finger, "ta-ble-s-p-oons," which Millie again repeated. Mrs. Adams had Millie copy recipes into a book, so she learned to write as well. Eventually she read Mrs. A. the headlines of the newspaper and before she knew it whole articles. Mrs. A. pretended it was the most natural thing in the world, but Millie never knew she could do it.

"I know Mrs. A. helping me to learn, and I be mighty grateful, but we was so scared someone find out," she told Abigail. Mrs. Adams would be in trouble with the law if someone caught Millie reading, and it would mean twenty-five lashes on Millie's back. "Figure she must have told her sister, Lydia Anauer, 'cause they watch me in the kitchen and whisper together and smile," Millie grinned. "But I never let on, lest I's wrong in that."

With Union troupes surrounding the plantations many slaves took that opportunity to walk away from their homes. Damien and Millie left the Adams Plantation, but the question was where to go? Some former slaves wandered over the countryside scavenging for food and shelter. Some ended up in contraband camps near the Union soldiers, but the army just let them starve to death. If they wanted out of the camp, they were told to go back to the plantation they came from.

So with a prayer to The Almighty but no destination in mind, Millie, Damien and the children headed up the road. Each carried a small sack containing their belongings–a flax and hemp shirt or dress, woolen socks, a shawl. The boys carried a chunk of smoked meat and a loaf of bread. Damien secured a hammer. The knife Millie took from the Cook House he stuck in his belt. Letty Ann and Millie carried jars of water. They all walked in silence, glad to be free, but frightened about their future. Soon the road-dust covered their faces and fatigue filled their already worn bodies.

After a few hours, they came upon Mrs. A.'s sister Lydia Anauer in her buggy with her son, Deagon L. his arm in a sling from a battle wound. Millie had heard many arguments before the war between Clive Adams and Lydia and her son. The first was heavily entrenched in his belief they had a right to own slaves, but the Anauers were against it. It had caused a rift between the families; though in private, the sisters, Delia and Lydia, remained loyal to each other.

Lydia, recognizing the family, waved. "Where are you headed, Millie?"

"Don't rightly know, ma'am. Up the way a bit, I guess."

Lydia spoke quietly to Deagon L then said, "Millie, come live with us. You can stay in the barn. We can't pay you because we don't have much coming in ourselves, but if you work the farm you'll have plenty to eat. Deagon L and I would be delighted for the company."

Millie grabbed Damien's hand. He nodded. "Thank you, ma'am. That be very kind," Millie said. They put their belongings into the buggy and walked to their new home on the Anauer farm. Millie cooked and took care of the house, while Damien worked the land and cared for the animals. Both families dug in the vegetable garden.

The Adams had been living on the farm for four years when just before supper, their oldest son Daniel, madder than a hornet and frightened out of his wits, with tears streaming down his young face, ran screaming from the soybean field to find his mother at the house. "They got Pa, Mama! They got Pa! Where's Deagon L?"

"Who got Pa, boy? Where?" Millie called out of the kitchen door.

"Deagon L!" Daniel shouted again in frustration and flew from the house. He got a horse and galloped away with Deagon L not far behind.

Damien had been weeding the crop when seven men holding ax handles and rifles marched into the field. He ran, but they knocked him down. "Niggah, where do you think you're goin'!" one said in a sickly sweet tone. They pulled him out of the field onto the road and took him into a clearing in the woods. The leader of the pack took his rifle butt and hit Damien on the back of the head. When Damien came to, his hands were tied to a tree branch, and his shirt was hanging at his waist.

"Black boy, you think you a free man?" the biggest one said. "Let me show you what you are, niggah!" He raised his whip high and brought it down hard across Damien's naked back. "No blackie's gonna be livin' next door to me like he's white," he jeered and turned to the other men. "Can you imagine some darkie thinkin' he gonna vote?" Then they beat him until one eye was closed and whipped him until his back was striped.

Deagon L and Daniel heard the sound of the lash hitting skin, a hissing breath, and a deep groan as they rode to where they held Damien. Damien had fainted and was slumped over with blood pooled around his knees. Deagon L gave Daniel a pistol and set him behind a stump, telling him to keep quiet, then he rode closer hidden by dense summer leaves.

"All right, gentlemen," Deagon L said from within the trees, his speech slow and steady sounding like a ghostly aberration. "Drop what you got in your hands and the gun from your belt. Slowly now, boys, if you want to live."

For a moment no one moved.

Deagon L cocked his gun. Daniel cocked his. In the silence an owl screeched and a bullet hit the dirt near where the men stood, its sound echoing against the hills. Then like claps of distant thunder, clubs and guns hit the ground.

"Hands in the air, gentlemen. Walk away from him twenty paces, face away from the road, and do not move. Slowly now, boys," he warned. "If one of you tries to turn around, the explosion of my gun will be the last thing you see."

Deagon L and the boy helped Damien onto a horse and the three of them rode to safety.

The Knights of the White Camellia, a Louisiana version of the Ku Klux Klan, rode with torches ablaze to set homes on fire and terrorize Negroes and Natives or their sympathizers, anyone they thought threatened the white man's way of life.

Millie prayed every night for the Lord to heal Damien's body and his heart, because for Damien to have his son see him beaten in this way was more than he could stand. For a while he kept to his own company, and only after several weeks when the wounds healed was he more like himself again. But it had changed him, and now all he thought about was finding a place for them to live out of harm's way. And the Anauers agreed; it wasn't safe to stay on the farm.

After much discussion, Damien decided they would go where the war had not touched, to California. With talk of gold in every stream, he knew as a blacksmith there would be plenty of money to be made.

Millie said, concerned about the journey, "First we gotta

get there. Seem like a long way to go. Couldn't we find somewhere in Louisiana?" she said, then shook her head. "No, suppose not."

When Damien and his family were ready to depart, Deagon L brought the wagon around to the front of the barn. "God bless his precious heart," Millie told Abigail. "Gave us their biggest rig."

Damien and Deagon L piled bales of hay around the edges of the wagon, leaving the center hollow. On boards across the top was piled more hay; sacks of beans and flour filled in the front; and finally inside were blankets, cooking pots, and a barrel for water. To hide from prying eyes, Damien, Millie, and the children stuffed themselves into the cave in the middle of it all. Deagon L filled in the back with more hay and sacks, threw a tarp over the whole thing lashing it to the sides of the rig, and tied his horse to the back. "I am surely not knowing how we gonna manage this undertaking," Millie said to her husband. "Good thing the children be slight 'cause it sure am tight in here."

Before they rode off, Lydia gave her son a long hug and handed him a large bag of soft toffee to give to the children along the way. The plan was for Deagon L to drive them into Texas, then ride back home. The Adamses would go on from there, taking the wagon to California. The family was to hide in this "hay house" for the next few days, till they were safely out of Louisiana and away from deadly nightriders and Klansmen.

Traveling through Louisiana was hard on the family, not only because of the close quarters, but because with the general hatred for freed slaves, they feared if anyone found them they could be shot or lynched. Millie tried not to be terrified, but she was not good at it. To let his passengers know when someone was near, Deagon L shouted out a hearty 'hello' or a 'good day', which made the entire family stop breathing.

"Dark as a cave, and hot as an oven," Millie told Abigail. "Children put up with it to a point, then got crabby and annoyed each other any way they could. And Damien, he tried not to complain, but his joints ached, stiffening from being cooped up." They couldn't sing for fear of being heard, so Millie held up the Bible Mrs. A. had given her to the little bit of light that peeked through the canvas. Quietly she read aloud while the family sweated and jostled in the dark.

At the end of the third day they heard three riders approaching. Inside the hay house the orange sunlight blinked on and off as their horses circled the wagon for what to Millie felt like an hour.

Deagon L reached for his rifle and set it on his lap. "Good afternoon, gentlemen," he said loudly. "How can I help you?"

"What you got in the wagon?" a man with a patch on his eye said and stared with his good eye at the piles of hay and bags of beans. "All this for you?"

"Supplies from town," Deagon L said and put his finger on the trigger. Sweat formed under his collar.

"I hear niggrahs is tryin' to escape," said another as he tried to peer into the hay. "You seen any?"

"Slaves, you mean?" Deagon L said. "Thought the war was over. No more slaves."

"I don't care if the war am over, no niggrah's gonna live near me." Another spat then jammed his bayoneted rifle deep into the center of the supplies. The blade darted in and out. Wide eyed, Millie ducked and wrapped her arms around Daniel and Letty Ann, while Damien reached for Timothy just in time. The blade caught Damien in the arm and left a two-inch slice near his shoulder. He gasped, but at the same time one of the horses whinnied and muffled his cry. With all the dust those hooves kicked up it was all they could do not to cough and give themselves away.

"Do you mind not making holes in my bags of beans?" Deagon L said.

"Got any chewing tobacco in there?" the one-eyed man asked.

"Don't use it myself. Sorry."

"You got whiskey?" asked another with a mind to cause trouble.

"Naw. Just going now to get some," Deagon L said. "You know a good place?"

"My uncle Johnny sells the best," the one-eyed man said. "Two miles up, road twists left. Come to a fork–left side. Take you to his farm directly. He'll set you up with the best corn liquor you ever had. Tell him Rafe sent you."

"You like sweets?" Deagon L asked. "I have some soft toffee I can share with you." One of the men grabbed the entire bag and rode off. The rest laughed and followed.

"Damien, Millie–you all right?"

"Still breathing," Damien responded while Millie tied a kerchief around his arm.

"Sorry about the candy, children. It was all I could think to do."

"Better they stole them treats than find us in here," Millie said.

The day finally came when they passed into Texas, and the Adamses could sit out in the open. Deagon L and Damien opened up the back of the hay house and attached a tarp roof overhead to keep off the sun and rain for the months it was going to take to get north. As he left, Deagon L shook Damien's hand, the children waved, and Millie cried.

Daniel and Timothy sat on the seat with Damien while Millie and Letty Ann rested in the back. Though they would always have to be careful, all were much relieved to have light and fresh air.

The Adamses rode on through Texas, and after a couple of

weeks the children didn't even fuss about having to sit in the rig or walk beside it.

When her stories got too rough Millie poured herself more coffee, took a bite of the sweet bread or made an excuse to retreat into the kitchen for a time, but she began again once she recovered. Millie had lived this life and now she wanted to shed its pain by telling Abigail all about it. She took a last gulp of her coffee, looked over the field and up at the trees, deciding if she was going to tell Abigail about the next part of their journey. "I needs to tell you just this one thing before I go back to make supper."

The Adamses stopped in a clearing for the night. The boys, Letty Ann, and Millie unloaded pots, mugs, and blankets and got a meal ready while Damien went deep into the forest to gather more firewood.

By the time Millie heard the leaves rustle and twigs snap, it was too late–a white man, a hunter, walked into the clearing. He eyed Millie like a bobcat ready for dinner, grabbed her by the hair, and pulled her to standing.

"What do we have here!" he said, his voice gravelly from too many cigars and too much moonshine. Millie yelled, but the hunter slapped her mouth shut. Timothy jumped onto his back, pounded him with his small fists, and kicked him with his hard-toed shoes, but the boy was so little, the man pulled him off like a bug. From within the woods Damien heard the cry and started back.

Just as the man turned to go at Millie again, a shotgun blasted. A deep red splatter spread across the man's chest, and he fell hard to the ground. Daniel, eyes wide and mouth slack, stood still in mid-breath. In his young hands was a smoking weapon.

"You all right?" Damien asked his eyes riveted on the white man's body.

Timothy and Letty Ann both threw themselves into their

mother's arms. "I be fine-thanks to my boys," she said and wiped the blood from her lip, fussing with her hair to hold back the tears.

Damien carefully lifted the firearm from Daniel's hands and put his arm around his son's shoulder. "It's all right now," he said. But Daniel stood as still as the dead man on the ground.

"He was hurting Mama. I had to stop him, Pa." He stared at the blood splatter on the man's chest.

Damien pulled the boy in. "Was the right thing to do, son. But we gots to get going before anybody sees."

Damien picked up the hunter and took him way into the woods. He placed the man's rifle across his chest so whoever found the body would think it was a hunting accident.

The next day Damien pulled up to the General Store outside of Union. Three white men stood on the porch talking. They studied Damien as he climbed down from the rig and ascended the stairs to the store. Millie's heart was in her stomach. It seemed each step he took creaked louder than the last. She thought for sure they would stop her man before the screen door closed on his backside, but then their voices swelled with excitement over the story they told.

"Damn fool got himself shot! Bet a hunter thought he had missed his prey," said one.

"Must a happened yesterday," said another. He spat tobacco juice out into the puddle he had made in the road. "Already cold when they found him." He spat again.

When Damien came out of the store he held a jar of molasses and a bag of sweets tight to his chest.

"Hey, boy! Which way was you coming?" one man asked. "Through San Augustine?"

The men went quiet and waited for Damien to respond. He held his gaze on Millie's face and shook his head. His face dripped with sweat. "Union," he lied and got into the rig. He snapped the reins and pulled the wagon into the road. The white men watched, then turned back to continue their conversation. Millie could hardly speak, and the children were wide-eyed and shivering for hours.

For Abigail hearing about to the harrowing trials of the Adams family left her unsettled. She decided to get some air to let those feelings shake off. It was raining as she went out the door, but she walked anyway. When the sun finally broke through, a rainbow hung in the sky above the barn.

# TWENTY-SEVEN

"The children can join Abigail's class," Preston said.
"I teach 'em some but they still not much good at reading," Millie said. "Sums neither."

"Abigail and I will help them," Preston offered. "They can enter the class when they're ready." The children were smart and quick to learn and soon were able to go to school.

Since there were several Negro families in the area, at least in Auburn, as well as Nancy and Peter Gooch, former slaves who in 1850 built a homestead in Coloma, Abigail did not expect the ill feeling the Adams children would cause in the class. She understood prejudice and had experienced it many times herself, but not the kind of intolerance based on the color of skin. And even though the students had been informed in advance there would be new members, when those three dark faces came into the classroom, all jaws dropped. There was a shuffle of nervousness and the word "slaves" was muttered throughout the room. Daniel and Timothy were understandably skittish. Letty Ann clutched the back of Daniel's pants.

"Joseph, move over and let Daniel sit with you. Patrick, slide over. Timothy, you sit with him. Letty Ann, there in front with Margaret." Terrified, Letty Ann, who nearly messed her drawers, slid onto the bench.

After the noon meal, while the children played a game of Run, Sheep, Run, Abigail heard a scuffle outside, but before she could get to the boys, the student in charge rang the bell, and the children returned to their seats.

Daniel had a bloody nose and the other boy a black eye, each blaming the other for the altercation.

"I don't care who started it, no more fighting," she said. "Go to the pump and get yourselves cleaned up."

The bloody nose and torn clothes from a schoolyard fight brought back memories for Abigail: *"You started it," Franklin argued. Abigail, dismayed at the lie, blotted the blood from her nose and stormed out of the room.*

The discovery that Abigail, who had been a madam, was to teach their children made the parents understandably suspicious. Now these new students challenged them once more and added fuel to glowing embers. The next day only half the class came to school, and the parents threatened to have Abigail discharged. But she could be mule-headed stubborn, and she didn't need their twenty-two dollars and fifty cents a month, so she held her ground.

"Their opinions about the color of skin hold no water with me," she told Preston. "My ladies were of all shades, and they got along just fine. Almost all learned to read, write, and do arithmetic–together. Besides, I believe anyone has the right to get educated if they want to, so to my way of thinking, if the Adams children are not welcome to join the class, then those folks' children cannot come into my classroom either." But it was a standoff for several weeks.

She went to speak with Marge and Grant Edgewood, neighbors who had been sympathetic to the Adams family when they first arrived and had brought gifts for the children–a tied bundle of sheets and blankets, some outgrown clothes and several pairs of shoes from their son Mark.

"What should I do?" Abigail asked.

"They'll get used to it," Grant said, but shook his head. "Prejudice, Abigail, I don't have to explain to you how deep a river that can be."

Marge stopped knitting and announced, "Prejudice is fed by ignorance and fear by people who do not know each other and have a need to feel more important than someone else. Besides, it's not the children's fault. It's their parents' doing. They taught them." She continued to knit at a racing pace. "You'll see. The children just need time to get used to the newcomers, then they'll be fine."

To ease the tension about Abigail becoming the teacher, Preston had talked with all the parents, but there was enough discontent about this that he met with them again at the church. Later he told Abigail, "No need to worry now. They were upset, but I spoke with them for a while, and they promised the children will be in class in the morning–most of them anyway."

But ultimately, what changed the parents' minds were the complaints from their own offspring, who found they had more chores to do since they were at home during the day. The children preferred school and begged to go back to class to sing songs, read stories, and learn how to count money.

Though the tension in the schoolyard was not gone, it was eased, and by the time the leaves fell off the trees, there were no more bloody noses. And not only did the parents have a better opinion of Abigail but she was less wary of them as well. To her great surprise, on more than one occasion when she arrived in the morning, she found a bundle of baked goods or a sack of apples at the schoolhouse door.

Abigail sat in the shade of the oak trees in the schoolyard and gazed over the golden grasses on the hills. Even though for the first time in a long time she felt useful and fulfilled, she still carried her ever-present concern.

She said to Preston later, "I don't want to go, but I'm afraid Franklin will find me. As you know, he almost did in Placerville–more than once. And now that you have help on the ranch, perhaps it's time for me to move on?"

"But you mustn't," Preston said dumbfounded. "Who would teach at the school?"

"You could have Millie help you here or hire someone to come and give you a hand, and I'm sure there are teachers available if you put an advertisement in the paper or a notice up at the mercantile."

"There aren't any here in Placerville," Preston stated flatly. "Millie is helpful, but she has too much to do as cook and housekeeper to be able to help me as well. I, I do not want anyone new. You must stay. Please, you must. I couldn't take it if you left."

So once again, Abigail let her concerns rest as best she could and filled her days with helping to care for Preston and teaching at the Coloma School.

# TWENTY-EIGHT

M illie stood behind Preston and stared at the large, four-hooved creature. Before the war, except for the blacksmith and the carriage drivers, the enslaved were not allowed to ride. It could mean a whipping or worse. Millie had a friend whose Master only thought he had seen her on the back of a horse, and to this day Millie could hear the hiss of the whip and her friend's cries as the lash left its mark on her back.

"Millie, you can't live on a ranch like this and not know how to ride," Preston encouraged.

"It's all right, Honey. Get up there," Damien said. "No master here. We free. We can ride a horse anytime we want."

Millie scrunched her face. "He awfully big."

Daniel held the reins and stroked the animal's muzzle. "Old Smokie am big, but he gentle. I promise to keep hold of him while Pa help you up. Hold the saddle horn, then set your left foot in his hands."

Millie swallowed hard and threw her leg over the animal's back. "Whoa!" she screamed when the horse shifted his feet, then she pretended to relax. "I so tall now." She smiled weakly.

"Look at you, Mama!" Timothy called from the chicken coop.

"Mama, you riding a horse!" Letty Ann screamed with excitement. She and Timothy ran to the paddock fence. "You gonna love riding. You see." Both children had already taken lessons from Daniel.

"Quiet now," Millie scolded. "You gonna make this animal nervous."

"You hang on to the horn and the reins, while Daniel walks you around the paddock," Preston said.

On the first circle Millie held tight to the saddle horn with both hands, but by the third or fourth turn she relaxed some and let go of one.

"Honey," Damien said, "when you more comfortable with it, we ride together. You hardly seen any of the ranch lands. Over this hill," he said, pointing to the ridge, "past the big meadow, a beautiful stream with a little brook running into it. Over that hill, the grandest mountains you have ever seen. And if you turn 'round you see the ocean from there. Well, almost."

"Don't know how soon we gonna do that," Millie said nervously. "Walking maybe, with Daniel holding the reins." She tried to laugh.

"With a little practice, you'll get the hang of it, Millie," Preston encouraged.

While Abigail and Damien drove to Placerville to pick up supplies for the ranch, Damien told her that when he first came he had found that as a blacksmith he had plenty of work. When the sheriff needed a repair on his wagon, he told him about how Mr. Hahl was not feeling well and could use someone to help him run his ranch. "Mrs. Wilcox, it like the sun breaking through after a bad rainstorm. Knew I had to go there." Abigail decided she would have Millie make a pie for Sheriff Bullock and his wife.

"Damien! Damien Adams!" a man called. An older gentleman with brilliant white hair, his arms full of items bought at the mercantile, ran as best he could to catch up to their wagon. "Mr. Adams, I have not seen you for some time.

Thought you might have gone on to Marysville."

"Hello, sir! How are you? Mrs. Wilcox, this be Fletcher Robertson. Worked on his ranch when I first come."

"How do you do, ma'am?" Robertson breathed heavily and mopped his brow.

"How is Mrs. Robertson?" Damien asked.

"Don't think she will be with us next spring. We are old, Mr. Adams."

"Sad thing to hear. But you quite spry, sir, from what I see."

"You look through kind eyes, Mr. Adams," he mused.

Robertson started to leave, then turned back. "Mrs. Wilcox, a cowboy asked about an Abigail Wilcox. Been a number of weeks now, though. Would that be you?" She explained and he agreed he would not divulge he had met her.

It had been more than three months since she left Auburn, and Abigail had hoped Franklin had given up by now.

# TWENTY-NINE

Daniel sat on the porch with Abigail and read his book aloud, carefully sounding out each word and trying to make sense of the sentence at the same time. Millie rode in, tied her horse to the paddock fence, and ran across the yard as fast as she could. "Mrs. Wilcox, Mrs. Wilcox!" Millie called as she ran.

"Very good, Daniel," Abigail said. "We'll finish up later. Please take your mother's horse to the stable." Daniel loved to work with horses, and he had a knack for training them.

"I cool him down for you, mama," he said.

Abigail pulled her scarf tighter around her neck to cover the sore that had just appeared.

"Mrs. Wilcox, you not gonna believe this! I practicing my riding, and staying on the saddle and everything, when my horse took off. Kept saying whoa, but he kept not hearing me. I's barely hanging on with my arms flapping and my legs, too, knew I was going to fly off the back and land on my head. Right then a white man come up beside me and grab my bridle. I knows I's free, but still I feel my hands tied to a tree and a whip's lash on my back. Just plain scared." She acted out the whole encounter, becoming the man and the horse. "'You've just learned?' the man said. I guess he saw I were not good at it. I panted and gasped, and slid my rear right off that saddle, glad to be with my feet on the ground. 'You do better you pull back the reins,' he say. 'He stop then. Kick him, he thinks you want to go.' Mrs. Wilcox, just then I got a square look at the man, thick blond hair, bushy mustache, fresh whiskey on his breath."

"Franklin?" Abigail gasped.

"Yup," Millie said. "Sure enough he say he looking for a friend, Abigail Wilcox. 'You know where she at?' he say. 'Heard she live nearby. She got long gray-blond hair, bright blue eyes–a beautiful woman.' 'Abigail who?' I say. What was I to do to get him off your scent? 'Oh, you mean Mrs. Wilcox? I met her a time back. Why, I heard she gone to Marysville.' 'Marysville,' he say. Helped me back onto old Smokie, then he ask, 'You want me to walk you back to home?' 'No, sir, I get there myself,' I say. 'To get him going, squeeze his sides with your legs,' he say, 'and ease up on the reins.' I squeeze and the horse walked forward. 'Well, how about that!' I say. 'Marysville. You sure?' he say. 'Sure as the sun shines, mister, and thank you for stopping my horse,' I called. He grunted, then rode off." Millie shook her head and fanned herself with her bandana. "He don't know how close he came to you."

Almost every day Abigail envisioned what would happen if he found her–the inevitable argument, his rough hands on her shoulders. Sometimes it was all she could do to shake off the thought.

# THIRTY

Timothy ran across the field to the path where Letty Ann and Abigail walked. Letty Ann attempted a handstand. Her dress came up over her head, and then she fell over and rolled onto her back.

"Mama says come to supper, and Letty Ann s'ppose to wash her hands b'fore she come to the table," Timothy said, and he ran back to the house.

"I know," Letty Ann sighed. Abigail brushed off the girl's dress and retied the sash. "Mrs. Wilcox, was your hair blond like Julia's when you was young?"

"My hair did not have all this gray in it back then. Why do you ask?"

"Just wonderin'," she said and kicked a stone.

Abigail held out her hand for the child to take. "Shall we see what your mama has made for our supper?"

# THIRTY-ONE

"This come for you." Millie handed Abigail the letter she had picked up at the post office in the mercantile. "Your face all pinched," Millie said. "What is it? What do it say?" Millie leaned in to read it over Abigail's shoulder.

"Marguerite. I didn't know she knew where I was." Abigail reread the letter. "She tells me Franklin got married just after I left. That man never could be alone." She threw the letter onto her desk.

"Just as well," Millie snuffed. "He no good for you. Let some other woman take on that bad temper, drinking and carousing. You ain't got no need of a man like that."

"Don't know why it hits me oddly, Millie, but it does, like a nail into a coffin. I suppose it's a fitting end to that part of my life."

Millie squinted. "Who'd he marry?"

"Florence Ritchfield," Abigail said flatly.

"That same Sacramento woman he say he not having affair with?"

"Yes," Abigail said, annoyed with Franklin all over again.

# THIRTY-TWO

The doctor came to see Preston. "How are you feeling, Abigail? While I'm here, I might as well check you over."

"No need," Abigail said. "Nothing to be done anyway."

She really didn't want to know the worst, and though she felt something troublesome in her chest, except for needing some salve for the sores on her skin, she didn't feel in vital need of the doctor's services.

Every afternoon, Millie read to Preston while he ate his noon meal. She noticed lately he was more tired and less able to take care of his needs, so when the doctor came to bring him medicines, Millie was not surprised to hear him say there was nothing more he could do. "He's in God's hands now." The cancer was in his bones.

It was a hard blow for all of them. Preston was a proud man who wanted to be self-sufficient, and that stubborn man would not let anyone tell Julia how bad it was for him because, "She has enough to handle with her family."

"How's your riding coming, Millie?" Preston called from inside the privy, his face pasty white and dripping with sweat.

"That horse ain't gonna get much exercise with me on it," she said. He opened the door and she helped him with his pants. Even when his back was a torment, and the pain of relieving himself had become unbearable, he never complained. With his hand on her shoulder, they walked back to the house. But when Julia came, Preston felt trapped in his denial. Before she arrived, he made everyone promise not to tell her the truth.

While Preston lay naked under the sheet and waited for Julia to come help him with his morning bath, Abigail poked the fire and added a few more logs to warm up the room. Julia poured water from the pitcher into the washbowl, then added boiling water from the kettle heated in the kitchen and dunked the cloth. Preston found the warm rag soothing. Millie brought in fresh clothes from the line and they got him dressed. Julia fluffed his pillow and opened the throw to cover him.

"I wish there were something more I could do for you, Papa."

"I'll be better in no time. Just lifted a log the wrong way and threw my back out, besides, the bath was just what I needed," Preston lied. "Now sit here and talk with me."

Abigail brought in coffee and biscuits and left them to visit through the afternoon.

# THIRTY-THREE

M illie and Abigail were in the kitchen when they heard voices at the front of the house. Nanny barked her hard bark. Abigail froze. Millie stood stock-still at the window, her mouth agape. "Franklin?" Abigail whispered.

Millie shook her head. "A Lee man," she said. "Got a gun aimed at Damien."

The memories of all those years in slavery tumbled back through Millie's body, and she began to shake uncontrollably.

The young man in a Confederate coat shouted with a heavy southern drawl, "Give me food!" To Damien it felt like a lash hit his back, and he was unable to respond. "Give me food!" the man shouted again, shoving his gun at Damien's face, his hand shaking with fatigue.

"What is it, Abigail?" Preston called, then came from his office to the drawing room.

"An intruder," Abigail whispered loudly.

Preston peered out the window, then slowly lifted his hunting rifle from where it leaned against the wall. He cocked it and pushed the door open with its barrel.

"Mister," Preston said in his careful style, his gun aimed squarely at the Confederate soldier's chest, "I expect it is hard for you to tell a free man when you see one even with the war over and all, but if you intend to stand on top of this earth, you had better drop that pistol and kick it over here. Otherwise, I'd be happy to help you reside under it."

The man froze. Unruly red hair stuck out from under his

cap. His woolly red beard and long oily mustache covered his mouth, his clothes hung on him like dead leaves, and he was in need of several good meals as well as a hot bath and a shave. The expression on the young man's face was not one of anger or hatred, but of a man tired and worn whose legs could hardly hold him up. The young man's arm dropped heavily, and the pistol fell to the ground. Damien kicked it away.

*But a starved animal will attack when it gets hungry,* Preston thought, so he held the gun squarely on the man's face. "Mister, go sit on that stump over there, and don't even think of moving." Millie stood in the doorway her mouth still open wide. "Millie, go fill a bowl with soup and break off some bread. Put it on the ground near him—not too close, though."

"Careful, Millie," Abigail whispered. "He might act like a fool."

While Millie brought the food from the house, Damien picked up the pistol and held it barrel down, his finger on the trigger. He watched closely as his wife put down the soup and bread. "Millie, go back inside and keep the children with you."

"All right then, mister," Preston said. His gun held firmly in his sure hands. "Eat your fill." The man lunged for the food, devoured the soup, and tore into the bread like an animal. "Now then, get on your horse and keep riding." The soldier did not need to be persuaded.

Exhausted, Preston sat heavily in the chair by the door. Millie took his rifle and set it down while Abigail let loose with a tirade of profanity just to ease the tension.

Except for her husband Bradley, Abigail had never seen a man shot and killed and did not want to start now. She hated guns drawn like this. It meant someone could get hurt. She was grateful it was not to be on this day.

# THIRTY-FOUR

F ranklin crossed the street and went into a saloon a few businesses down from the Bradley. He was restless and on edge. The night's drinking had not blotted out Abigail's face as he had hoped, but instead left him feeling more anxious. It didn't seem to matter how much time went by, he still longed for her, particularly in the night when he remembered the warmth of her body and the sound of her breathing. Unfortunately, however, the bitter fruit of his upbringing, always just below the surface, kept him from looking more closely and understanding why she left.

"Whiskey. Leave the bottle," he told the barkeep. He downed several shots and turned to scrutinize the crowd. "Anyone here seen Abigail Wilcox? There's money in it for you if you tell me where she is." The men in the saloon had gotten used to this request, so as usual no one spoke up. Most of the men only turned their heads for a moment before going back to drinks, cards, and conversations. Franklin only half expected a response because he had all but given up hope of finding her, thinking she must have gone to San Francisco.

But the next day he told Sam, "I know she is somewhere near. I can feel it."

"Sir," Sam said, "as I have told you many times before, I don't know where she is. She didn't tell any of us where she planned to go, and as far as I know she has not contacted anyone here. By now she could be in Massachusetts for all we know." Then Sam stepped back so as not to get hit if Franklin took a swing at him.

Franklin walked over to the doctor's office.

The doctor felt pity for him, for any man who had syphilis because he knew how it would play out. "We'll just have to treat each symptom as it comes, Franklin," he told him. "Try to get enough rest. Let your men do the heavy work. Hold off on your drinking and remember to eat."

"Doc, is Abigail sick like me?"

"Well," the doctor sighed, "this disease presents in many ways, so I can't say, but chances are she has some symptoms by now." That Abigail was ill, and that it was his fault, weighed heavily on Franklin. Even so, he couldn't help himself, his resolve to find her hardened once again, and he went to the Bradley to shake the truth out of Marguerite. He just couldn't imagine Abigail had not told anyone where she was heading.

As soon as Marguerite saw him, she pulled the pistol from under the till and laid it on the bar. When he went into the kitchen, Cheng raised his cleaver, and before he even knew what was happening, Sam had again walked him out of the hotel.

"No one knows where she is, Mister Clayborn," Sam told him. "You'd best go home now."

But Franklin never wanted to go home. The only thing he could ever expect to find there was an over-cooked meal and a cold shoulder.

# THIRTY-FIVE

I n late summer a buggy pulled up to Hahl Ranch. By this time, Abigail had been gone from Auburn almost a full year. So she was surprised and happy, but also unnerved to see Marguerite's face at their door. She was slimmer, better dressed, and had a new carriage, and though Abigail had missed her boisterous, good-time charm, she knew Marguerite would only have come to see her if it were about something dire.

"Franklin boasts he will bring you back," Marguerite told her.

"I know he's asked around," Abigail said, "but I had hoped by now he'd given up."

"He just can't let it go. He and his men rode out yesterday heading to Marysville. His men tried to tell him it was the wrong way, but you know Franklin-especially when he has had a few-stubborn as a jackass mule. He'll be angry for having made that mistake. I thought I was the only one who knew where you were, but word has gotten around. Thought you should know."

Abigail had been waiting for this.

"His wife must be pleased," Abigail said. By now no part of her longed for the old life, but it was nostalgic to see a familiar face. When Marguerite turned to go, she said, "Come in. You've come a long way. Please, stay a little longer." After Abigail introduced her to Preston and Millie, they sat close to the fire for a couple of hours and talked about what had happened to each of them.

"Are you still singing in the saloon?"

"Only on occasion, and not Hanna either, her voice no good. We have a new girl." She lifted her arms and shouted like a carnival barker with her still thick French accent, "Straight from the Mississippi Queen, the rage of the river, the songstress who captivated audiences from Baton Rouge to N'Orleans. Put your hands together for our very own queen, Miss Ginger Lee!" They both laughed, as Ginger had never lived in New Orleans. "The men like her."

"Not as much as they liked you, I imagine."

Marguerite shrugged as only the French can do. "She's not French," she said and tossed her still brilliant red hair. She pulled the comb from her tangle of curls and brushed the hair away from her face. "Jiau Ju got married to Nuttermeier. Joseph. Remember him? Came to town to open a saloon but someone ran off with his cash? They have a baby now. Lilah opened the café and it is very popular. Ruthie and Elizabeth live in Sacramento, so Consuela keeps the place clean. Adrienne, well she died from a stomach infection, and Françoise," Marguerite shook her head and sighed, "she took too much opium."

"Sorry to hear about Françoise and Adrienne; they were dear friends." Abigail noted the fine jewelry Marguerite wore, and her green silk dress seemed new. "I can see you are prospering." Even though many of the mines had closed, men still came by buggy, by rail or on foot to dig for treasure, so there were still plenty of customers. "Are you in love, Marguerite? I only ask because you seem so happy."

"*Oui*, the business she thrives," she said proudly. "You were a good teacher." Abigail took a bow. "*Eh...oui,*" she said in the characteristic way Marguerite would tell you something but not disclose more than she wanted.

"Anyone I know?" Abigail asked.

Marguerite hesitated, then said, "Hanna."

"Brinson? I can see the two of you together," Abigail smiled. "She is a wonderful woman. I am very happy for you."

Within the confines of the brothel, two women together would be safe from prying eyes and harm, but out in public it would be a different matter. Most miners were men, but Abigail knew that it was not only for lack of women that there had been gentlemen who danced the woman's part.

"You look well yourself, Abby," Marguerite said.

"I have my good days and my bad days. And–no–I am on my own, but I am glad you think of me as looking well," she laughed. "It's peaceful here and I have my friends on the ranch who are good company."

It was clear to each how much they had both changed. They walked together arm in arm out of the house and stood on the porch and gazed over the land. The flower and vegetable gardens were in full bloom, and the yellowed grass that covered the hills glowed in the sun.

"It is beautiful, Abby. I never would have thought it could be, but this life has done you good. I enjoy running the Bradley, but I do miss you," she said with a wisp of sadness in her voice.

"It's wonderful to see you, too. Wait, before you go, come with me. My dresses. They're all in the barn. Take them back to the girls since I don't need them anymore." They loaded the dresses into Marguerite's buggy, as well as some of Abigail's hats and shoes. Then she gathered a bunch of roses and snapdragons from the garden, which gave her a moment longer with her friend. "For you and Hanna."

Marguerite looked at Abigail for a long while, hugged her then got into the buggy.

"Cheng asked me to give you these. They're some more recipes for your favorite sweets," Marguerite said. "Take care of yourself, Abby."

"I will. Thank you for coming. It's been so very good to see you."

"Be careful. You know how Franklin can be when he drinks." Marguerite snapped her reins.

Abigail kept her eye on the buggy until Marguerite drove past the big oaks at the top of the hill and rounded the bend, for she knew this might be the last time she would see her.

Marguerite's visit had reminded Abigail of the happier moments in her life at the Bradley, but now she was concerned about what to do, since Franklin still wanted to find her.

# THIRTY-SIX

T welve-year old Timothy ran past Abigail and barely stopped to say hello. "You're all wet, Timothy," she said. "Have you been swimming in the rain barrel?"

"I had him," Timothy said with his lower lip pushed out in a pout. "I did, Miss Abigail! A big one! Ran back to haul him in, fell over a rock into the river."

"He get away, your big fish?" she asked from rocker where she continued to knit, hiding a smile.

"No, ma'am. When I got him to shore, Nanny got all tangled in the line and ran. Chased her all over b'fore I catch her. But the fish were chewed up like the dog had played with it. Wouldn't bring that home. Y'all laugh at me," he admitted sheepishly, his shattered pole in his small hand.

"Too bad," Abigail said. "It would have made a nice supper. What happened to your pole?"

"Broke when I fell, ma'am. Pa is goin' to be right mad."

"Timothy, no one ever caught a fish by just looking at it," she told the boy. "And you mustn't worry about your father, son. I am sure he has done the same thing once or twice in his life."

"You ever done something you wish you hadn't, Miss Abigail?"

"More than once, son, more than once. Go on now and put on some dry clothes."

That night Abigail took paper from the persimmon wood box and wrote:

When I fell, it was not over a rock but down a cliff, or so it seemed.

And about Timothy she said, *It takes some people longer than others to find what they do best. Fishing did not seem to be the way for this young man. Even at his young age Timothy is good with numbers and can calculate distances easily. Maybe he'll help build the railroad when he is grown.*

# THIRTY-SEVEN

Julia and the two-year-old twins had arrived in the afternoon, then rode into town to look for material for clothes and sweets for the children. Abigail went into the garden to pull weeds. The day was balmy, and she was happy she had gotten more done than she thought she could. Millie came out with a jar of water and gathered vegetables, then went back in to start the evening meal. Just then Nanny gave her warning bark. Three riders rode down onto the property, dust billowing up as the horses danced around the trunks of the shade trees. Damien came around the barn to see who was there.

"Good girl, come here, Nanny," Damien said. Nanny stood between Damien and the men. "Can I help you, gentlemen?"

"Where is she?" a man snapped.

Abigail's heart stopped when she heard his voice.

"Who you looking for?" Damien asked, though he knew who the man was.

When Franklin saw Abigail, he ran toward her like a rabid dog ready to bite. Seeing him coming for her brought a torrential rain of memories–their screaming arguments, his constant belittlement, and the loss of her child. Whatever love she might have had for him had finally disappeared.

"Darling, there you are," he said tapping his horsewhip against his leg. "Come here, honey, let me see your pretty face." He was thinner and his skin was pasty white, not his usual ruddy tan.

"What the hell are you doing here?" Abigail said, holding the garden hoe across her chest. "Go away."

"Honey, you can't mean that?" he said, winded from the exertion.

"What do you mean riding in here like you own the place? You've got your nerve. What do you want?"

"Abby, honey, after all our years together, why did you leave?"

"You know perfectly well why I left you, and I am certain you found out how I got here. Did you beat it out of Marguerite?"

"Marguerite?" He shifted from one foot to another. "Come-come on now, honey, you–you know I love you."

"Well, I do not love you, Franklin. Take your men and go back to Auburn. I don't ever want to see you again. Do you hear me? Go!"

Damien scanned Abigail's face, then Franklin's, not sure what he should do. Nanny took her fighting stance and growled.

"How did you find this ranch in the first place?" Franklin tapped his leg again with his whip. "It's in the middle of nowhere. You're no farmer, and besides, you barely know one end of a steer from another. Seriously, you can't possibly like living here."

"I am fine where I am," Abigail said in a measured tone. "Franklin, leave me alone."

"Now Abigail, come back with me. You belong with me in Auburn!" he bellowed, his anger rising.

"Calm down, Franklin." Abigail tried to step away, but Franklin lunged for her. Damien stepped between them, and Franklin's whip flew up across his cheek. Damien, with eyes bulged and nostrils flared, a man who had been whipped too many times in his life, went for Franklin. He seized him by the collar, pulled him away from Abigail, then drove his fist straight into Franklin's jaw. Franklin pulled his gun, but Damien tore it from his hand before he could shoot. But by this time, Franklin's men had their guns drawn, barrels pointed at Damien.

"That's enough!" Abigail roared in a tone she had never heard come from her own mouth.

Suddenly the front door flew open, and Millie swung up the heavy shotgun that was as tall as she was, and she pointed it straight at Franklin. "You best leave here now, Mister Clayborn."

"Marysville, eh?" Franklin snarled.

Abigail felt more confident with her friends by her side, and for the first time was not afraid of anything, not of Franklin, not even of death. "I don't care what you want," she said. "I am not yours anymore. Do you understand? Go back to your wife."

He put one hand to his swollen jaw and dusted himself off with the other. "You'll come crawling back. You will," he mumbled. "Come on," he barked to his men, then mounted his horse.

Franklin galloped up the road and stopped at the top of the rise. Just then Julia and the children rode past in their buggy. He shot a look at Abigail, then watched as Julia rode down the hill. He turned his horse and disappeared over the ridge.

"You can put the gun down now, Millie." Abigail put her hand on Millie's trembling shoulder.

Millie handed her the gun, then ran into the house to get a wet cloth and ointment for Damien's bloody face. "Gonna be a scar, honey."

"No matter. Was worth it."" Damien said and finally opened his clenched fist.

Preston called from his bedroom, "Everyone all right?"

"We're all fine now, Preston," Abigail said. "Julia and the

boys have returned. I'll be in in a minute."

Abigail began to breathe heavily and sobbed from the tension.

"Sit down, Abigail. Catch your breath," Damien said.

There was no way that Franklin could ever understand why living at Hahl Ranch was like being in heaven.

# THIRTY-EIGHT

M illie fixed a hearty breakfast of scrambled eggs, sausage, and fried cinnamon apples. Abigail made coffee, and Preston sat by the fire to read Mary Shelley's Frankenstein. Damien and the boys would be in soon from morning chores. A winter rain mixed with snow had fallen all night, let up for a moment, then started again at daybreak and pounded harder than ever. There was a knock on the door. Abigail stirred the fire, while Millie and Nanny went to see who was there.

"What the–Mr. Preston!" Millie called, disturbed. Nanny barked but wagged her tail.

In the doorway stood a bedraggled young man who stared at the ground, hat in hand, drenched to the bone. His boots were nearly worn out, and his clothes the same. "Sorry to bother you, sir," he said.

"No gun this time?" Preston said as he recognized the redheaded Confederate soldier who in the fall had demanded food at gunpoint.

"No, sir," the young man said quietly while fingering the brim of his soaked hat.

"What do you want, then?" Abigail barked.

Unsure what to say, he shuffled his feet. "If I could work for food and lodging, ma'am, sir," he said and steadied himself. The rain poured even harder, muffling his answers. "I worked on my father's farm before the war. I'm real good with horses. Can do 'most anything," he said, his southern drawl as thick as the rain-clouds in the sky.

Millie edged toward the shotgun kept by the door, and Abigail held onto the fire poker, neither one sure if this man really wanted to work or had come to cause more mischief.

"What's your name, soldier?" Preston asked. "And how old are you?"

"Edward, Edward James Mill-ar, from Pea Ridge, Arkansas, sir…Twenty-three…sir."

The young man was so thin and hungry he could hardly stand. To Abigail he looked like some of the men from the mines that had come into the Bradley, exhausted and starved. "How long did you fight in the war?" she asked.

"Two years, ma'am," he said.

"It's a long way to Pea Ridge, Arkansas, Mr. Millar, and the war has been over several years now," Preston said.

"When I left Brownsville, Texas, I wanted to get as far away from the war as I could. Seen enough killing for any man."

"We still have your gun," Preston reminded him. "It was empty."

"I know, sir. I apologize," Millar blurted. "That's not my way normally. I was just so hungry I didn't know what to do."

"But you came back," Preston said.

"Others have not been so generous, and I am hoping you might hire me."

"I don't remember being generous," Abigail shot back.

"Yes, ma'am…I mean, no, ma'am. But you did give me food and others did not." Edward fingered the brim of his hat. Rainwater dripped off his clothes onto the floor, soaking the rug.

Abigail could read a man after working the hotel for so many years. To her this fellow did not look like someone who meant to cause harm.

Just then Damien's big frame filled the doorway, and when he saw who was in the entry he stood in front of Millie.

"Have you had time to fix those fences in the far pasture, Damien?" Preston queried. Abigail knew he had not. "You think this boy could handle that job?"

Damien squinted, then nodded. "Maybe," he said.

"Millie," Preston said, "give Mr. Millar some cheese and a hunk of bread." Meanwhile Damien quickly ate some of the breakfast that was on the table.

Preston told Edward James Millar from Pea Ridge, Arkansas that, "Mr. Adams will tell you where to work and when to stop. And he'll take a look at what you have done to see how good it is." Damien, who appreciated the irony of the situation, tried not to smile. "Come back here for your supper when you hear the bell."

"Thank you, sir," Edward said and tipped his hat. He opened the door and followed Damien out into the rain.

Later he told them, "I kept thinking all the way here it was gonna be easy money. Rumor in the south was that gold lined the streambeds, and all you needed were big pockets to hold all you could put in 'em. But the closer I got to California the more truth sifted through the rumor. I tried it for a couple of months, but it turned out to be more bending over than picking up." Like so many, he barely found enough gold to buy food, let alone pay for a roof over his head.

Edward Millar's journey to Hahl Ranch had been a test of his inner and outer strength. After he deserted his Confederate unit at Brownsville, Texas, and he saw there was nothing left of his hometown to go back to, he began the long and exhausting trip to northern California by foot with another Confederate soldier from Arkansas. There were long scorching hot days on the road with bandits stealing their food, Indians his horse, and a mudslide that sheared off the mountain and nearly took him and his companion with it.

Edward liked the company but found that almost every morning the man woke from nightmares of cannon fire and screams of wounded soldiers, his clothes sweated through and rank from the fear that filled his body. By the time they reached the southern part of the state, both were rail thin. Edward thought he would never get enough food or rest, but he was determined to go where he thought he might make his fortune. They parted company at the turn-off for San Francisco with a goodbye that was hearty if unsentimental. Edward wished he could have caught a stagecoach north, but his pockets were as empty as his stomach.

# THIRTY-NINE

## Auburn

B ertie unpacked shirts, pants, hats, and the like at the back of the store. It was just before closing when she heard Mr. Sawyer call to her. A man had come in who needed new clothes and Sawyer was busy with another customer. When she pushed open the curtain, she could not believe her eyes. "Edward Millar!" Bertie exclaimed.

"Oh, my Lord, Bertie! Mrs. Wilcox told me you worked here. I just thought it couldn't be true." Edward was ecstatic to see the girl he loved. "I thought you must be–"

"Dead?" Bertie said.

"Well...yes," Edward replied.

"And I can't believe it! You are alive and well."

"A few bullets came my way. Thankfully nothing I couldn't dodge." He took a handful of his thick red hair and tied it back with a leather strap. They went for supper at a nearby cafe and talked till the wee hours of the morning.

But the next day when Reggie, the ex-slave boy Bertie had adopted, saw Edward in his Confederate coat, the boy ran out of the store as fast as he could. Bertie didn't see him for weeks. But late one evening there was a knock on her door, and there stood the young boy, hungry and cold, soaked through by the winter rain. She wrapped a blanket around his small shoulders and brought him inside. After supper, he climbed onto the pallet and went right to sleep. They talked as he ate his breakfast in the morning.

"I promise you," Bertie assured him, "no one will take you back; besides, the war's over. There are no more slaves. Edward's a good man. I've known him for years. Yes, he was a Confederate soldier," she told him, "but he had to join or be thrown in jail."

"Miss Marguerite say all Confederate men is mean and ignorant," Reggie countered.

"I know Miss Marguerite does have strong opinions," Bertie said. "But you'll like him. I know you will if you give him a chance."

Bertie arranged for Reggie to meet Edward face-to-face. Neither was sure it would go well. The boy, skittish as a cat, hid behind Bertie's skirt.

"You have slaves, Mister?" Reggie shot out at Edward.

"No," he said. "We had a small farm on the edge of town, raised chickens and vegetables."

"But you was a Lee Man! Your coat!" Reggie's jaw jutted out in defiance.

The remnant of a Confederate jacket was the only coat Edward owned. "I was taken," Edward explained. "To catch us off guard, they come in the middle of the night–four armed men on horseback. Killed my ma and pa and took all our livestock. Next thing I know I am wearing this coat and holding a Confederate rifle. I shot my gun, but never tried to hit anybody," he said. "Was another two years before I had opportunity to get away."

The boy's history was also painful. He told Edward that the Overseer had sent a posse to follow after his two brothers as they tried to escape and shot them while they ran through the woods. The man hanged Reggie's mother because she'd helped her two sons. That night Reggie dug his way under a fence, and raced to freedom running for miles through riverbeds, jumping onto a wagon filled with cattle bones, and rubbing the cow blood all over his skin to mask his scent from the dogs. Then all the way across the Texas Panhandle and north to Auburn, the eight year old traveled as cook's helper on cattle drives.

When they finished he and Edward sat in silence for a moment. "They have some fine sweets at the counter. Would you like a piece?"

"Yes, sir. Like them mint drops," Reggie said.

"Me, too." And they both went to find the candy. From then on Reggie and Edward could not be pried apart.

# FORTY

## 1871

"Abigail, you step aside now, don't want to burn you." Millie got the chocolate cake from the oven, a special dessert to celebrate the birth of Julia's third child, Helena, and set it on the rack, its sweet aroma filling the kitchen.

Preston opened up his pocket watch. "Hmmm. It's stopped. What time is it now?" Just then the grandfather clock in the hall began to chime.

"Precisely three," Abigail laughed.

"Julia promised me they would be here by suppertime," Preston said.

"And we be ready for 'em when they come," Millie told him. "Now don't you worry yourself, Mister Preston. Stagecoach coming any minute now. Daniel'll go for 'em."

Millie, Preston, and Abigail went out onto the front porch to sit for a while. Bertie Hetch, who was visiting from Auburn, took Edward's hand as they walked from the barn across the yard. Bertie went to the chicken coop, and Edward headed toward the paddock. "They be as tight as a vine to a fence," Millie smiled. "He get along fine with her young charge, too. What do y'all think?"

Preston answered with a wry smile, "I think we might have a wedding soon."

# FORTY-ONE

Julia, Bernard and the twins, and the families on Hahl Ranch returned from the Placerville Methodist Church and Helena's baptism to have coffee and dessert and reminisce about the day. They sat at a table set up under the oak trees in front of the big house. A gentle wind blew the tablecloth. Petals from blossoms of a nearby peach tree sprinkled over the table and the surrounding grass.

"She didn't fuss too much," Julia commented.

"A little angel, wasn't she?" Bernard said.

"Well, I am ready for a nap," Preston put his cup down and rose unsteadily. Millie cleared the dishes while Damien walked with Preston to the house. The twins and Letty Ann played on the rope swing in the field, while Julia and Bernard sat with Abigail at the table. Helena began to whimper.

"Let me take her," Abigail said. She lifted the child into her arms. With her little head dropped against Abigail's shoulder, she fell right to sleep.

"My father doesn't seem like himself," Julia said. "He's thin and pale and seems so tired all the time. Is he all right?"

"Has he seen a doctor?" Bernard asked. "I swear he has lost more weight since we saw him just a few weeks ago."

"He worries about the ranch," Abigail said, without divulging the whole truth. "Though truly he needn't. We make good money now. I do encourage him to rest, but he won't take my suggestion. As you already know, I'm sure, he can be stubborn." Abigail thought, *Stubborn as a bloody fool.* It was all she could do not to speak of his ill health, but she had given Preston her word.

"Can be a mule, for sure," Julia concurred. "You would tell me, wouldn't you, Abigail, if there were something to worry about?"

"Miss Julia!" Millie called from within the house. "The bottle's warm."

"Coming!" Julia called back and took the baby.

Abigail walked with Bernard arm in arm toward the house. Her legs were heavy as logs. She was out of breath.

"You seem a bit peaked yourself, Abigail," Bernard said. "Are you unwell?"

"Just a little tired. I've had a few bad nights. Need a good night's sleep, that's all."

"You have been 'a little tired' often lately. Maybe you should see the doctor yourself?" he suggested.

They continued to walk in silence as Abigail worked out what to say. Bernard was a man who could see the truth in front of him when others could not. But she lied.

"Doc gave me an iron tonic to brighten my spirits," she said.

"Let's hope that does the trick. My wife has grown extremely fond of you, Abigail. We all have." He hugged her arm tighter. "We don't want anything to happen to you."

"Thank you for saying so. I am rather fond of all of you, too." she said, feeling as if she were naked.

Bernard knew Abigail was not telling him the whole truth but he did not press her, and they walked back to the house together in silence.

# FORTY-TWO

Franklin's horse knew the way to Hahl Ranch, and once they came to the bend in the gorge, knew to stop under the tree at the top of the hill above the property. Sometimes Franklin would wait there for a good hour in hopes of just a glance of Abigail.

With so much time alone he had begun to look at his life, and he didn't like what he saw. He was only beginning to understand what it meant for him that his mother had been as distant as his father was mean, and that after his brother Joe died he shut himself off from everyone. But with Abigail he'd been able to feel a connection with another human being. A longing for that closeness pulled at him hard. He knew she had felt the same, but he still didn't understand why she had cut him out of her life.

When he was sober he could leave the ranch without much effort, but once he had been drinking he could barely tear himself away.

# FORTY-THREE

"It's taken a while, but the war's finally fallen off him, hasn't it?" Abigail remarked. "Doesn't even seem like the same fella, does he?"

"Who?" Millie asked, her attention coming to focus late.

"Edward," Abigail said.

The ladies were sitting on the porch for their afternoon ritual when Edward came to the bottom steps. "Good afternoon, ma'am. Miss Millie. Damien said you wanted to see me?"

Letty Ann, now twelve, jumped onto the landing and ran to Abigail with glee. "Edward's getting married!" she sang.

He was no longer the starving and exhausted ex-soldier who had barged onto the property, who looked at the ground while he talked, and shuffled his feet out of nervousness. Edward Millar was now a self-assured and steady man. He had become a strapping fella and a good worker. He was tall, handsome, and clean-shaven. His shoulder-length red hair is held away from his face by the leather tie. Even the Adams family saw the goodness in him and had settled into an easy relationship.

Edward had helped Damien with many of the repairs on the ranch. They rebuilt part of the barn that had rotted and added a couple of bedrooms onto Millie and Damien's house for Letty Ann and the boys. Along with sharing the daily chores on the ranch, he fixed the kitchen roof and to everyone's delight hung a swing on the front porch. He was gentle and kind, good with cattle and uncommonly comfortable with the horses. He did whatever was asked of him without hesitation. Today, he grinned with irrepressible joy.

"Afternoon, Edward," Abigail said. "Come up here for a moment. I want to speak with you about something." He jumped up the steps, full of vigor. "So as Letty Ann tells us you plan to get married?"

"Yes, ma'am! Once Bertie and I are hitched, we're gonna have a house full of children!" he grinned, hardly able to contain his happiness.

"Sounds delightful, Edward," she smiled. "Mr. Hahl is awake from his nap and would like to speak with you."

"Ma'am?" Edward said, slightly concerned. He called out to Reggie, who was in the yard pushing Daniel and Timothy on the rope swing, "I'll be right there, son." Reggie waved. "The boy and I are going into town later to buy some tins for baking."

Preston sat in his easy chair in front of the fire reading.

"Big surprise, Preston," Abigail told him with a wink. "Edward's getting married."

"That so?" Preston smiled and set his book on his lap.

"Yes, sir," Edward said. "I asked Bertie last night!"

"The boy seems all right with it?" Preston asked.

"Yes," he smiled. "He's the one who pushed me to ask her. I would have done so anyway, of course, but I was glad to know he was in favor of it."

"Congratulations then." Preston shook Edward's hand. "Do you have a date in mind?"

"Not yet. Bertie's going to the church this afternoon to see when we can have the ceremony."

"I expect you'll need a place to live," Preston mused. Then gazed at Abigail. Edward had been living in the bunkhouse with the rest of the cowboys.

"Bertie went into town yesterday. Didn't find nothing though. You know how women are about wanting everything to be just so."

"Edward..." Preston hesitated in order to savor the moment. "Abigail and I have talked this over, and we think..." He stopped to light a pipe. "We think we could find a spot to build a house for you here on the ranch. Down the hill on the other side of the pasture near the little creek, under the grove of bull pines might be a nice place for it, that is if you and Bertie and her boy would like to live on the ranch?"

"Really, sir? Here? Yes, sir! Yes, ma'am! Bertie and I would be proud to live here on the land with y'all. I'll send her a telegram." He flew through the door and called back, "Thank you. Thank you!" and disappeared down the road at a full run.

"We'll want to get the house started as soon as possible, will we not?" Preston smiled at Abigail. "Best to get it done by the end of the summer before fall rain starts."

Damien and Millie went to make arrangements with the neighbors; a week from Saturday there would be a house-raising.

*Most people had gotten used to the idea of a madam and some ex-slaves living on Hahl Ranch. We were not asked to tea or anything, but when help was needed, the neighbors pitched in. And besides they all like Edward Millar and his soon-to-be-wife, Beatrice Elizabeth Hetch.*

With the memory of Franklin's drunken proposal, Abigail's pen became heavy in her hand. She secured the writings in the persimmon wood box, put her pen back in the jar, and called it a night.

# FORTY-FOUR

The morning's cool temperature was good for the hard work to come. Friends, neighbors, and the ranch wranglers were already at the site with nails, hammers, saws, and boards for the framing of Edward and Bertie's new home.

Edward and Damien lifted the first of the three heavy tables from the barn onto the rig, stacked the others on top, and placed the chairs all around.

"All right boys, up you go and hang on," Edward said. "Keep your hands on those chairs so they don't fall off." Timothy and Daniel climbed up onto the end of the wagon.

"Edward," Timothy exclaimed, "we's making you a house!"

"I feel so lucky." He clucked, the mare whinnied and took off. "Slow up there, Rita," he said tightening the reins. "We want to get there in one piece."

While Edward, Bertie, Millie, and the boys set up tables under the pines near where Edward had dug the foundation for his new home, Damien went to get Preston and Abigail.

"Are you ready, Mr. Preston?" he called.

"Grabbing my hat just now." Preston limped to the door, cane in hand. "How do I look?"

"Fine, sir," Damien grinned. "Fit for a party."

"I wish I could still swing a hammer, but I'm afraid enjoying the company and encouraging the men as they go will have to suffice. Reggie, you coming with us?" he called back into the kitchen.

"No, sir. Bread's not ready," Reggie responded.

Damien helped Preston into the wagon. "All right, son, see you there," Preston called.

"Miss Julia and the family already waiting for you down the hill." Damien called back into the house, "How 'bout you, Miss Abigail? Ready to come with us?"

"Be right there," Abigail grabbed her shawl.

"This will be the third wedding we've had on the ranch since I've lived here," Preston remembered. "Helen and I had our reception in front of the house. Julia and Bernard's nuptial party was held here, too. It was such a hot day the flowers wilted. Helen had been in such a twitter to get ready for it, I thought she might expire from the excitement."

Preston had been quite forgetful of late so Abigail reminded him, "You do know we are just to frame their house today."

"Yes...yes, I know," Preston said, more animated than he had been in weeks.

Ten families whose children attended the school, plus the ranch's five wranglers and their wives or girlfriends, all came together on a sunny morning in August. Hammers pounded nails, saws ripped through wood, and men grunted under the weight of heavy planks. While the men worked, the children played in the stream, picked wildflowers and caught bugs, and the ladies set out the food.

The guests brought hot dishes, which Millie arranged on a table with a vase of flowers, and desserts were put on another. Marge Edgewood was the first to arrive with fried chicken.

"It's a wonder, Millie, seeing a house shoot up from the ground." Marge said. "Like a plant growing out of the earth in spring, all of a sudden it appears. It's so thrilling!" Where Millie came from, the enslaved did that work.

Maryanne Ridgeway brought her heavy iron pot of potato Croquettes. Mrs. Semple brought her favorite pork-apple and onion-smothered, along with cornbread dumplings.

Reggie brought down his bread. Millie had made blackberry pies that made your mouth water, and of course, everyone loved her pot of beans with ham. There was lemonade for the children, with hard apple cider and jugs of beer for the rest.

At sundown all hammers were put aside, and there it stood, the miracle of a new house. It needed plenty of work on the inside, but the frame was up.

Preston knocked his glass with a spoon. "It's my honor and pleasure to lift a glass to you, Edward and Bertie. May you live long and happily inside your new home."

After supper Bernard called to the fiddlers, "Boys, how about a jig for the betrothed couple!" Men, women, boys and girls all danced on the dry, summer grass.

Edward would work every free moment he had during the next month to be able to finish the inside before they were married.

When the day arrived, the ranch was humming with the excitement of the nuptials.

"Millie," Abigail called, "can you brush Mr. Preston's jacket while I buff his boots?"

"Surely," Millie said. "Letty Ann, run get the clothes brush." The girl ran back from the mudroom off the back of the kitchen. "Honey-girl, help Miss Abigail with Mr. Preston's boots. Boys! Boys!" Millie shouted. Daniel, Timothy, and Reggie stood in front of her for inspection. "Reggie, you're not ready?"

"Going to change after I put something over the cake like you said—to keep off them dang flies."

"Don't swear, young man. Use your vocabulary," Abigail reprimanded, laughing inwardly at how easily she had succumbed to the use of foul language while at the Bradley.

"Those irritating flies," he said.

"Much better. I understand completely your desire to dang them, however," she said and shooed them with her handkerchief.

Millie and Reggie had created the wedding cake, a molasses confection with a honey and sour cream icing. On the top, in the center of a circle of white and pink rosebuds, sat the two carved doves Damien had whittled for the occasion.

Abigail told them, "You and Reggie have done a beautiful job."

"Looks right pretty don't it?" Millie smiled. "Hurry now, Reggie. Change your clothes. We off to church in no time. 'Member to brush your shoes," she called.

"Yes, ma'am." Reggie ran over to the Adams' house where he was to change.

Bertie was in Julia's room. Abigail put the last pin in Bertie's hair, then Bertie slipped on the bridal gown she designed. She had picked out white silk for her dress and had just finished sewing it with help from Millie and Abigail. It had lace at the cuffs and the collar, and rosettes down the front of the jacket.

"Let me put this on your wrist," Abigail said. Bertie's eyes widened as she slipped onto Bertie's arm a gold bracelet, the one with the amethyst stones that Franklin had given her. "You keep this to remember the day."

After Millie tied Bertie into the dress, she tucked a lace handkerchief into the sleeve. "If you like me, honey, you gonna need this b'fore the day over." Bertie gave Millie a hug.

Julia and Preston knocked on the door. "My wife wore this on our wedding day," he said. "Something borrowed, something blue. This sort of covers it, I think," and he latched a delicate aquamarine necklace around Bertie's neck.

"This came from England," Julia said and unwrapped her gift, a silver pin topped in gold and pearls. "I thought it might be just the thing for your dress."

"They are just beautiful!" Bertie gushed.

The Adams family gathered in the parlor. With Bertie's help, Millie had made a green dress for Letty Ann, blue gingham shirts for Damien and her boys, and a white shirt for Reggie. Millie fluffed the skirt of her new yellow dress, then put spit on her hand and wiped her temples to tame the frizz. Abigail's dress was silk, a dark peach, and new for the occasion.

"How do I look, husband?" Millie asked.

"Like a sunflower lighting up the garden," Damien told her.

"What a day!" Preston said.

"Yes, sir, quite a wonderful day," Damien agreed. "Shall I help you into the wagon?"

"Not quite yet," Preston said. "Damien, you look right handsome yourself, but there's something missing."

"Sir?" Damien inspected his clothes.

"You need this." Preston pulled out a pocket watch from his jacket. "As you know, my father collected pocket watches from all over. The one I carry every day was his. I thought you might like to have this one. Come here so I can fit it to your vest."

"My own watch," Damien said. "I never had one. Thank you kindly, sir." Damien put his hand to his vest pocket, pulled out the gift, and opened it to check the time. There was an inscription on the inside, *Freiheit*. "What do it mean, Mr. Preston?"

"It's German. The watch was my grandfather's. It means freedom, Damien."

Damien slid it back into his pocket and smiled. From then on he called it his "freedom watch".

When they all came together for the ceremony at the Placerville Methodist Church, Bertie was radiant and

Edward striking in his clean white shirt and newly polished boots. The two were as happy as any pair has ever been. The preacher prayed, they sang hymns, and Bertie and Edward were united in marriage. But during the service Abigail got lost in the memory of her own wedding to Bradley, a man she had known for only six weeks:

*"Are you nervous, honey?" Bradley said. He took her shaking hand and led her toward the front of the small church.*

*"Oh, darling," was all she could say.*

*Ruth and Ezra Ledler, the owners of the Migrant Saloon where Bradley gambled, stood as their only witnesses. Ruth had made her a bouquet of wildflowers, and Ezra held the rings.*

*Even though Bradley's steady eyes calmed her, and she knew vows had been exchanged, she couldn't remember if she said them. Her new husband kissed her with joyous passion.*

The applause and cheers that erupted when Edward kissed his bride brought Abigail back.

After the ceremony everyone was invited to the ranch to celebrate. They sat in front of Edward and Bertie's new house, and ate roast beef, baked squash, potatoes, and Reggie's bread. They drank whiskey, lemonade, and mulled apple cider. While fiddlers played the guests danced, and there was gaiety all around.

Franklin stood at the top of the knoll near the entrance to the ranch and watched as the joy bubble up from the field below. He could see Abigail in her peach dress. He wanted to ride in because a deep longing to be a part of Abigail's life again pulled at him, but he held that desire in check. Instead, he took a slug of whiskey from the bottle in his saddlebag and struck a match for a cigar.

Damien caught sight of him standing on the top of the hill, and the scar on his face stung for a moment. "Do you think he come to cause trouble?" Damien asked Preston.

"Let's hope not," Preston said. "Keep an eye on him."

"Come on, Reggie." Timothy pulled at the boy's arm. "They gonna cut your cake."

Edward took the knife and with Bertie's hand on top of his, cut a small piece and fed it to his new wife. She fed some to her husband, and all cheered.

"They're so happy," Abigail said as she and Julia walked in the evening air.

"So sweet together," Julia answered. "I'm reminded of our own wedding. Bernard was nervous, afraid he would drop the ring, and I must admit between the heat and my nerves I felt a bit faint myself."

"I'll bet you were beautiful," Abigail said. "I would have liked to see you get married."

"It would have been good to have you there, Abigail." Julia squeezed her arm affectionately.

A pink-orange blush filled the darkening sky. Bertie cupped Reggie's young face in her hands. "Your cake was delicious." The boy smiled a toothy grin. "You have what you need for tonight?"

"Yes, ma'am," he nodded.

"You mind Millie now. We'll see you for breakfast in the morning. I love you." She hugged him. He smiled and ran off to join the other children.

Soon candles were passed around, and the guests formed two lines. Preston lit Abigail's taper with his, she in turn lit Julia's, Julia Damien's, till all candles were aglow. Edward and Bertie, hand in hand, walked slowly toward the door of their new home. He lifted his bride into his arms, walked over the threshold, and they began their life together.

When Franklin saw the light of the candles, as hard as it was for him to leave, he turned his horse to the road and away from Abigail. The pull to Hahl Ranch was almost as strong as his need for whiskey.

# FORTY-FIVE

## 1872

Abigail opened the persimmon wood box, took out some fresh paper and inked her pen:

*I relish the times when Julia and her children come to visit. It does make me wonder what kind of mother I might have been had I not lived at the Bradley. I grew up on a ranch and had fun with my friend Maria Marsalas and her two brothers, but what would it have been like with a mother and father who adored their children? Through Julia, Bernard, and the Adamses I can see how much I missed.*

*Marisita brushed my hair and got me dressed in the morning. At supper, I ate alone in the kitchen while Marisita cooked. When my mother and father were there father would be drunk and mother would do nothing to hide her annoyance with him. Even now it gives me a stomachache to think about it.*

*It never ever occurred to me this simple life could satisfy me as it does—a meal with my friends, to read to Preston in front of the fire, or sit on the porch with Millie and old Nanny. Everything at the Bradley needed my attention at all times, particularly Franklin. There was no opportunity to stop, to relax, and enjoy.*

# FORTY-SIX

Millie called into to the kitchen, "Boys! Stop snitching dessert!" Then to Abigail, "They eating my cookies." Timothy and Daniel ran out of the front door past the ladies. "Boys, almost time for supper. Put them chickens away. Tell Letty Ann wash her hands." Millie picked up the broom and quickly swept the porch.

Damien came in from the fields and ducked into their house to change into a fresh shirt and pants. "Be right there, darling. Evening, Miss Abigail."

"I know it's a southern thing," Abigail told them, "but it sounds like I'm your mistress when you call me 'Miss' Abigail. Call me Abigail or even Abby–everyone else does."

"Abigail. Abby," Millie said but strained to leave off the habitual miss.

"How did you do with the downed fence? Do we need more wire?"

"Should hold fine now, ma'am," Damien said. "We need a bag of nails though." He helped her up the steps and into the house for supper. "By the way, Clayborn been sniffing around again. Town folks saying he wants to buy property near Placerville."

Abigail's stomach clenched. "Did they say where?"

"No. But he take over bank loans, what I heard."

"Oh, Christ, what is that son of a bitch up to now?"

"You didn't eat your breakfast this morning," Millie said.

"You feeling all right?"

"Wasn't hungry." Abigail shifted uncomfortably in her reading chair.

"Now this something I want to say to you. It pushing at me so hard if I not say this to you out loud, I meet my maker sooner than I want." She took a breath. "Abigail, I seen all kinds of things on the plantation, things passed around, if you know what I's saying. Things a man can give to a woman, sickness and all."

"What do you want to say, Millie?" Abigail was annoyed at being confronted with the truth.

"Just saying–don't keep what happening all to yourself. A terrible thing, syphilis. So you say what you need, and I do it. You hear me?"

"I don't know what you are referring to," Abigail huffed and turned her head.

"You do know what I refer to. I seen those sores you cover with your scarf. I just say, you ask me, and I do it."

# FORTY-SEVEN

Abigail came into the drawing room to find Preston staring into the flames, his face drained of color. In his hand was a letter from the bank.

"What is it, Preston?" Abigail asked. "Something wrong?" Just under the letterhead was stamped *"Foreclosure"*, dated *November 1, 1872.*

"What is this about?" Abigail said. "Foreclosure-Preston?"

"When Diefman and his men took my cattle they-they took every cent I had. After he took off with my money, the bank let me take out a mortgage on the ranch to help us get by. I restocked the cattle and started to build a herd again, but there were some rough winters, some of the cattle died and some were stolen. It was all I could do to pay men to gather what cows we had." He stopped and stared into the fire. "My herd dwindled to the few I had when you came."

The ranch was Preston's, so she had not inquired about its solvency, and so had not been unaware of the dire straits it was in.

"But we make good money now. How can this be?" she asked.

"The bank is calling in the loan," Preston said. "It seems there is someone who wants to buy the ranch and is willing to pay well over what it's worth. Harold says the bank will hold off if I can come up with the money by the fifth and this is the first."

"What can I do?" Abigail said. "You know I do have resources and could help you pay off the loan."

"No, no. Let me think on it a while. I am sure I can come up with a suitable solution." He slumped back into his chair, his eyes intent on the flames that popped and crackled in the fireplace.

Preston took a bad turn and was too ill to even talk about the foreclosure. When he was able to give it his attention they had lost four days. He was in bed when he called Abigail to his room.

"Sit down, please," Preston said slowly, his voice weak.

Abigail slid the chair close to his gaunt face, his body so frail now it was as if there was nothing on the bed but clothes.

"Doc tells me I...I don't have long to live." Abigail began to speak, but he lifted his hand to stop her. "He cannot say how long, so I thought we had better get this foreclosure business taken care of right away. You know, of course, I wanted to leave the ranch to my daughter, but I...I certainly don't want to lose it to the bank before I die."

"But Preston–"

He raised his hand again. "At the same time I want to be sure you and the families here are taken care of."

"You're not responsible for us, Preston."

"True, but I want to be. Without all of you the ranch would have been lost long before this." He shivered and pulled his covers higher onto his chest. "Now hear me out. But first bring me some paper and a pen...please." He let his head fall heavily onto the pillow.

Abigail had no idea what he was going to say, but his mood had lightened, and he had a twinkle in his eye.

"I have thought this through," Preston said carefully. "It seems I can leave something to my daughter, pay off the loan, and take care of you all as well." He took a labored breath and began again, "What I will do, if you agree to it, Abigail, is to sell you the ranch at a fair market price. The money from the sale will pay back the bank and will, with what is left, give my daughter a financial inheritance at my death. Not what I have wanted, but the loan will be paid off, and the ranch will not be lost." He looked up at the painting of his wife above the fireplace and took a labored breath. "Hahl Ranch will then be yours. The families can stay on here if you choose." He looked at Abigail for the first time. "How does that sound?"

"What about Bernard and Julia? Certainly they could help you with the loan?" Abigail exclaimed. "You wanted to leave the ranch to her?"

"I don't want Julia to know–not just yet." His humiliation at his circumstances was certainly understandable to Abigail. Through the years, she had seen that look on many a miner who had hoped for riches but was forced to beg for food. "Julia and Bernard live on a sizable ranch," he said, "with a beautiful home that more than meets their needs. And most likely she would sell this property rather than live on it."

Abigail tried to talk him out of it, but he was steadfast in his decision. When he turned his face away, she knew not to press the issue any longer.

She had the money to buy the ranch plus much more, but it was the thought of Preston dying that overwhelmed her. She had gotten used to his gentleness and kind bearing; caring for him had become a joy for everyone on Hahl Ranch.

"Preston, I..." she stammered. "That would be perfect."

"Good. I know I have waited till the last minute. Now we only have until the bank's closing today before they call in the loan, so you'll need to leave right away. Give this to Harold. He'll get the papers ready for you." He finished his letter and put it in an envelope. "It'll put my mind at ease."

It was a little before four o'clock by the time she arrived into town. The bank vault was secured, and the guard had already locked the front door. She pleaded with him to let her in, but he refused. She went around to the side of the building where she knew Harold Brockweiller's office was and looked in the window. She rapped on it and called out for him to let her come in. Harold was putting on his coat, ready to leave. He looked up at the clock, which read two minutes to four. Normally, he would not have acquiesced, but he let her in.

"You have certainly waited till the last minute, Abby." He put his hat on his desk. "I was afraid Preston would lose his ranch. You have cut it very close."

She signed the papers and handed over the payment. "Harold if you don't mind telling me, who is the prospective buyer?" She could feel her heart pounding against her chest.

"Sorry, Abby. I am not allowed to share that information."

"Not allowed or won't?"

"We're done with our business, aren't we? You have control of the ranch, and the bank won't take it over. " Harold walked her out of his office.

Back at the ranch she told Preston, "It's done."

He was much relieved, but in the next few days while she looked over the ranch's financial records, pulled weeds in the garden, sewed on buttons, drew sketches of the fields, and a myriad of other chores, Abigail was nagged with curiosity. She wanted to know who had tried to take over the ranch. Even Millie told her she should let it rest, but she couldn't. She headed back to the bank and by the time she arrived, had worked herself up into a fury. She pushed past Harold's secretary and opened his door.

"We'll go over this later," he said to the teller, who quickly gathered his papers and exited the room.

"Now, Harold, you know you have all my money in your bank and we both know it's practically holding it together. So I want to know right now what slithering varmint tried to take our home."

"Now Abby, calm down. I promised the buyer I would not

divulge his name."

"I'll bet," she barked. Just as she was about to embark on another tirade, Harold's secretary looked in the door. "I'll be right there, Emma." He straightened a stack of loan documents and he laid one on top, then excused himself from the room. When the door shut, Abigail leaned in to read what was written at the top of the page. Even upside down she could see it said "Franklin Clayborn."

# FORTY-EIGHT

Edward and Bertie were expecting their first child. Though the sun had yet to make a morning appearance when Edward poked his head in the door, Abigail was just coming out of her room.

"Bertie's breathin' hard, Abigail. Where's Millie?"

"In the kitchen finishing up the breakfast dishes."

"Water broke, Millie," he called. "Can you come now?"

"Edward, honey," she called back. "Got plenty of time b'fore that little thing say hello to us all. Now you go to the house and hold your wife's hand while we pull together what we need to help her." Millie went to the cupboard and pulled out some clean cloths. "First babies always make 'em nervous," she told Abigail, and grabbed a bottle of scented oil. "Mrs. A. give me some of this. Put it on my babies, each one of 'em. Keeps their skin soft. Can you carry these?" She handed Abigail the bunch of cotton pieces.

"Preston," Abigail called out. "Bertie's having her baby. We're going to the house."

"All right," he called back.

"Hold that lantern higher so I see the road, Abigail," Millie complained as she hurried to the house.

Millie walked straight in without knocking. "How are you doing, darling?"

"When the pains take ahold of me, I think they will never end. Catches me right in my back," Bertie said, trying to breathe slowly.

"How long between 'em?" Millie asked.

"Oh!" Bertie gasped as another contraction hit her.

"All right, darling, I put these under you. Lift yourself a bit." Millie slid the cloths under Bertie's buttocks.

"Is it time?" Edward asked.

"Honey, let me see how open you are." Millie checked between Bertie's legs. "My guess is your baby be coming any minute," she said.

*I felt apprehensive and could not keep myself from worrying. With all the commotion I went right back to the birth of my boy and those terrible, sad words. 'I am sorry, Abigail. The cord was wrapped around his neck.'*

"Millie, is everything all right?" Abigail asked.

"Don't you fret 'bout nothing. She doing fine."

Feeling dizzy, Abigail sat down in a chair. *"What do you mean she is gone, Franklin?"*

*"It's for the best,"* Franklin had said. *"What would you have done with a baby at the Bradley anyway?"*

Millie fanned Abigail's face. "She must have blacked out." When Abigail awoke, Edward and Bertie had a new baby, Anthony Moses Millar. "I declare, Abigail. You think you was the one having a baby." Millie wrapped the little newborn in several of the soft cotton cloths and handed him to Bertie.

# FORTY-NINE

*I*t had been several days that Preston lay on his bed and stared at the painting of Helen that hung above the fireplace. I tried to feed him soup, but he couldn't eat. He looked at me with his kind, hollow eyes and watched as I went about his care. I brushed his hair, fluffed his pillow, and helped him shift from one side to the other, then I read to him some. Julia visited a few weeks ago when he had been stronger and more like himself, but even then we had to help him bathe and get dressed for the day. Now he would not let me send word to her.

"Hand me that photograph, the one of Julia," Preston said. The picture in a silver frame was of his daughter when she was quite young. He held it to his chest.

Millie came in to give Abigail a break, while Abigail went to the kitchen to heat some water. She was gone only a few minutes when Millie called out. Abigail dropped the kettle and ran back into the bedroom.

"I was holding his hand. He smiled, the breath left him, and that was that," Millie said. Tears filled her eyes.

The skin on his face was a tight alabaster covering over bone. Millie gently laid some coins on his eyelids. They stood by his bed for a long time before they could move again.

*The rhythmic pumping of lungs, no matter how small or quiet, tells you someone lives. When death comes a cavernous stillness fills the room.*

*It was heart wrenching and unbelievable to me that Preston was dead. And I could see my own grief in Millie's sad face. Even though I thought I had prepared myself for his end, it still seemed sudden, like it snuck up on us. Now the stillness knocked the life out of me.*

Daniel came to the door.

"He gone?" he asked so quietly only the angels could have heard him.

"Yes, son," Abigail said. "Tell the others, will you?"

Damien sent a telegram to Julia. She came the next day.

Reggie and Timothy rode for the preacher. Millie, Bertie, Abigail and Julia prepared Preston's body and dressed him in his good suit. Daniel drove the wagon up to the site where Damien, Edward, and the cowboys had dug the grave next to Mrs. Hahl's.

The weather was crisp, and the breeze swirled the fallen leaves while all stood and listened to the preacher's graveside prayers. Letty Ann laid some fall flowers on top of the mound while the group sang a hymn.

That afternoon Abigail went to the bank to look at Preston's will. She and Millie gathered the items Preston wanted to give to Julia. "We've boxed up what your father wanted you to have–their two portraits, the sterling silverware, the family bible and of course, anything that you want that he didn't mention, just tell us," Abigail told Julia. "Damien will put them in your buggy."

*Preston's graceful and loving presence saturated the entire ranch. He was the glue that had held us together. We did adjust to life on the property without him but getting used to it took some time. I knew I'd miss him, we all would, but I didn't know how much. He was such a good man.*

# FIFTY

"Now, Abigail, you keep turning that ring you gonna wear a hole in your finger," Millie chided.

"It's just my nerves." Abigail shook her hand. "Julia comes this afternoon, and I have something I want to tell her."

"Well, rubbing a hole in your finger not gonna help you get it out."

"Edward!" Abigail shouted out to the paddock where he and Daniel were working a horse. "Will you please pick up Mrs. Brown and the children? You have about a quarter of an hour before the stagecoach comes."

When they arrived, Letty Ann lifted little Helena and took her into the house. Jeremiah and Henry yelled with excitement and ran into Abigail's open arms.

"Hello, boys! How are you this fine day? Millie told me she has a surprise for you in the kitchen. Julia, my dear, it is always so nice to see you." Abigail gave her a kiss on the cheek. With the death of her father, Julia was quite subdued.

She put her arm around Abigail's shoulders in greeting. "It is so nice to see you, too. I have looked forward to this visit for weeks." Then she broke down and cried on Abigail's shoulder.

"Let's walk up to the grave site," Abigail said, "so you can see how nicely the new headstone sits above the house." Arm in arm, they hiked the hill. "Come on, Nanny," she called. Nanny followed along, the hitch in her step a little more pronounced. "You'll want some time with him by yourself.

Why don't I meet you back at the house?" Nanny turned several times and with a deep groan curled up for a nap. "The old girl gets herself up here and naps with her head against his stone—done so since the day he died."

That afternoon, after they had eaten, Abigail and Julia sat on the porch and watched Julia's boys play in the yard. Helena napped on a blanket at her mother's feet, and when she woke the child began to play with her own little toes. The women sat and chatted into the late afternoon.

"Bernard is away quite a bit," Abigail noted.

"I used to travel with him," Julia said, "but once the babies came I didn't feel the urge quite as much. Did you ever have children, Abigail?" The question caught her off guard. She was surprised they had not spoken of it before, or at least that Preston had not informed her.

"Yes," Abigail answered, "a boy then a girl."

"Where are they now?" she asked.

"The boy was strangled at birth. Came out that way," Abigail answered.

"Oh, dear. And the girl?"

"I guess it was just not meant to be either."

"How terribly sad," Julia said, taking Abigail's hand. "I can't imagine the loss of one child, let alone two. If any one of my children were to die, I don't know how I would ever get over it."

"You don't. You just get through each day," Abigail said flatly.

Julia's boys chased each other in the yard below, one tripping over the other in play. "Careful, boys!" Julia called out. They grabbed onto the rope swing and gave each other a push. "The ranch certainly is beautiful this time of year."

Abigail, still caught in the memories of her own children, didn't hear Julia. "It is amazing how fast the children are growing," she observed.

Julia noted the sadness on Abigail's face. "I can hardly keep up with their clothes before they burst their seams."

"Like dough rising," Abigail said softly. "Come here, son," she called to Jeremiah. "Let me tie your laces." The boy ran onto the porch and leaned against her, his hand securely holding her knee. He poked out one foot, and when that lace was tied, poked out the other. Julia told the boys to go in and get ready for supper

"Wash with soap, and take Helena with you," Julia said.

Henry tapped Jeremiah on the head and shouted, "You're it!" They both ran off into the house, but then Henry returned sheepishly for the two-year-old. "Sorry, Mama," he said.

"Thank you, Henry." She winked at Abigail.

"Is it lonely for you with Bernard away so much?"

"I am not all alone. We have several people who work in the house, but some days I do find being by myself a challenge. When I am not caring for the children, I paint. But yes, it can be hard. Especially the nights, sleeping in a half-empty bed."

Abigail suggested Julia come to the ranch while he was away. "The children can play together, and they can join my classroom. And I'll not take your time if you want to paint. We'd all love your being here. Think on it, will you?"

Julia was taken off guard by the suggestion, but Abigail noticed the suggestion brightened her spirits.

While the ladies conversed, fifteen-year-old Daniel, who with Edward's help had become a horse breaker and trainer, worked a stud in the paddock and was riding him in circles.

"He seems to sense what they need," Julia said. "The animals trust him."

"Millie told me on the way to the ranch they stopped overnight at a Comanche village where he watched the Indians with their horses, but truthfully, it comes to him naturally. He doesn't even use a whip." She looked out at the field while she found some courage. "Julia, before we go in, do you mind if we chat for a moment longer?"

"Certainly. Is there a problem?"

"No. No problem. It's just I want to tell you something."

At that moment the horse in the paddock reared, and his head showed high above the top of the fence. Daniel's body flew up into the air, and his arms flailing. There was a thud, and dust billowed where the animal's hooves slammed onto the earth. Daniel screamed.

They ran toward the paddock. Julia grabbed the horse's reins and tied him to the fence while Abigail went to the boy's side. Daniel lay on the ground, his face contorted in pain. A blood circle grew on his pants at the break in his thigh.

Abigail ran to the bell at the front door and rang it with all her might. Damien came from the barn, and Millie's head popped out of the doorway.

"Daniel's hurt!" Abigail shouted.

"Hold still, son," Julia said. "Don't try to move. Your father is on his way." Daniel, frightened and in great pain, only moaned.

Abigail caught the Brown children as they came from the house and held them close to her to keep them from seeing the worst. Millie ran to her son. Damien, Timothy, and Letty Ann followed right behind.

"Lordy, sweet Jesus," Millie said when she saw Daniel's leg.

Damien gave Daniel a reassuring smile. "Gonna take good care of you, son." Then he took his knife and split the pants. The smile left his face when he saw the bare leg. Blood flowed from the deep gash onto the dirt below.

"Is it bad, Papa?" Daniel looked for the answer in his father's face.

"It's broke, son," he told him. Millie felt frozen to the spot.

Damien took Millie by the shoulders. "Honey get me a board, size of his leg. Letty Ann, a sheet." Millie and Letty Ann could barely pull themselves away.

"Miss Julia," Damien said, "hold the boy down. Lean onto him, ma'am, keep him still."

Julia put her arms around his back, leaned into his young chest and held him tightly as if he were her own son. Daniel breathed in fits and starts and fought back tears.

"Boy," Damien said, "not gonna lie to you. Gonna hurt."

Damien took hold of his son's leg, and with his full weight, pulled as hard as he could till there was a snap and the bone popped back into place. Daniel screamed and blacked out.

In the barn, Millie threw boards right and left till she found the right size, then ran out with it. She desperately wanted her husband to give her some sign her child would be all right.

"Timothy, go get the Doc," Abigail called.

"Do you think he will come for us?" Millie asked.

"Say it's for me," Abigail told Timothy. "He'll come, and that's all I care about right now."

Timothy mounted his horse and galloped out of the gate past Edward.

"What happened?" Edward yelled as he ran in from a field.

"Broke his leg, bad," Timothy shouted as he rode off.

"Now, honey, we gotta tie his leg to the board." Damien spoke in measured tones to calm his wife. "For the bone to heal right, he gotta keep it like that for at least six weeks. Pray no infection set in."

Millie and Letty Ann ripped the sheet into ties. Damien took a length of it and wound it tightly around the thigh to stop the bleeding, then worked quickly to tie the leg to the board. He and Edward carried him into the Adams' house, where Damien stitched him up.

It felt like hours before Timothy returned with the doctor.

"It is not me, Doc," Abigail said. "It's young Daniel."

The doctor examined the leg and the stitching Damien had done to close the wound.

"You will need to watch him through the night," Doc said. "He's already feverish. Keep his head cool. Boil the dressing rags and change them every day. And if you keep that wound dry and clean, it should heal just fine." Then he turned to Damien. "You did a fine job. We'll have to see, but you might have saved his leg."

"Thank you, sir. Not much doctoring on the plantation," Damien explained. "Had to do it all ourselves."

"I see," Doc said. "Lucky thing, then." The doctor packed his bag. "I'll come by in a few days. Let me know if things get worse." He added, "Abigail, I would have come anyway."

Frightened for Daniel, they all took turns through the night to wipe his brow and watch him breathe. Luckily, the fever broke early and the next morning he ate a full breakfast.

"Did you want to speak with me, Abigail?" Julia said as she carried dishes back into the main house.

"Yes, but it can wait," she replied and went to get books for Daniel to read.

Letty Ann or Timothy sat with Daniel to help pass the time. Millie read to him every day. Abigail helped him with his schoolwork. But for that young man it was a long six weeks.

The first thing he did with the crutches Damien made for him was to get to the paddock fence to watch the stallions. The horse that threw him was in the corral with the others.

"Didn't mean to hurt me. Really he didn't" he told Edward. "Rattler come 'cross. Bucked b'fore I was ready, trying to kill the snake with his hooves, only my leg was in the way. He a good horse, and quick to learn. And fast? Whew!" he said with great admiration. "Edward," he asked, "how long b'fore I ride again?"

"At least two more weeks, son. The doc will tell you when your leg is ready. Then you will need to build some strength in it just to walk correctly. But you'll be on a horse in no time," he said, though with such a bad break he was not sure that was true. Even the doctor had been concerned he might be lame.

When the brace was removed, he took his first steps. Though he was weak, and the leg was a bit shorter, and he had a hard limp, Daniel could walk, and in a few weeks, he was back on his horses.

# FIFTY-ONE

"I am so tired. Can't keep my eyes open," Abigail told Millie. She had struggled to get through the school day, something that happened more often now.

"Go outside and sit. I bring some coffee and warm bread," Millie said.

Abigail sat heavily on the porch swing and waited. Just then the sky clouded over, but where the sun shone through, the clouds and the tops of the trees were golden.

Millie came out with a pot of coffee and a plate of sweet strawberry jam bread.

*You would think my waist must have expanded with all the wonderful things Millie cooks, but truly I cannot eat much of it and find I am getting thinner than I like. And Millie is so sweet to me. I know I'm not the easiest company, but still she is kind and generous with her caring. What have I missed all these years, not allowing myself to have a good friend? Franklin always discouraged me from fraternizing with anyone at the Bradley. He told me I would lose control of the business if I did. Sadly, I believed him. Now I think he just wanted me all for himself.*

# FIFTY-TWO

## 1873

*T*he warm sunlight bathed our faces as Millie and I walked along the boardwalk in Placerville. I thought of the momentary happiness I had felt when I walked with Franklin during our trip to Sacramento. Was it really six years ago? But I was shocked into the present when I caught a glimpse of my face in the glass of a store window. My cheekbones were more prominent, my complexion ashen, and there is weariness in my eyes I don't remember seeing before. On the other hand, Millie's face was filled with the joyous anticipation of buying something new, something just for herself.

They stopped at the Placerville Dry Goods for Millie to look at the items in the window. Her eyes widened as her hand covered her mouth. "Do you think I could get me a new pair of shoes?" she asked. "Party shoes, not them old work boots. Ain't never had no party shoes."

Abigail had taken Millie's arm while they strolled, and normally Millie was careful to be unhurried, but in her excitement, she pulled on Abigail and nearly sent her to the ground.

"Sorry, I go slower," she apologized. "I wanna–want to try them on." She pulled on Abigail again, more gently. "Is it all right we go in here?"

*Even though Millie knows she does not have to ask permission, the habit is still heavily ingrained. Sometimes I lose my patience, but Millie just ignores my agitation.*

Millie decided and said proudly, "Wanna try that hat another time, but today a new pair of shoes."

They both tried on several pairs, but nothing interested Abigail. Millie, on the other hand, found just the right party shoe, red satin with a slight heel and a red satin ribbon in the shape of a flower on the toe. She straightened out her legs, clicked her heels together, then got up and tried to dance. "These just fine," she glowed. "Would you teach me the waltz? I wanna dance with Damien in these red shoes."

"I'd be glad to. How about Damien? Do you think he'd want to learn?" Abigail asked, if only in jest.

"He do it if I ask him to," she beamed.

When they got home, Abigail had Millie practice with Letty Ann in front of the fireplace in the drawing room, and when Damien came in at the end of the day, they showed him a few steps.

*For a big man Damien was quite graceful. While they danced, I played a waltz on the pump organ, and all the children cheered.*

# FIFTY-THREE

## Auburn

F ranklin thought for a minute. *Let's see. I was born in 1824. That makes today my fifty-first birthday.* While they were together, each year Abigail had arranged a party to celebrate his birthday, inviting his men and the girls at the Bradley. She had served local sparkling wines, oysters from the coast, and cheeses from around the world. Abigail had lifted her glass to him: "Here's to a long, happy and healthy life for the both of us." He recalled how the firelight lit her face and glowed on her yellow hair. It had warmed his heart. For a moment the memory lifted his spirits, until he realized he was without her and it would never happen again. He loved her, but he could never tell her the way he wanted, and somehow it always came out awkwardly or worse, in a way that hurt her.

But he was not one to celebrate on his own, and now that he remembered, it made him feel empty and alone. "The usual," he said to the bartender of what had been the Union Saloon and now was Gardner and McGuire's. He set down a glass and pulled out the cork of the whiskey bottle, poured a drink and toasted himself, "Here's to you, sucker," then he finished the bottle and fell asleep with his head on his hands.

# FIFTY-FOUR

With Damien and Edward's hard work, the ranch prospered, and now they needed to hire more men.

"We supposed to meet a couple of men in town at noon," Damien reminded Abigail. She told him she was not feeling at all well, and if he liked what he saw to take them on. Long ago she had given him this kind of responsibility and had only promised to accompany Damien to get out of the house. But today she was grateful not to have to make the effort.

Later, he introduced her to the two new cowboys. "Abigail, this is Seamus and Sean O'Brian."

The O'Brian brothers were strapping young men in their early twenties, with hands well calloused and a brogue of just-off-the-boat Irish. Sean came forward with a strong muscular handshake. His brother was gentle and quiet. Both were polite, she thought.

"Where are you from?" she asked.

"From Dublin we are," Sean said affably. "Lookin' for a grand bit of land to make our own, but in the meantime we have come to be of service to you." He bowed robustly.

"Well, welcome to the ranch, gentlemen. We are glad to have you with us. I am sure Damien has shown you the bunkhouse?"

*It was wonderful to be in the company of men who were not desperately digging for gold. These steady fellas were good hearty stock and I was glad they had found us.*

When Damien and Sean went out the door, Seamus stayed behind.

"Mrs. Wilcox?" Seamus began, "Damien might have mentioned you have a library of many books? I'm wonderin' if I might choose one t'read."

She was surprised he could read till she heard his father was a deacon. "You don't want to join the cowboys at the saloon?" she asked. At the end of a long workday, the boys usually gathered at the El Dorado Saloon in Placerville for a drink and a game of cards.

"Canna hold me liquor, ma'am. One drop and me legs get ricketier than me granny's knees," he said. "Not much of a gamblin' man neither."

"You are an anomaly, Seamus O'Brian."

"This word anomaly? What's its meanin'?" he asked.

"Most Irishmen drink," she told him.

"Me ma told me I broke the mold," Seamus said. "Is that your meanin'?"

"Close enough," she said. "You wanted a book? Then you had best come in and browse." She walked back toward her room. *My son would have been his age had he lived*, she thought.

"Ma'am, in your bedroom? Em, 'twould not be proper for me to go in there," Seamus said.

"I suppose you are right. I'll stand at the door, that suit you?"

"Me ma would approve, ma'am," he smiled then walked over to the bookcases and read titles with avid interest.

"Take what you like, Mr. O'Brian. Bring it back when you are done."

"Might you have a volume on veterinary medicine by chance?" he asked.

"I don't believe so. Is that your interest?"

"I like understandin' how all the parts work together," he

said. "Mrs. Wilcox, who helps your animals when they be ailin'?"

"We've done well with Doc Harding in Salmon Falls."

"Would you be a grand woman and introduce me to the man?"

"Certainly," Abigail answered. "Do you have more family in Ireland, Mr. O'Brian?"

"Practically a town-full," he laughed. "Aunts and uncles and their broods, me grannies and grandads, too, two more brothers and three sisters. With meself bein' the eldest."

"Your mother must not have wanted you to go so far away."

"She passed, ma'am, but me da was a bit of a mess at the boat landin'. Tore me heart. Sean and me, we write him every month or so as we promised." Then he asked, "Did you paint these glorious paintings, then?"

"Mr. Hahl's daughter, Julia. You'll meet her. She and her family come to visit often."

"And the beautiful charcoal drawings, too?" he asked.

"Those are mine."

"Me sister, Caitlín, she's good with colors. Don't have the gift meself." Seamus pulled *Moby Dick* off the shelf, opened it to the first page and read. "This one," he said. "Da told me it was a rollickin' tale." *What is it about men and Moby Dick?* she thought. It had been one of Preston's favorites.

"That one is about a whale," she told him. "When you bring it back, you must tell me what you think of the story, and, Seamus, if there are words you don't understand, you can ask me about them if you like."

"Thank you, ma'am," he said, his nose already in the book.

Dizziness took Abigail for a moment, and she caught her balance on the doorjamb.

"Are you feelin' proper, ma'am? Here let me help you." He took her arm and guided her to one of the chairs by the fireplace in the parlor. "Mrs. Adams is in the kitchen, is she not? I'll get you a spot of tea."

Millie heard and poked her head in the door.

"It's nothing," Abigail waved. "Thank you, Mr. O'Brian. Your father has raised you well."

"Me da would be laughin' heartily to hear you think so," he said as he left to find Damien and Sean.

# FIFTY-FIVE

## 1874

Reggie has become a tall and handsome sixteen-year-old and is well-settled on the ranch. With Millie's help he is quite the baker. Today he stood in the kitchen with arms white to the elbows in flour making us a cobbler for dessert.

Reggie stole food when he first visited the ranch even though he was fed more than he could eat. "Dang it," Millie had told me," That boy gonna be the death of me. Soon's I get a pie from the oven and set it to cooling, he sneak it out to the barn and eat it all by his self. Yesterday he had all the ginger cookies you and me made."

The day was chilly and damp with a drizzle. Millie had caught a chest cold and sat by the kitchen fire wrapped in a blanket. Since she had taught Reggie all she knew about baking, she watched his every move.

When the kettle sang out, the boy dropped the dried black leaves into the teapot, poured in the hot liquid, stirred the brew, and then refilled their cups.

"You're doin' good there, New Boy," Millie said, using his old nickname. She took out her handkerchief and blew her nose.

"Thank you, Miss Millie. I done learned from de bess," he

smiled then turned to Abigail. "How are you today, Miss Abigail?"

"I *have* learned from *the best*," Abigail repeated. It was not a good day, and she felt crackly like burnt toast, but truth be told, a hug from Letty Ann or a smile from Reggie could lift her spirits.

Slowly he repeated, "I have learned from the best," and smiled at Millie. "You'll like this," he coaxed Abigail cheerily. "Your favorite–blackberry."

Millie blew her nose hard and hacked a chest-splitting cough. "What the name on that book you ordered?"

"*Outlines of the Veterinary* Art by Delabere Blaine."

"Dela bear. That's a fancy name," Millie said. "Vit-trinary what?"

"*Veterinary Art*. It's for Seamus. Only took four months for it to arrive. Don't tell him it's here, though! I want to see his face when he opens it."

"Maybe he can help me with this croup I has." Millie blew her nose again.

Abigail wanted to correct her English but thought better of it. Seamus walked by the kitchen porch, and Abigail called out to him. He bounded up two steps at a time and almost flew into the kitchen.

"Millie, pass me another cookie," Abigail said. "Seamus, would you like one of Millie's excellent sand cookies?"

He wiped his soiled hands on his pants, took one, and popped the whole thing in his mouth, the sugar topping lingering on his lips.

"Have the heavens parted? This might be the best cookie I ever ate, but don't tell me auntie! She thinks she's the best baker in Ireland," he laughed.

"Have another," Millie offered and coughed.

"Mmmm, delicious," he said as he inserted another.

Abigail asked him to bring in the package from the dining

room table.

"It's for you," Millie said, unable to contain herself. "Come in yesterday morning."

His eyes opened wide when he tore off the paper wrapping. "Glory be, Mrs. Wilcox." He cracked open the book and began to read one page after another.

"You said you wanted a book on veterinary medicine," Abigail said. "I hope it meets your expectations, Mr. O'Brian, or should I say Doctor O'Brian."

"Mrs. Wilcox, you could not have given me a grander present. Thank you with all me heart." He continued to leaf through the pages, eventually reading and re-reading every page whenever he had a spare minute. "You're not feeling well, Miss Millie? May I listen to you breathe?" He reached for the kitchen funnel and put it against her chest. "Your lungs sound hearty, but I do hear that bad cough. Put some menthol in hot water and breathe in the fumes, and me ma always had me drink lots of liquids."

But Millie's cough got worse. After several days, even though Millie insisted she was fine, Abigail had Edward go for the doctor.

In private he told her, "I believe she has influenza. I've seen this before. Because slaves were not fed consistently, their bodies in some cases became constitutionally weak, and therefore can't rebound quickly from an illness. Keep a close eye on her. We don't want it to become pneumonia." He left them with some menthol.

Seamus came every day to listen to her lungs. Abigail was beside herself with worry because her father had succumbed to pneumonia. What would she do if they were to lose Millie? She would not only lose a friend, but she was also concerned that when syphilis ravaged her body, until now the possibilities of which she had put out of her mind, who would care for her? For two weeks Abigail sat with Millie, read to her, watched her sleep, and made sure she drank enough liquid.

After Bertie made supper for everyone, she and Abigail walked arm in arm from the main house toward the Millars', across a stretch of grass new-green from the spring rain. "Millie seems better today," Bertie said. The rustle of their dresses matched the rhythm of the flicker of the soft gray-pink white oak leaves that had begun to fill the branches above.

"She's fussing because she wants to get back to work so I'd say she must be feeling better," Abigail said. "Doc made her promise to rest another day or two. Thankfully she's out of the woods."

The baby asleep in a sling, which hung across Bertie's shoulder, was their brand new second child, Sara Lynne. In her tiny hand, she held the little rabbit Daniel had whittled for her.

Smart and quick, Bertie talked freely of what she thought and felt, so was easy company especially when Abigail did not feel her best. She was sympathetic and seemed to anticipate Abigail's needs when she was slowed or quieted by the illness.

The Millar home had a rough-hewn charm about it. Edward had built most of their furniture: the bed, table, and benches. Abigail gave them a rocker, and Millie's wedding quilt lay on the end of their bed. It was small, but still adequate for the growing family. Mostly, it was filled with the warmth of the people who lived there.

"Let me hold her," Abigail said and took Sara Lynne, who nestled against her shoulder and melted Abigail's heart.

Bertie disappeared into the house and came out with a shawl she'd knitted, which she wrapped around Abigail's shoulders. "I thought this color would match your eyes."

"For me? It's lovely, Bertie. It's just perfect. Thank you,"

Abigail beamed.

Edward came out to take Sara Lynne into the house and put her in her cradle.

"Shall I bring 'round the buggy to take you back?" Bertie asked.

"No," Abigail said. "Let me sit here for a moment. Then I'll be just fine."

The pain in Abigail's stomach was strong now and constant. Though Bertie never asked her about her health, she could see Abigail didn't feel well and went into the house for some soothing tea.

"Is she all right?" Edward whispered.

"She's pretty uncomfortable," Bertie said. "Doc told Millie there wasn't anything anyone could do. He gave her some laudanum to ease the pain, but Millie says Abigail won't take it. Usually, if she rests for a while, she seems to feel better."

Bertie came out with the tea and some choice ginger molasses cookies made from one of Cheng's recipes. The two women sat there for a good long while and chatted about the children.

Eventually, with her hand on Bertie's arm Abigail was able to walk back home, though it felt like a long way to both of them, each pretending to the other everything was all right.

*The shawl was the color of the sky—and Bradley's eyes—and the wool felt warm and soft. Franklin would not have liked that Bertie had given me a gift. He would have belittled her—and the gift. I would have thrown my shoe at him, slammed the door on his backside, and thought less of myself for having accepted it. But now I've finally learned to appreciate thoughtfulness.*

# FIFTY-SIX

"I leave a couple of men here to help you while the boys and me is away," Damien said to Abigail, "You likes Seamus, so I asked him and his brother to stay b'hind to take care of the barn. That Sean likes to talk a bit. Tells a good story. Thought he make the time go by. Seamus bring in firewood and take you to town if you a mind to go. If you need anything, Abigail, you ring the bell, one of those boys'll come."

Damien kissed his wife goodbye and rode off with his sons and the men to gather the cattle for market.

"Letty Ann!" Millie called. "Take old Nanny down to the river and give her a good wash. Poor thing smells a bit, and them fleas is making her scratch herself bald. Take a stick of lye soap. That should do the trick."

"Ok, Mama. Come with me, Nanny girl." Letty Ann skipped to the barn to get the soap. Nanny, with her stiff hip, waddled her way alongside.

"It seem like Nanny has taken on the job of her name," Millie commented. "Wherever Letty Ann go the dog right there by her side. When I ring the bell for supper, Nanny herds her back home. Children been insisting she sleep by the fire in our house just like Mr. Preston had her do."

"She's a good old dog," Abigail said. "I suppose she has earned her place by the fire. Just glad it is your fire and not mine."

"Now Abigail. You don't fool me none. I see you giving

her scraps when I ain't looking. You's attached to that dear old thing as any of us," Millie said.

"I suppose I am," Abigail agreed.

The poisonous diamondback snake wove its way through the grass undetected. The hot sun warmed its triangular head and the brown diamonds surrounded by tan lines on the long spine as it slithered its way toward the river's edge. Over four feet long, the snake curled up in the sun in the middle of the path the girl and the dog would take home.

Letty Ann sang a song and waded in deep enough so Nanny's belly was dampened, then she cupped her hands to splash water over the dog until she was good and wet. "This make you feel better, Nanny," Letty Ann said. "Get all those fleas drowned so they don't bite you no more." She took the lye soap and scrubbed it throughout the dog's fur. Every so often Nanny shook splashing water and suds all over. Letty Ann wiped the soap from her face, rinsed the dog, and brought her back up onto the shore. When they started back home, Nanny shook herself again, broadcasting droplets of water, and startling the snake.

"Good morning," Seamus said as he stood on the porch with a novel in his hand. "Just returning this. 'Twas a grand read. Thought I might find me another. Have you a thought of one you think would suit me?" They went to the bookshelves. "Little Letty Ann, she is a dear thing," Seamus commented. "Will be a pretty girl, me thinks, with the two eyes of her shining like the diamonds in your ring. But some young gent's gonna have his hands full. A mind of her own, that one."

Abigail looked over the selections and pulled several books off the shelf. "I think she enjoys working with the animals as much as you do," she said and handed him the books. "You and your brother doing well?"

"We certainly do appreciate working for you, ma'am. Beauty all around us, and good friends, too. Of course, as you know, me and me brother Sean want to find just the right place to buy, but 'twill be a while before that happens."

Off in the distance Nanny barked and kept at it long enough for Millie to be concerned.

"Seamus," Millie called. "Go see what that dog barking at. Possum, most likely, but take the rifle anyway."

Seamus took the gun by the door and ran toward the sound.

"How he like his book? Vitrinary medicine."

"Veterinary," Abigail corrected.

"Every time I see him he got his nose in it. Vet-er-in-ary," Millie said. "Bet he has it memorized by now. Seem to have a mind for taking care of animals, don't he?"

Seamus got there just in time to see the long snake lunge and hear Nanny yip. He quickly took aim and blasted his gun, the echo carrying back to the house.

"Oh, Lordy!" Millie cried and ran toward the sound with Abigail just behind her. They arrived to see Letty Ann and Seamus standing over Nanny with the long snake dead at their feet.

"Letty Ann, you all right?" Millie pulled her daughter to her breast, then quickly inspected her arms and legs.

"Fine, Mama." Letty Ann wiggled away. "Nanny saved my life. That snake was on the path shaking its rattle. Nanny got between us and started barking and barking, and now it killed her." Tears began to stream down her cheeks.

"She is hurt something terrible," Seamus said, "and we do need to take care of her, but she's not dead yet, honey."

The dog had been bitten on the back of the neck, leaving two puncture holes from the snake's fangs. Seamus picked her up like a baby and carried her to the barn. "We need to keep her quiet. She has a lot of fur on her neck so if she's been lucky, the snake didn't inject much venom, or if God be with us, none," he said. "But we won't know till we see if she..." But he didn't finish the thought because he knew if Nanny quit breathing there had been a lethal dose of poison. "If she had just a gash, well, I've stitched up a lamb or two back home. Been peering over me pa's shoulder, he thought enough of me to teach me how–but a snakebite," he said and shook his head. "Letty Ann, my book is on the end of my bed, would you be a dear and go get it?"

"Shall I bring Nanny some whiskey?" Abigail asked. "It's what we did in Auburn."

"Keep 'em from meeting the Lord, did it?" Seamus asked.

"Well, yes and no. Some lived, some died."

Millie jumped in, "I'll go mix up some gunpowder, salt, and the yeller of an egg. That's what Master always used on the plantation, but now I think on it, more men died than lived."

Letty Ann returned with the book and Seamus looked up remedies for snakebites. "Seems nothing really helps." Nanny tried to stand, but Seamus held her tight. "There now, precious dog, you keep still. We don't want that poison moving through your body any quicker than it has to." He turned to the ladies and said, "I hate to disappoint, but we'll just have to see if she gets up in the morning and wants breakfast."

Abigail and Millie sat on the porch and listened to the loud, constant chirp of the tree frogs at sunset, then each in their beds slept fitfully till morning. Letty Ann and Seamus slept in the barn. Every time Nanny made a noise or stretched her legs, one or the other would check to see if she was all right. In the middle of the night, they found Nanny had become feverish and weak and the bite swelled her neck to twice its size.

"Seamus, what's the matter with her?" Letty Ann asked.

"Her body's fightin' with the poison."

The dog was panting, and her nose was clammy. Seamus felt for her pulse and found it slow.

"Did the Sierra Ice Company make their delivery?"

"Yes, last week," Letty Ann said.

"Good for our Nanny." He handed her a clean cloth. "Go to the icehouse and bring her back a chunk of ice on this towel." When she returned he placed the cool cloth on the dog's neck. "It's to keep our girl more comfortable," Seamus said, but he didn't tell her that with the poison in her system Nanny might not live. He wrapped the dog in a horse blanket and watched her closely throughout the rest of the night.

The next morning Abigail found all three asleep. Seamus was leaning against the wall with one arm around Nanny and the other holding Letty Ann. Abigail had brought a small amount of meat and some water.

Letty Ann woke suddenly and reached for the dog. "How is she?"

Millie crowded in just behind Abigail. "How is our girl this morning?"

"All right, Nanny," Seamus said. "You'll be wanting to stand." He helped the dog to her feet, but she lurched from one side to the other. "Getting her sea legs now," he said to Letty Ann. "That a girl, Nanny." The dog started to scratch her neck, but Seamus took ahold of her paw. "Best let that be, miss."

Nanny licked Seamus's hand and leaned into Letty Ann, then slowly walked over to the meat and sniffed it. At first she took only a small bite, but then finished the rest.

"Good girl," Seamus said, much relieved. "Best to keep her quiet in the stall for a day or two. She'll be needing all her strength for mendin'."

Letty Ann ran back to the house to get a book, and she stayed with the dog for the rest of the day.

"Mr. O'Brian, would you and your brother join us for Sunday dinner? Bring your girls if you would like," Abigail said.

"We would like that, ma'am" he answered.

*I can't help but compare that snake biting the dog to Franklin's giving me syphilis. You're not aware of it till it jumps out and bites you. I sure wish our Seamus could cure me of this dastardly disease.*

# FIFTY-SEVEN

When Franklin woke at first he wasn't sure where he was. And he couldn't move because he was overwhelmed by his dream of Abigail and the understanding it brought. *Tears the color of blood streamed from her eyes and her heart cracked open, spilling its contents down the front of her chest.* A horrifying if not revealing look at how Abigail felt about losing her child. As his mind cleared he found he was at the Bradley in Abigail's rooms, though oddly not with Abigail's things.

It was a hot day, sweat poured off his emaciated frame, and it was all he could do to get out of bed. He pulled on his pants and tightened his belt several notches shorter than he normally had worn it, then sat down heavily. He could barely get his shirt buttoned, let alone tuck it into his pants. His socks, white to start with, were now brown with ground-in dirt, and he couldn't remember when he had last bathed. It all seemed like more effort than he could rally.

The door opened and Marguerite came in with bread and tea and some of Cheng's stew. The sight of it made him nauseous.

"Try to eat something, Franklin, and drink some tea. Mint. It'll settle your stomach."

Finally he asked, "How did I get here?"

"Sam found you calling up to my windows. I told him to bring you in. Drink the tea." He tried to but couldn't force himself to swallow anything. *"Drink it, Abigail,"* Franklin remembered saying. *She threw the cup at him. It missed and crashed into her vanity leaving a crack in the mirror. She pitched a hairbrush, which hit him on his hand, but before anything else could come his way, he ducked out of the door.*

"I have sent someone to find one of your men," Marguerite said. "He'll take you home."

*Home,* he thought, *This was home.*

His foreman picked him up by the arms, but Franklin's legs buckled, so he had to put him over his back to carry him down the steps.

Hanna looked around the room, "Oh dear. Let me help you clean this up." She took the sheets to the laundry and Sam carried away the privy bucket. Marguerite opened the windows wide and left her door open to air the room.

"He knows she's not here—when he is sober anyway," Marguerite said. "Something is not right about him. He seems addled and it's not just the drink."

# FIFTY-EIGHT

Millie called to her eldest, who was playing with the dog in the yard. "Be gentle with our Nanny. No rough-housing now. She best get her rest. And get your brother and sister to help me in the kitchen."

"OK, Mama." He ran off and returned with Timothy.

"Where is Letty Ann?" Millie asked.

"In the barn with Seamus," Daniel answered as he leapt onto the rope swing

"Did you tell her to come?"

"Yes, Mama, but she say she in the middle of something."

"What are they doing out there?" Abigail asked.

"Looking at rabbit guts," Timothy said and joined his brother on the swing.

"I declare," Millie said to Abigail. "We throws that stuff away, and he be inspecting it. Boys, tell her to wash her hands b'fore she come into my kitchen."

The ladies went into the house, and Abigail sat down stiffly on a chair. "You're right, Millie." She waited a full beat before she continued. "It is what you said. And we both know syphilis is nothing but a death sentence."

"Well, you dead yet? From what I see you got more living to do. So you best search for them roses," Millie said. "Tell me what you need. Like now. What's hurting you?"

"I can hardly breathe—my stomach is in such a knot, and my mouth tastes like yesterday's socks."

"Warm tea will soften your belly," Millie offered.

The thought of it turned her stomach. "No, not just yet."

Millie stood behind the chair and rubbed Abigail's shoulders for a moment.

"Doc gave you laudanum," Millie said. "Take a bit of that."

"No, I've told you I don't want to get started again. You know what happened before."

"Abigail, it just hard for me to do nothing for you. Surely there's something could ease your discomfort?"

Abigail thought for a minute and then said, "Tell me more about your travels to get here. It's always a good distraction from my aches and pains."

The boys returned to the kitchen, and Letty Ann ran back from the barn.

"You wash those hands been feeling rabbit guts?" Millie scrunched her face.

"Yes, Mama," Letty Ann said.

"Stir my stew, all right, girlie?"

"Yes, Mama." She took her position at the stove.

"Boys, one of you peel the potatoes, and the other bring in wood for the fire."

"Wood!" Daniel sang out and ran to the woodpile.

"Mama! I always peel them potatoes," Timothy objected.

"Never mind," Millie said. "Daniel will peel 'em next time." She turned back to Abigail and began one of her stories, this one about an Indian named Puuku.

"We was hot, thirsty, and tired riding through Texas with nothing but high stone cliffs and sandy trails before us."

The last watering hole had been the day before, and they were not sure where the next one was. They had been traveling for weeks and all were exhausted. Timothy had a terrible fever and was lying in the back, wet with sweat. Letty Ann, now too tired to cry anymore, had streaks from tears running down her dusty cheeks. Daniel stared out at the trail, his head wig-wagging with the motion of the rig.

Suddenly, an Indian, a Comanche warrior, rode in. Before Millie could reach for the rifle behind her, the Indian's horse stepped into a gopher hole and sent the man flying, landing him squarely on some rocks. He was badly injured and couldn't move.

Damien jumped down with Millie not far behind, her gun raised and ready. He took his kerchief and pressed it over the gouge in the man's side. Millie, not sure if she should help the injured man or shoot him, decided on the former and brought him water. Damien sewed up the gash.

While they made camp for the night, Daniel gathered what few pieces of wood he could find, and Millie added water to the dehydrated vegetables and meat called portable soup. Timothy's fever did not improve.

The Indian spoke no English, and Damien knew no Comanche, but somehow they talked to each other. "He say his name is Puuku along with some other Comanche words. I think it mean a man who sits tall on his horse," Damien told Millie. "I told him I be taking my family to find a place to live in California." But Millie, sure they would meet their maker any minute, worried that either they wouldn't find water or else the Indian would kill them.

The next day, when Puuku could ride again, he told Damien to follow him.

"Husband, are you sure we should do what he say? What if that Sits Tall Puuku want to trap us and take all our things or...or worse...kill us?" Despite the fact that Deagon L had warned them that Comanche, Kiowa, and Apache Indians attacked settlers who invaded their Comancheria, stealing livestock, or taking them as slaves, Damien decided to trust the man.

Half a day later their horses pulled hard to get the wagon up to the crest of a hill. Down below, Puuku and his stallion stood in a cool stream.

Letty Ann and Daniel ran down and splashed in the water. Damien laid Timothy close to its edge, where Millie could dip a rag and wipe his face and hands to calm his fever.

Damien clucked at the mules, while Millie fretted and kept her eye on Puuku/Sits Tall On His Horse. He expected to see his tribe, tipis and horses when they went down a steep trail to the bend in the river, but instead there were only dark spots on the ground where their fires had been, and horse's hooves chewed up those marks.

"White settlers," Damien said. "Says his family left in the night before the attack."

"What we gonna do now, Mama?" Timothy asked, his face shiny with sweat and lips cracked from dry air.

They followed their guide to a secluded canyon where they were to rest and wait for dark. It would be cooler for the animals then and safer for the family to travel.

Puuku let his horse rest for a while, then ran it through some intricate moves. He clicked his tongue and flicked a piece of cloth tied to his lance to guide the animal in the direction he wanted him to go. Daniel, fascinated, watched his every move.

As the sun went behind the rocks and the temperature dropped, the Adamses set out again. It was a long night under a full moon. Finally, the morning glow began to illuminate the vast desert valley. In the distance were gigantic red cliffs bigger and taller than anything any of them had ever seen.

Off in the distance, dust began to billow from around an outcropping of rocks. Puuku, concerned, circled around the back of the wagon and came alongside Damien, who pulled the wagon to a stop. Unfortunately, they were out in the open with no time to find cover. Three white settlers rode toward them.

"Don't think they hurt us," Damien told the family. "But

Puuku say they kill him. Children, stay in the back and don't say nothing. Pretend really hard everything all right. Answer if they ask a question, but don't say nothing else." Puuku climbed into the wagon. "Cover him over with your blankets, and don't move. Y'all understand?" With eyes wide, all nodded. The Indian curled himself around the bags of beans and coffee, and the children covered him over with their blankets.

While Damien pretended to fix a wheel, Millie sat up on the buckboard, barely able to breathe.

"Where you folks headed?" the leader asked as he wiped his face with a black bandana.

"California," Damien responded. "Just stopped to check this wheel. Thought it feeling loose. Nothing really wrong with it though. Guess we'll be on our way."

The leader started to peer into the wagon when Timothy hacked a raspy cough that came deep from within his congested chest.

"What's wrong with him?" the leader asked.

"My boy, he's right sick," Damien said. The leader backed away from the rig. Consumption, yellow fever, bubonic plague, influenza, smallpox, chickenpox, typhus–all kinds of infectious diseases were prevalent and would kill.

"You seen any Indians?" asked another. "Where's the one who owns this horse?" The horse's back was wet with sweat, and the settlers saw it. The third man began to check the rocks above, then all around.

"We bought him from a white fellow a ways back," Damien said. "Been riding him to give my beasts a break."

"Where'd you come from?" the third man asked, then eyed Millie.

"Louisiana," Damien said.

"You're a pretty thing," the man with a red bandana said. "Bet you had the eye of your master back there in Louisiana.

Bet you had a lotta men who took a liking to you. Come down here, darling," the leader said. Millie, terrified, slowly stepped down from the rig.

Damien reached for his rifle, but not before the three white men cocked their guns and pointed them at his face. The leader put his gun to Damien's head. "You got no say in this, mister."

"I know you don't mind if we take turns, do you honey?" the second man jeered. He slid off his horse, grabbed Millie by the arm, and pressed his pelvis against hers. Millie tried to get away, but the man held her tightly, ripped open the bodice of her dress and pawed her breasts, grinding his hips into hers.

The children, terrified, froze. But the Indian, hidden by the canvas roof, crept to where the man held their mother, and from inside the wagon Puuku ripped through the canvas with his knife and ran the blade across the man's neck. The body silently crumpled to the ground. Puuku flew out of the wagon and dove for the leader. With an upward thrust, he jammed his knife into the man's gut. Damien grabbed his gun and turned to shoot the third, but the Indian, fast as lightning, had already thrown his knife into the man's eye.

Damien put his arm around Millie's shoulders, but she couldn't speak. "Children?"

"We's ok, Pa," Daniel called out.

Puuku tied their three horses to the wagon. "Good gift for my brother," he said. They left the three bodies for the vultures. The next few days were blessedly uneventful except for the recurring nightmare Millie had each time she tried to sleep.

With much relief they came to the riverbank where a tribe of about a hundred men, women, and children camped with lots of dogs and a herd of more than two hundred horses.

Puuku took Timothy into the tipi belonging to the tribe's

medicine man. Millie followed closely with Daniel while Letty Ann hung onto her skirt. Inside was dark and smoky and smelled like a mixture of tanned hide and damp dirt. An old woman with feathers woven into her long black braids, wearing a necklace of bones, gave Timothy a gourd filled with a hot liquid that to Millie smelled like rotting vegetables, boiled tree bark, and sage. The old shaman, with braids wrapped in fur, shook his rattle over Timothy's head and down his body and sang. After a while Millie felt woozy, then her head began to bob back and forth, and before long her insides relaxed. Timothy closed his eyes and fell sound asleep.

At dark they returned to their wagon and settled down for the night. But Millie woke with every birdcall or the sound of leaves rustling in the breeze and kept her hand on the rifle. At daybreak Millie opened up the back flap to see that the whole camp had was being dismantled. The tribe never stayed in one place too long because they wanted to follow what was left of the buffalo herds, but more importantly they had to keep away from cavalry soldiers and settlers who would just as soon kill them as breathe. Puuku brought them breakfast. To everyone's amazement Timothy's fever was gone, and he ate a whole bowl of Indian porridge.

While the men rounded up the herd, the women attached a travois to the horses and piled on their belongings. The very young and the very old climbed onto the heap, and the rest rode or walked down the trail.

Suddenly, they were alone in the clearing. Puuku had stayed behind to hang a piece of buffalo-hide with feathers woven into the beading from the top of the post of their wagon, then gave each of them a small bag hung on a leather strand. They were to wear it till they got to California.

"Good medicine," he said in English. "Comanche friend."

Millie didn't have anything to thank him with except the

dirty red ribbon from her hair, but Daniel gave Puuku the small deer he'd been whittling. After they parted ways, Damien headed the wagon north while the Indian turned south to find his family.

Millie took a breath, looked around the ranch, then said to Abigail out of the blue, "You gotta know if that Clayborn fella ever come here again and try to hurt you, I shoot him before he get off his horse, and if I don't get to, Damien or young Daniel will. We ain't gonna let no one hurt you no more," she said, still shaken by her story.

# FIFTY-NINE

*T*oday Millie jumped right into telling me one of her tales. She does that when I am feeling poorly and can't see my way out of it.

*Hearing about Millie's past has at times left me quite ragged. Some of her memories leave me filled with joy, but others bring on anger or break my heart. That she has gone through such hardship and still remains generally cheerful certainly attests to her strength.*

"Does Daniel know Damien's not his father?" Abigail asked.

"He started asking questions after some white children on the plantation teased him 'cause his skin's so much lighter than ours. Master was his father, but Damien tell him he were the light of his life, held him for a long time to let him know he mean it, then took the boy fishing. My boy sure is a flower among them thorns." Millie sat back against the chair. "The day he were made be a dark day for sure. No amount of sweeping or cleaning or weeping gonna wipe away that memory. It there and that's that. Every once in a while," Millie said, "like a carriage that lost its driver, that day runs through me, knocking me down. It like one of them whipping scars on Damien's back, always there even if it don't hurt every day."

*Millie felt better, but it opened a prickly door for me. When my own nightmare began, I was eight years old:*

"*Stop, Papa. Stop.*"

"*Quiet now, Abby. Don't wake your mother.*" He undid his pants and entered her. The first time, she screamed from the pain and he slapped her hard. From then on she bit her lip and looked out the window till he was done.

"*Now this is between us, honey,*" he said. "*You don't want to upset your Mama.*"

The next day there was blood. When she showed Marisita, the disappointment on the woman's face told her all she needed to know. But it didn't stop until she was thirteen, and her bloods started. She thought her father was afraid he might get her pregnant.

She couldn't tell Millie about it, because she never talked about it with anyone, and most of the time didn't bring it up to herself either.

Franklin, barely able to stay upright in his saddle, took a drink from the bottle of laudanum he kept in his saddlebag. He knew how often he was supposed to take it, but he paid no attention to the doctor's instructions and took it whenever the pain got too bad. If nothing else, it made living easier, momentarily lifting his spirits, but when it dropped him into a dark pit he took another swig. Soon his moods began to swing like a flag in a bad storm.

# SIXTY

D amien came into the office in the evening to go over the ranch books with Abigail. He found her at her desk with her head in her hands. "You feeling all right?"

"Just a little tired," she lied. The knot in her chest had not let up its hold for most of the day.

"Let me see those." He picked up Abigail's reading glasses and took the books to the lamp. When he first arrived Damien couldn't read or write. Abigail had wanted to teach him, but she also knew to be careful not to hurt his pride. While she added up the receipts from the Feed and Grain she would point to each item and name it with its price. Eventually, he began to connect the words on the paper with the things they bought, and once the children were asleep Millie worked with him while he read aloud to her. Though it was not yet easy for him, he had learned enough to get along.

"Now see here?" he pointed to one column. "Last week four sacks of flour were a dollar and a half each, this week a dollar and twenty-five cents." He slowly scratched the numbers on a piece of paper. "Minus twenty-five cents. We saved a dollar," he exclaimed happily. "Have to keep our eyes open when we go to the store next, see what else we buy for a bargain. But now, ma'am, you get some rest. You look tired as a possum."

"I feel tired as a possum," she said.

"Good night, ma'am," he said and closed the door.

It was a warm fall Sunday afternoon and there was a knock on the door.

"Who is it, Millie?" Abigail called from her bedroom, always fearing Franklin would come back.

"It's a Mr. Irwin Barber," Millie answered. "Say he a photographer and want to take your picture."

"What for?"

"Good afternoon, ma'am," Mr. Barber called. He explained he was taking portraits of all the ranchers in the area to show at the Historical Society at the County Courthouse during the county fair.

She wondered if Franklin would also be in one of those pictures. Mr. Barber leaned his big camera against the doorjamb and mopped his brow.

"What do you think, Millie, is this cadaverous face worth saving in a photograph?"

"You're too silly, Abigail," Millie answered. "Go put some rouge on them lips."

"All right, I'll do it, Mr. Barber," she called, then insisted that he take the portrait with everyone who lived on the ranch. He sighed.

"Come out when you are ready. The light's changing. If we could get together soon before the sun goes behind the trees?" He set up his camera in the open yard.

"In time, Mr. Barber. There are a lot of us," Abigail called out. "Millie, gather everyone. Edward and Bertie's brood, too. Someone go get the Browns. They're at the river. Damien, bring out two more chairs for you and Millie," she said. "The three of us will be in the chairs, Mr. Barber."

"I see." He mopped his brow again.

"Gather 'round, everyone," Millie instructed. "Tall ones in the back. Miss Julia, you and your family stand behind Abigail. My children will sit here in front of us," she added.

"Seamus, you're the only cowboy here?" Abigail called.

"Well, come on then. Stand in the back."

There was a confusion of moving bodies as all found their places.

"On three. Don't move till you see the flash," Mr. Barber said to the children, who wiggled and poked each other. "All right, everyone, think of something pleasant, on three." Mr. Barber lifted the flashgun. The flash went off and it was done. There they were, Abigail and her family, frozen in time.

That afternoon, Millie made biscuits. "Miss Julia, please pass me the tin of flour."

Julia reached for the tin, but it slipped from her fingers and landed squarely on the counter, sending flour up in every direction.

"Oh, I'm so sorry, Millie," Julia said. "I've made quite a mess."

"Never you mind," Millie said.

Millie picked up the canister, only to have it fall through her fingers and send flour across the countertop and onto Julia's dress. Her own was white with it as well. Then she began to laugh, which made Julia dissolve, and a cascade of giggles filled the house.

"Well, this is quite a picture," Abigail said when she came into the kitchen. "Now where is that Mr. Barber when you need him?"

# SIXTY-ONE

Franklin winced as he gingerly buttoned up his shirt and carefully tucked in the shirttail so as not to press the material against his inflamed skin.

"Put this salve on your back a couple of times a day. It will ease the pain," the doctor said. "I know I don't need to tell you alcohol is not doing you any good. And, Franklin, you must remember to eat," the doctor chided.

"I'm all right," Franklin growled though he was having difficulties remembering what was said even just a few minutes before.

Franklin stepped out into the street across from the Bradley Hotel and grabbed the hitching post to keep his balance. He never went to the Bradley anymore. It held too many memories. And though there were other brothels to go to, with his body covered in sores he was no longer welcome at any of them. Even the saloons hesitated to give him whiskey, so he carried a bottle with him in his saddlebag.

He started to return home to his ranch, but he didn't want to go there either.

# SIXTY-TWO

How could I know the introduction I had arranged for the Irishman to Doctor Harding would take our dear Seamus away from Hahl Ranch so soon?

"My dear lady," Seamus said to Abigail, "I am sure you will understand the gracious gift this invitation is."

"Invitation? To what?" Abigail said.

"The one from Doc Harding, ma'am. I thought he might have spoken to you of it? He has asked me to come work with him at his veterinary clinic. I know it will be leaving you with one less man, so I can wait till after spring calving," Seamus said. "Doc Harding will be teaching me everything I've been longing to know. And Salmon Falls is a mere twelve miles away. Ma'am, might I continue to borrow your books?"

"Yes," Abigail said solemnly. "Of course." The day for him to move away came too soon. "Are you all packed, Seamus?" Abigail asked. "You have your books?"

"All right here," he said and patted his case. "You've been an angel, Mrs. Wilcox. I can never thank you enough, you and everyone here," he said as he opened his arms to Millie, who waited to say goodbye. Then he put his arm around Abigail's back and hugged her gently. "May the sun always shine on your shoulders, Mrs. Wilcox," he said. She held him for a moment, then kissed his head. "Now where's our charmer Letty Ann and old Nanny?" he asked.

"They waiting for you at the gate," Millie said.

"You promise to come by and see us?" Damien offered. "We wanna know how you getting along."

"We will that for sure, Mr. Adams."

"We'll miss you here, Seamus," Abigail called. "You're welcome to come for Sunday dinner anytime you can."

"I look forward to it. Tell Sean he's to come to see me soon," Seamus called.

"You tell him yourself," Daniel called and waved from the door of the barn. "He out there with Letty Ann."

Timothy held out his hand, but Seamus grabbed him and pulled his head to his chest.

"You boys are a wonder. God was surely makin' the best when he made you." Then he jumped on his horse and rode away.

"I don't know why it's so sad to have him leave. After all, he's just a ranch hand, but it has me all teary," Abigail told Millie.

"If your boy had lived, he be about his age?" Millie said. "Abigail, you know you took him on like he was your son, so it be like your son moving out of the house, ain't it?"

"I guess so." Abigail watched until Seamus had disappeared over the hill.

# SIXTY-THREE

Abigail stepped into the street in front of the Placerville Mercantile and looked up and down for any sign of Franklin or his men. Reassured he was nowhere in sight she walked back to the rig with one hand on Millie's shoulder and a cane in the other.

"You drive home today, Millie," she said. "I want to look at the scenery." This was only partly true. The thought of running into Franklin had left her feeling weak.

"You ever have a gentle man after Bradley? Seem like all I hear is about that mean man. How come you stayed with Franklin so long if he were always so bad to you, Miss Abigail?" It was something Millie had wanted to ask her for some time. Millie shook her head and clucked the horse to a trot. "Now my Damien, he a gentle man," she said. "'Cause I was jumpy-scared of any man coming too close after Master had his way with me, he knew he best be kind. Even after we was married, it be many months till I let him know me that way, but he were patient. I needed healing, and he knew it. Most men, you know, force their way, but not my Damien. He the kindest man I know." Millie turned to look at Abigail. "But why'd you stay with that Franklin?"

Abigail thought to herself, *That goes into my heart like a bullet into prey. I've asked myself that question over and over. Why had I?* "He was not bad to me all the time. Many times he was gentle, kind, and affectionate. So the best answer I can give you is I got used to his ways. He was familiar. And why is it you call me Miss Abigail when you ask a question you know will be difficult for me to answer?"

"Familiar. Familiar like the master's lash, if you asking me. Even when you know it be coming, still pains you when it bites your back. How come a strong woman like you let that man sting you so many times?" She puckered her face in disapproval and continued, "Master keep me as his woman if I let him. But a free woman like you with money and a hotel, you don't need no one like that. Franklin be keeping you on short reins, and for a long time."

"I loved him," Abigail said, trying to answer the question honestly for herself as well as for Millie.

# SIXTY-FOUR

*L*etty Ann, now tall for a fifteen-year old, pleads with me to write down everything I can remember about my life. Though she never says it out loud, she is concerned I won't have enough time to get it all down.

"You always been telling me you like to write, so it be easy for you," Letty Ann said. "You like writing, and I like reading. For me then, write it for me."

Abigail thought it was sweet that Letty Ann was so interested, but she also found her own attachment to the young girl had grown stronger with each day.

Abigail coughed in an attempt to clear the phlegm in her throat. A head cold had overtaken her midway through the afternoon and had taken its toll on her resilience, and now she was fatigued. She put down her pen, covered the ink bottle, put the pages with the others in the persimmon wood box closing its lid. She picked up the heavy box to set it on the mantle, but before she could catch her balance, down she went, the contents of the box covering the floor like autumn leaves.

Millie heard the thump and came. "You all right?"

"I think so," Abigail said, "but my box fell to the ground, and now the hinge is broken."

"Letty Ann," Millie called, "come help Miss Abigail."

"Oh, my goodness, Miss Abigail. You made a right mess."

Letty Ann gathered the pages and put them back in the box. An hour or so later Millie went in to check again and found the whole floor, the desk, and most of the bed was covered in small piles of paper. Letty Ann grinned, both hands filled with Abigail's writings.

"You should be in bed," Millie said.

"We are trying to put these in some semblance of order," Abigail said. "Careful there, Millie. Don't mix any of them. It has taken us forever to get this far."

"Abigail, go sit in your chair. I have brought you something to eat. You not had a bite since this morning. Nearly time for supper."

Abigail collapsed into the chair and let her head drop against the doily on the back of the seat.

"Letty Ann, honey, put the ones on the bed in their proper order." Letty Ann stacked the papers and set them on the nightstand. "Now these, Millie." Abigail pointed to the papers on the floor. Millie picked up the stacks and added them onto the bottom of the collection.

"Am I supposed to consume that food or just look at it?"

"Now don't you fuss with me, you the one sick." Millie stepped over the papers still on the floor.

"Letty Ann, go tell your father to come for supper. He's down by Winding Creek. Tell them boys, too." Then she changed her mind. "Oh, just ring the bell like always. If they don't hear it their stomachs will tell them what time it is."

"Yes, mama." Letty Ann went into the kitchen.

"It will be just a few minutes," Millie said. "You rest some." But as soon as Millie left Abigail leaned over her writing desk and inked her pen.

*Even while I lived in Auburn I loved the first snow of the year with its crisp chill that filled the evening air. Off in the distance the mountains dusted white loomed like winter ghosts. The other evening, when I chopped kindling at the woodshed, my breath lingered like a cloud at my mouth. More and more I cannot exert myself without paying heavily for it, but it was a good day, and so it was particularly satisfying to be able to split wood. And thankfully Damien knew when to come take over for me.*

*Rain mixed with snow had fallen for an hour or so. Edward and the boys rode the fence-line in the pie-shaped field behind the barn, then put away the horses before they returned home for soup. This time of year the wind can be brutally cold, going right through your clothes and stiffening your joints.*

"Come on in," Millie shouted from the front stoop. "Take off them wet clothes and sit here in front of the fire. Got some good hot soup to warm your bones."

"Sure cold out tonight," Damien called. "Looking forward to your delicious soup." Millie always some kind of potage to warm them after chores.

Damien jumped onto the porch, kissed his bride, and went in the door to strip off his soaking-wet hat, gloves, and jacket.

"Daniel, pass me some bread, will you?" Damien said. "Abigail, would you like another piece?"

"No, thank you, Damien. I'm full." Abigail patted her stomach though she had only eaten a few bites.

"How 'bout you, Letty Ann?" Damien asked.

"Me, too, Pa. Full," Letty Ann rubbed her tummy.

"Pa, what are we going to do about the mare?" Timothy asked. "She's 'bout ready to drop her fold."

"Her foal, Timothy," Abigail corrected.

"Her *foal*–'bout to come any minute," Timothy grinned.

"Best check on her through the night," Damien said. "You boys get some sleep. Edward and me will take turns going out. Ok by you, Edward?" He reached for another piece of bread and refilled his bowl.

"Yes, sir," Edward said and finished a third bowl of soup.

"Had my eye on her all day. Might be any time now. I'll tell Bertie, then meet you in the barn in a couple of hours. That all right?"

"Are Jeremiah and Henry comin' soon?" Reggie asked. "They want to see the new foal."

"In a week or two. Julia will let us know when they plan to come." Abigail always looked forward to seeing Julia and her family.

The garden had a bounteous yield of vegetables and fruits. Except for what they sold at the mercantile, all that Millie, Bertie, and Abigail had canned was stacked high in the cold cellar. They had a hefty pile of winter squashes and potatoes. There was plenty of meat from the cows and chickens raised on the ranch. Damien and the boys went into the woods to hunt deer, quail, turkey, rabbit, or whatever else they could find to shoot.

Abigail rested in the knowledge their basic needs were met, and her family was safe.

# SIXTY-FIVE

*I*t has been more than six years since I left Auburn. I haven't dared go visit because I'm afraid to run into Franklin. I don't have the strength for that anymore.

Edward tells me the town has changed quite a bit in my years away. There are new stores—haberdasheries, bookstores, and the like—not so many saloons and brothels. He told me didn't hear the usual angry words and guns blasting or see fights over nothing at all because the miners had found a gentler way to make a living since gold had run out.

I have thought long and hard about my life in Auburn and longed to come to terms with myself about my time there, not about owning a brothel, because I have accepted that once Bradley's money ran out I would have starved, but why did I stay with Franklin for so long. After all, the way he treated me no one should think is acceptable. I certainly don't now. When we were passionate it was the most beautiful thing in the world, and that was a hard drug to release. But now I see the passion never lasted, and I spent most of my time hoping the good times would return.

Franklin often blamed me for his destructive behavior: his hitting me was my fault, and his drinking was definitely my fault. But I am the one who stayed, and that was my problem.

I recognize as I write this now there is a difference between the need to be with a man and being loved by one. The first is a compulsion like some people have for liquor or drugs, and the second? That is a feeling of safety and warmth that I now can feel from my friends here on Hahl Ranch.

I have come to understand that between the haze of alcohol and the horrible memories of his father, Franklin really didn't have a chance. And now when I think back on my parents in Marysville, I see that my father was as much of a drunk as Franklin, and he treated my mother with the same disrespect that Franklin had treated me. And since my mother hardly gave me any time at all, my life there was terribly lonely. If it had not been for our cook Marisita, I never would have learned what love is.

But I am glad I never returned to the Bradley. I really didn't want to see the changes on the inside. I am sure it is attractive, but I realized it was more important for me to keep the memory of what the hotel was when it was mine.

# SIXTY-SIX

Abigail had worked hard to pull up the remainder of the bounty in the garden while ranch hands Shiffy and Enos hoed the rows. Now too fatigued to continue, she sat on a chair wearing a beat-up straw hat and holding a parasol to keep off the sun. The two men took forkfuls of aged manure, threw it across the turned soil, and dug it in with their shovels in what, in the spring, would be the start of a row of potatoes.

Daniel rode in on his palomino.

"What is it, Daniel? You look like you have eaten something sour," she said.

"I seen him again, ma'am," Daniel said through gritted teeth.

"Again? Who?" Abigail asked, but she knew who it was.

"Clayborn." Daniel could hardly abide even the sound of the man's name after Franklin had not only held a gun to his father's head, but also left a scar on his cheek. "The one who come here a ways back and is always watching us from the hill."

"What? He's been watching us?" Abigail felt like she had just been punched. For a minute she thought she might faint.

"We all seen him up there watching us. Now he sitting on a stump at the front gate," he said. "Something about him ain't right. He alive, but he ain't moving."

"Ask your father to come with the rig and bring his gun."

"What do that man want?" Damien asked as she stepped up onto the wagon.

"I wish I knew," Abigail said.

Along the side of the road, the late spring ice had collected on the dense leaves and pulled down branches. With the day's warming, water dripped heavily on the hard ground and drummed the earth like thick tears. As they came up the hill and around the bend, she saw that Franklin's horse was loose by the side of the road and he sat slumped on a rotted tree stump. He was much thinner, and his face was drawn and gray. The sores at the sides of his mouth, on his hands and neck were inflamed and bleeding. His eyes held a haunted gaze, which told the truth of him. Damien could see it as well. Syphilis had run its course through his body like a charging herd and left every part of him weak and torn. Franklin was dying. Abigail's ears began to ring, and she could not catch a good breath.

"Help me take him to the ranch," Abigail said, "then we-I-will take him back to his wife."

She held the horses as Damien and Daniel lifted Franklin's all but lifeless body onto the boards, then she climbed onto the back next to him. She knew she loved him, not in a romantic way anymore, but because they had shared so much life together. Even with all the rough times, Abigail could not help but feel compassion for the man. And for all the anger she held for him, when she saw him like this, weakened to almost unrecognizable, she was sad, but also discouraged. And if she was truthful with herself she was terrified; she wondered if this might be what the end of her life would look like.

"Abby," Franklin whispered, his eyes filled with tears. "I just wanted to see you before... Can we go home now? I'd like to go home."

"Don't try to talk, Franklin. We'll take you to my ranch and get you some water," she said.

"I'm sorry. I just didn't realize...can you ever forgive me?"

he choked. "How could you not truly hate me?" He had finally understood the immeasurable pain he had caused her. He coughed deeply; his breathing labored. "Never thought I'd really lose you," he said. She was surprised to hear him say this because neither of them had been much for reflecting on the past. Then he gazed at her intensely. "How did you find this...?" but he began to hack again and couldn't stop.

"Easy now. We can talk later."

Franklin's mind skimmed over his life, and he talked about their time together jumping from one memory to another, but in no particular order.

Damien drove the rig back to the ranch slowly so as not to jar Franklin's weakened body. Millie came to the door to see, then inspected Franklin with annoyed curiosity. Even the children stopped playing in the yard.

"Honey, please bring Mr. Clayborn some water and a couple of blankets," Damien said.

Millie and Abigail put his head on a pillow and tucked the blankets in around him.

Franklin slit his cracked lips enough to take in a sip from the jar. "So good to see you," he said. "Sorry to be trouble." He took another mouthful. "You look so beautiful. I've missed you so."

"That past is behind us now. Best to leave it there," Abigail said curtly. "Does your wife know you've come?" With a look that beseeched her not to scold, he scanned her face again and turned away. "All right," Abigail said. "Do you think you could eat a little soup?" He tried to swallow, but he was only able to take in a little of Millie's broth.

"You'd better let me go with you," Damien said. "It's a long drive."

The wagon pitched awkwardly over the deeply rutted road. When his ranch house appeared on the horizon, Abigail took a breath, ready to endure whatever was to come.

Damien, however, cocked his rifle.

As the wagon approached and his men saw Franklin, they quickly gathered around the rig to lift him off the wagon.

"Mrs. Clayborn know you're coming here?" one asked.

"Leave him," a female voice called from behind. "He doesn't live here anymore!"

Florence Ritchfied Clayborn stood in the doorway, the narrative of her life written in the sores that covered her face and the thinness of her arms crossed tightly against her chest. His men held Franklin's limp body but didn't know what to do next. "Ma'am?" his foreman said.

"I threw him out, and I see he went straight to you, Mrs. Wilcox," she said coldly.

"Mrs. Clayborn, Franklin and I parted company many years ago, and our paths have not crossed since, so I had no idea he was coming. One of my men found him at our gate. He's your husband and needs to be with his wife–especially now."

"That man's not welcome here. Take him away." She started to close the door.

"Mrs. Clayborn, please, let me come inside so we can talk for a minute." Florence Clayborn relented and opened the door. "Stay with the rig, Damien," Abigail said, and the women went into the house.

Mrs. Clayborn took a chair off the hook on the wall and set it near Abigail at the dining table. She barked an angry laugh, the fire illuminating her boney cheeks, "The only person he ever thought of was himself. As you can see, he couldn't stay away from you people and brought it home to me."

"He's dying. He should be with you at the end."

"No," she said and turned. "Apparently, he needs you." She was silent for a moment, then said, "I thought when we got married six years ago, he would eventually stop thinking of you, and for a time I think he did. But when the disease took hold of him, and shook him like a rabid dog, and he was out of his head with fever and pain, it was your name he called."

"Do you have children?" Abigail asked.

"No, Franklin didn't want..." she started to explain. "We had none. Just as well," she said quickly. Then she reflected, "In the beginning, he was so sweet and kind, but when his drinking took him over, it was as if I had married two different men."

Abigail could see this was not a home love had touched. The room was spare, with chairs hung on the wall and only brought down for dining. No doilies on the table or curtains at the windows. Not even a rocker by the fire, just a bench. No evidence of feminine softness was to be found anywhere, only hard-edged necessity.

Franklin had always complained that there were too many things in Abigail's rooms, but she didn't realize this would have been his choice. Had she married him this grim existence might have been her own. After a long silence Abigail asked, "May I tell the men to bring him into the house?"

"No!" she barked. "You can take him anywhere you want, just away from here."

When Florence Clayborn locked the door behind Abigail, Franklin's men looked to her for what to do. They put him back on the rig, and his men, speechless, watched the wagon roll away. The clip-clop of horse's hooves sharply accentuated the hardness of the ground as the sun began to set behind the hills.

"That man ain't no good even dying," Damien hissed and turned the horse toward the ranch. The rest of the trip was made in silence.

"I'll tend to him, Damien, but I'll need help to get him into the barn. Where are the wranglers?"

Damien paused before calling them.

It made her feel depleted that Franklin was in her life again. But one thing she knew, even though he was gravely ill, she still did not want him in her home. He had hurt everyone he loved and corrupted everything he touched.

Damien, Shiffy, and Enos lifted him off the rig and carried him into the barn. She spread a blanket and hung the lantern on the nail above his head. Millie helped her clean him and make him comfortable before she went back to the house to serve supper. Abigail was caught between hating the man she knew and wanting to be kind to a dying man. Then she realized she no longer hated him. How could she? The look on his face, with skin ashen and cheekbones pronounced, had a softer tone to it. He gazed at her with kindness, something she had seen only a few times in their relationship. She realized he was no longer the same man she used to know.

Franklin slept, then woke with a start and called out, "Honey?"

"Right here," Abigail answered.

"In my satchel." He pointed to his saddlebag. "The book." Along with the accounts of his cattle sales was a small photograph, the leather frame casing old and worn at the edges.

"You've had this a long time."

When Abigail stepped out into the yard for some air, Letty Ann went in to take away the dirty dishes. It was all she could do to tear her gaze from this man who had been so abusive to Abigail and to her father.

Franklin, awake, watched her move about the room. "Who are you?" he asked with difficulty.

"Letty Ann," she answered quietly.

"You're a pretty girl," he said. "You like living on this ranch? Better than the plantation, I reckon."

"Yes, sir," Letty Ann said as she picked up the dishes. "Mister, how come you so mean to Miss Abigail? She so nice, and you treat her so bad."

"I realize that now. Too late though," he said and began to cough.

Letty Ann shook her head. "Mister, you is a mean fool and a liar," and she pulled the barn door shut behind her.

Franklin talked with Abigail into the night, which left her with some understanding about their life together. In the morning, they spoke only a few words before Franklin lost consciousness. His hand was in hers when he drew his last breath.

*Damien and Edward dug the grave and I helped to cover the body. Here he would be, a reminder of my past, dead and buried. The dead part of it was good to remember. There are other regrets I would like to bury, but they have not died quite yet.*

# SIXTY-SEVEN

## 1875

Though it had been a year since Franklin died, the memory of his last day had been with Abigail all afternoon. He was with her in the classroom as well as in the buggy ride to the Edgewoods.

The sun was still bright, but the afternoon wind felt bitter cold. She wrapped her coat tighter at her waist, pulled the scarf up to her ears, and snapped her whip. Mark, Marge and Grant Edgewood's son, had been ill and needed books to finish his classwork. Their log cabin lay ahead. Lining the drive were dormant flowerbeds, and a row of stately trees whose leaves swirled in the late fall breeze. Before she could get to the house a pain began in her stomach, chest, and shoulders, a deep shooting pain that stabbed hard and almost knocked her off her seat. She had had discomfort before, but this time it felt like it would finish her. She could barely get a breath, let alone steer the horse. Luckily, the steed went right to the house and arrived before she collapsed.

Mark called out to his parents when he saw her buggy come up the drive. Grant carried her into the house. Marge brought her a glass of water and put the kettle on for tea. She put some honey in the tea and held it for Abigail to drink.

"Really, I am fine," Abigail said. "If I sit for a while it will pass. There's no need to bother the doc." Grant insisted and went for him anyway.

The doctor had told her this might happen, for her heart had been severely affected by the illness. Now no matter how hard she tried, it felt like her lungs could never get enough air, she got winded doing the least little thing, and she was tired all the time, and at times her joint pain was crippling. For the first time she allowed the doctor to give her laudanum, but even after she took it the pain remained the same, though she didn't seem to care about it as much, which was an improvement. Grant helped her into the buggy and tied his horse to the back. The ride home gave Abigail time to think about the school and whether she could continue to teach, for it was clear she needed to make some changes.

When they started down the hill into the property, Millie ran out of the house and called for Damien. He lifted Abigail into his arms and took her inside, and Millie put her to bed.

The next morning Abigail announced to Millie, "I can't stand in front of my class any longer. It's a hard truth to accept, but this God-damned disease has completely taken over my life." She held that thought suspended for a moment before the enormity of what it meant struck her like a boulder falling from atop a mountain hitting her squarely. To Millie's surprise Abigail said, "Tomorrow morning you will go to the school for me."

"Me, to do what? I ain't no teacher," Millie exclaimed. "Who gonna be cooking and cleaning here, may I ask?"

"Bertie and Reggie can take over the cooking for you," Abigail said, "and Letty Ann is old enough to help with the cleaning. I don't think Edward and his children will mind eating here."

"Abigail don't know if I can do that. My speaking ain't perfect like yours. Teaching my children am one thing. Teaching other people's? And who gonna take care of you?"

"I'll tell you how to instruct them as you go. The children will be rowdy at first because you're new, but they'll settle down once they read their stories. They always do. Bertie can be here during the day, and if I need anything Letty Ann can help me when she comes home."

"But Bertie would be perfect for the school."

"Bertie has very young children to look after," Abigail said. "Your children are grown now."

Millie sighed knowing it was useless to argue with Abigail once her mind was made up. "Then you have to help me with my speaking. You say when something ain't right."

"All right," Abigail said. "You *tell* me, not *say*, you tell me."

"You tell me," Millie said. "You tell me I can teach, but I knows I can't."

"I *know* I can't. No *s*," Abigail said, "but I know you can."

"I *know*," Millie repeated and sighed, "but I do not know I can," she said, shaking her head on her way back to the kitchen. "Still think Bertie be the best one."

Millie was fair and compassionate, and knew how to guide children, especially when they avoided learning something new. With her help, the school could stay open. So in the evenings Millie and Abigail went over class lessons together and checked the students' writing. Much to Millie's surprise, she took to it.

"Timothy!" Abigail called from her bed, where she had spent most of the day. "Come add some numbers for me, will you? For the price of our cattle."

"Yes, ma'am," his deep voice called from the drawing room.

Abigail heard a shuffle and looked up from her reading to find the sixteen-year-old standing at her door with the account book and a pot of ink in his hands. "So you don't have to yell," he grinned, then sat down at the writing table, rolled up his sleeves, dipped his pen, and waited, ready to write.

"Now, how much have we made on our cattle since January," Abigail began, "taking into account the price change at the beginning of the year?"

He scratched numbers on the paper, thought a moment, then wrote some more. They had sold their beef in Auburn during the first part of the year, and in the fall, Damien, his boys, and the wranglers drove the large herd to Sacramento. Abigail was proud of her handsome men, and sight of them touched her heart as she watched them ride away.

"Each cow brung us–"

"Brought us," Abigail corrected.

"*Brought*–nineteen dollars in January, and then twenty-two dollars in October," he said. "For two thousand head, it comes to forty-five thousand dollars." Then he added up the sales from Millie and Bertie's jams.

Timothy suggested they build up their almond orchard to sell the nuts in Sacramento. "Need to plant more trees, of course, but in a few years they'll produce. We can sell the hulls for feed. What do you think, Miss Abigail? Here am–are the numbers. We make–could make good money from it." He handed her a list: cost of rail, workers' wages, and hauling.

"Timothy, how many hired men do we have now? For the life of me, I can't remember."

He looked at her oddly, but replied with kindness, "Well, ma'am, there's Rufus, Leroy, Enos, Shiffy, Willy-Boy, Thomas, and Sean. Edward makes eight."

"And Seamus," she reminded him.

"Ma'am," he said. "You remember Seamus is in Salmon Falls with Doc Harding?"

"Of course, how silly of me," she said. "Timothy, I want you to keep track of our spending–from now on. Help your parents run the ranch. You'd be the manager. Do you think you could do that, son?"

Concern washed across his face. "Yes. All right. If you want me to, but nothing's going to happen to you till you are a hundred and ten," he told her.

"In case I only get to be ninety-nine, will you do it for me? Starting now, I mean," she said.

*I need someone with a clear head to work through the spending, as now my thinking is not always straight. Timothy is good with numbers. He is able to help his parents with their bookkeeping and has learned to keep the accounts on the ranch. Damien handles the cattle and Edward and Daniel the horses. Now Timothy will take care of the finances. I have rested more easily since the day he said yes.*

The rig climbed to the top of the hill overlooking the pasture. From there she could see the whole ranch and the golden hills beyond. Rufus and Shiffy put down her chair and small writing table so she could enjoy the view while they mended the fences along the horse pasture and a newly cleared field. It had been several weeks since she had even been out on the porch.

"You want us, ring the bell," Damien said. "Your shawl gonna be enough?"

"I'll be fine. You go on now." Abigail settled into her chair and pulled the blue wrap, the one Bertie had knitted for her, closely around her neck. She loved this view with its vast expanse of the land, the round mountains, the groves of gnarled and irregular white oaks with their winter brown and yellow leaves, and the madrone's rusty branches. The sun danced between the clouds, and the air was fresh and clear. Even though the mountaintops were dusted with snow, for a winter day, it was pleasantly warm.

Below, Bertie and the children returned home while Millie

walked to the henhouse and Daniel and Edward worked a horse in the paddock.

Nanny had followed the rig up the long hill and had just arrived, puffing hard.

"Come here, old girl," Abigail said.

The dog circled several times and eased herself down next to Abigail's chair, warming her foot.

"You're good company, Nanny." The dog wagged her tail, brushing the fallen leaves. She put her head down and sighed heavily. "What is it, girl? Preston nearby? Feels like he might be," she said. "We're doing all right here, Preston. With Damien and Edward's help, the ranch has made good money again. Julia and her family come to visit often, and her children grow like weeds." Abigail's throat tightened. "I wish you could see it–but then maybe you can. I truly hope so."

Though ahe had brought a book to read, but she knew most likely she would fall asleep, and after a time she did. When she awoke the whole sky was a spectacular swath of crimson, orange, and lavender, a magnificent display of the end of a day. She wept at the beauty of it. In that moment, as she gazed over the land, Abigail felt close to a God she was just beginning to believe in.

Millie came out of the house and rang the bell for supper, so Abigail gathered her things to be ready for the men to take her home. Damien helped her into the rig while Shiffy and Rufus put the furniture back onto the wagon.

"Damien, we live in a beautiful place."

"Yes, we do," he responded.

"Gentlemen," she said, "lift old Nanny onto the back. Neither one of us can get to the house without a bit of help."

*Damien is such a good man, a comfort and a shoulder to lean on. But in all my life, except when I was young, I have never had a friend to talk with as I do with Millie. We share anything and everything. And even though she is quite a bit younger than I am, she is such easy company that I truly enjoy our time together. I have appreciated how Millie has always told me the truth even if it is not to my way of thinking. She has softened my temper, helped me understand my life, and made it easier for me to let my worries slide away. And Letty Ann, my dear Letty Ann, she has become my shadow. I notice I look for her when she is not at my side.*

*When I walked away from the Bradley Hotel, I had plenty of money. But I had not planned what I was to do or where I was to go. I only knew I had to get away from Auburn and Franklin, and head toward an unknown something that had to be better.*

*While I grew up I always felt alone, especially after Bradley died. The feeling no one could be trusted, or would care for me, has colored my whole life. Then I met my friends on Hahl Ranch. Even though I feel wretchedly ill at times, I have felt more love for and from them than I have in all my life.*

*One thing has led to another in unpredictable ways. There have been difficult times I thought I'd never get through, but now I feel at ease. And I can see how it all fits together, how each piece adds to the whole of who I have become.*

*I would never have left Franklin if I had not gotten syphilis. Preston Hahl, the Adamses, or the Millars would not have become part of my life. And I never would have met Julia and her family.*

*Through all the years Franklin and I were together I worked hard to keep my figure trim, but he still chided me complaining on more than one occasion, "You've become fleshy. You're eating too many sweets. Getting heavier than a cow." What would he say now? I'm too bony.*

Damien carried Abigail from the dining room to her bed, as he did each evening. With her arm around his broad shoulders and his arm under her legs and back, he lifted her as if she were a piece of cotton wool. As he got her settled on her bed, some intense whispering came from the dining room.

Soon the Adamses all gathered at the end of her bed.

"Abigail," Damien said, "we come to a decision–the family and me. Our last name be Adams, but that were Captain Adams' name. Made us use it so everyone know we was his. Now we free and wanting to change our name. Make it something we all like."

"Sounds fine, Damien," Abigail said, bemused by their eagerness and the smiles on their faces. "You'll need to go to the county courthouse and fill out the papers, but then you know that. What name did you choose?"

Letty Ann couldn't contain her feelings any longer and shouted, "Wilcox! We want to be called Wilcox!"

"If it be–is–all right with you," Millie said, two fingers lifted to cover her smile.

*To say I was not touched to the deepest part of my soul would be a lie. They have become my family, and now I am truly a part of theirs. We can't choose the family we are born into, but we can choose the family in our heart. These folks for sure are the family in my heart. After so many years I feel I am finally, truly home.*

*I stay in bed now, and I have lost interest in food, but I make an effort to eat to keep Millie, Letty Ann, or Bertie from scolding.*

*And it's strange that vanity should return after all these years. The only thing I have put on my face practically since I have moved to Hahl Ranch is some cream to soften my weathered skin. But I caught sight of my gray, sallow complexion in the looking glass.*

"Millie," Abigail called, "come in and make repairs."

"Now, you look just fine." Millie stretched the truth.

"You know, Millie, you don't lie well. Hand me my talcum. Put some on my face before the children come in to eat." As Letty Ann pushed open the door, Millie dusted Abigail's face, then started to put the lip rouge on her mouth.

"Let me do that," Letty Ann said and took the pot of rouge,

tenderly applying the color to Abigail's pale lips.

"Let me have some on my finger for my cheeks. I may be dying," Abigail grumbled, "but I don't want to look like I am." With trembling fingers she applied it to her cheeks.

"I'll do that," Millie said. "You is—you are making a mess of it." She dabbed her cheeks. "It's cold in this room. You want your wrap?" Letty Ann stirred the fire and added a log, then went out to get another load of wood.

"I thought maybe you were trying to freeze me to death so the illness wouldn't take me. Give me the one Bertie made for me." The tone Millie ignored, for Abigail was often irritable these days, and took it out on her best friend. "I am sorry, Millie," Abigail said. "Never mind this cross old biddy. She doesn't mean what she says."

"I know, honey. My ears go deaf when you get going. Just that illness taking a hold of your tongue."

Letty Ann returned with the wood and a book.

"What are you going to read to me today, sweetheart?" Abigail asked.

"*Alice In Wonderland* by Lewis Carroll." The girl sat upon the bed and curled up in the crook of Abigail's arm.

"'*What a curious feeling!' said Alice; 'I must be shutting up like a telescope.'*

*And so it was indeed: she was now only ten inches high, and her face brightened up at the thought that she was now the right size for going through the little door into that lovely garden...*" Abigail missed most of the rest of the chapter, though, because she fell asleep almost immediately.

# SIXTY-EIGHT

A bigail and Damien drove into town for supplies. It was the first time in weeks Abigail felt she had the energy or the inclination to leave the farm let alone her bed. The horse had thrown a shoe and was ready to be picked up from the blacksmith. She sat on a bench across from the livery waiting for Damien, then she decided to walk across the road. All of a sudden Placerville Main Street began to swirl, sounds muffled, and she fell onto her hands and knees. She heard a man's voice above her and looked up. With the sun behind his head, he seemed to glow.

"You all right, ma'am?" The man offered his hand.

"What are you doing, Bradley?" she asked thinking this man was her husband, and she was eighteen again.

'Abigail, now you wait right here,' Bradley said. 'And honey, you keep your eyes front. I'll come and get you when I am ready.' Bradley jumped off the rig, grabbed the picnic basket, and ran off behind her. She listened to the birds chirping and watched the butterflies float over the field of yellow flowers. It was all she could do not to turn around, but before long she heard, 'Now close your eyes, darling.' With his hands securely around her waist, Bradley lifted her from the seat and gently set her on the ground. 'Keep your eyes closed. Keep them closed.' He steadied her steps. 'Now-open!' he said. Before her was a breathtaking view of the still green mountains and a waterfall that cascaded down through the rocks into a pool. On the ground in a grove of trees, he had set out a red checked cloth, with bread, cheeses, dried fruit, and a bottle of wine with two glasses. They kissed for a moment, drank the wine, and ate his picnic. Then he pulled out a little box tied with a gold ribbon and put it into her hands. 'Open it,' he said, his face radiant with joyous expectation. Abigail loosened the ribbons and lifted the lid. 'I hope you like it,' he whispered and kissed her ear. In the box was a gold ring with a large brilliant diamond, surrounded by smaller ones. It twinkled like a starry sky. 'Will you marry me? Abby, will you become my wife?' Abigail nodded, the tears streaming down her face. He kissed her gently, and they loved each other under the clear sunny skies.

Above her head she heard a voice, which brought her back. "You all right, ma'am?" The sun behind him silhouetted his face. "Ma'am, are you all right?"

"Is that you, Bradley? I fell down. Help me up, will you? Where have you been? I've waited for you."

"Give me your hand, ma'am." After the man helped her to her feet, she saw the gentleman's face and felt confused.

"I'm sorry. I...I thought you were someone I knew. Thank you for stopping."

Damien walked the horse out of the livery. "Your dress all soiled. You all right, Abigail?" he said.

"I seem to have fallen," she said, still in a daze.

"Why you not stay put!" Damien scolded. "You knew I were coming back. Abigail, you have to take care of yourself or I won't let you come with me when I come to town."

"Damien...what town are we in?"

"Placerville," he said, surprised at the question.

She brushed off her skirt so she didn't have to look at him. "For a moment I thought I was in San Francisco."

Millie called into the bedroom, "You asleep?"

"Well, I am not now with you yelling like that." Abigail

pulled out a piece of paper and a slice of charcoal. "Come sit and let me draw you."

"Can only stay a minute. Got a stew on the stove." Millie pushed the loose strands of her hair back under her kerchief and sat. She was surprised when she saw the drawing. "Why, you made me pretty."

"You are pretty. I just drew what I saw. Now put it up there with the others." The faces of Preston, Julia, the Adams family, Bertie, Edward and their children all looked down at her from the mantel.

When Millie came back she found Abigail asleep, the pen still in her hand resting on her writing with the ink smeared across the top of the page.

Millie stood in the doorway of Abigail's bedroom several times during the afternoon to watch her sleep in the chair, but when the sun began to set and she had not rung for supper, Millie became concerned and almost went in, but Abigail yawned and shifted her seat.

"You hover there like a vulture that waits for dinner," Abigail said.

"You was—were so quiet, but I see you breathing. Someone here to see you." And she tidied the papers on the desk and then began to tidy Abigail.

"Who would be here to see me? The only people who care about me live right here."

"Now quit angling for compliments. I don't have to tell you plenty of people—oh, for heaven's sake," Millie said and dropped her concern. "It's that handsome Irishman."

"Seamus?"

With his ever-ready smile, he greeted her like a son to his mother.

"Just seeing your face lifts me spirits." He sat down, smiled, and took her hand. "Takin' good care of you, are they, Mrs. Wilcox?"

"Yes, of course, but they needn't. I'm merely a bit tired. I do feel much better for seeing you though." Seamus glanced at Millie, who shook her head. "You mustn't pay her any mind. I'll be fit as a fiddle before long," she said. "How are you and Doc Harding getting along?" It was hard for Abigail to catch her breath now and Seamus saw it.

"He's a most generous man, as you said. And he tells me I'm his right hand. Says when it comes time for him to retire, I can take over his practice. Wouldn't that be a wondrous thing?"

"He is lucky to have you," Abigail said. "Tell him I said so."

"I will, ma'am," he laughed. "Now you need your rest, so I won't keep a-jabberin'." He held tight to her hand, and she gazed into his green eyes. Then before he joined Doc Harding in the barn he told her, "Ma'am, you are as good as they come. May God himself be smiling rainbows over you, Mrs. Wilcox."

"You send for him, Millie?"

"Damien. He thought it might cheer you up," she answered.

"Thank him for me. Now hand me some paper, and ink my pen, will you?" Abigail's hand had a slight tremor now, which made it awkward to dip the pen into the bottle.

"How come you don't let yourself rest?" Millie said as she rewrapped her headscarf across her dark brow then straightened the shawl around Abigail. "You know what the doctor say."

"Don't fuss at me, Millie," Abigail said. "I need to get some things down on paper before it's too late."

"If you just be quiet some, it would not be too late," Millie snuffed. "Now, I am going to the kitchen to stir the stew. The family'll be in b'fore long. When it's time to eat supper Damien will come get you. So close your eyes for a spell."

"Millie, hand me my pen."

"All right, but don't blame me if you asleep before your favorite dessert." Millie went into the kitchen shaking her head. "Stubborn. Just plain stubborn as a mule."

Sundays the families at Hahl Ranch gathered together for the afternoon dinner. Abigail was feeling stronger than she had in a while, so she joined everyone, including Julia, Bernard, and their children. Even Seamus, with his girl, Dorothy, came for the day, along with his brother Sean and his girl. Bertie and Millie served roast beef with sweet potatoes. After apple pie, Daniel and Reggie cleared the plates. Then Timothy took his turn to read from a book by Hans Christian Anderson, called *The Golden Treasure*. Julia held Helena. Her boys at Bernard's feet played with a stuffed toy. Anthony, a squirming four-year-old sat in Bertie's lap. Sara Lynne Millar, three years old, lay asleep in her rocking crib next to the fire. Letty Ann, now a tall girl of nineteen, leaned against Abigail's shoulder. Millie held Damien's hand, while all listened. Timothy read slowly, with determination, *"'My golden treasure, my riches, my sunshine!' said the mother; and she kissed the shining locks, and it sounded like music and song in the room of the drummer; and there was joy, and life, and movement.'"*

*Yes, '... joy... life...and movement...'*

*As I write this, I know in the deepest part of my heart, this family is the reason I am still alive. Had they not been here, I would have ended my life long ago. There have been days when the discomfort in my gut was so acute I could barely breathe, but the pain of separation from all of them felt greater. I wanted to watch the boys grow into men, the girls into women, to have Letty Ann read to me one more time.*

*Then there is Julia. Thankfully after her parents' deaths, she and* her family became a part of ours here at Hahl Ranch. In the beginning her visits were infrequent, but now she comes regularly, and I have enjoyed her company more than I can say. Jeremiah and Henry love playing with Bertie and Edward's boy, and they follow Daniel and Timothy around like old Nanny does Letty Ann. Bernard and Damien take the young men hunting or fishing, or for rides into the hills. Letty Ann cares for little Helena while Julia and I sit on the porch and talk. I have relished each minute we have had together.

These days while Bertie and Reggie are in the kitchen making supper, Millie sits by my bed while I rest, and we have tea. I cannot imagine leaving her behind or Damien. At times the joy of it all brings me to tears.

I thought I understood what love was, but for me it always brought uncomfortable consequences. After all I had sold what some people called love, but of course, love was not really what I sold. I had been for sale, too, bought by Franklin, and I paid dearly for that security. Though a distant woman, I know my mother loved me, and my father, in his frightening way, also loved me, but theirs came at such a price. Even Bradley's kind and tender affection came with sadness. It was not until I embraced what I felt for this Hahl Ranch family, including Preston's friendship that I really felt how encompassing it could be. Like a warm wave, it has washed over my soul. There must be something or someone to thank for this, but thanks hardly seem enough.

Outside our kitchen in Marysville stood a persimmon tree. Its big green leaves, thick and full in the summer, turned brilliant colors in the fall. Throughout the warm months its fruit of large oblong balls grew and took on a red-orange glow. Because they were so pretty I was tempted to eat one too soon, but when I did, a harshly sour, unpleasant, crushed-velvet fur would cover my tongue. Waiting for them to ripen to a delicious ambrosia-like jelly took all summer and most of the fall. The fruit of the persimmon would only be ready when the leaves had fallen off its branches. Only when the tree appeared barren and lifeless would it bestow its sweetest yield. My life seems to have been like that persimmon tree. Its most precious gifts have come to me at its end.

You think change comes in an instant. It doesn't. It comes over time after you make a series of small, individual choices. The result is like the root of a tree that slowly breaks through the ground. Eventually, long before you notice, it causes upheaval in the path.

And no one else can truly understand why you are determined to follow a particular path. You may not even understand it yourself, but you know you must. So even though I have not gone far in miles, only eighteen or so from Auburn to the ranch, I have traveled far from what my life had been–a tight shoe I was ready to take off. To leave Auburn and yet stay near Placerville is one decision I have never regretted.

It was not until I began my lodging at Hahl Ranch and the damn syphilis took over that I had the urge to write what I could remember of my life, with Letty Ann's encouragement, of course. I could never see myself as a dancer on a stage or a singer of songs like Marguerite, but words come easily when I ink my pen. These stories of my friends and loved ones that I have put down on paper, have kept them alive for me, kept them close.

Yes, we all have scars–some visible on the outside and others hidden beneath a smile, but they are part of the landscape of who we are. Writing this has helped me realize who I have become on this journey.

"Morning, Abigail," Millie said cheerfully as she opened the curtains and let in the morning sun. "We got a telegram from Julia. Shall I read it to you?" She tore open the envelope. "Oh," she said, then read:

"Dear Abigail. Stop. I know I promised to come see you this week but both twins have come down with a cough. Stop. Will come as soon as they are well. Stop. Love to all, Julia."

"I'll telegram her back and let her know you ain't feeling all that well either," Millie said.

"No, don't. It's enough for her to care for two sick boys."

"All right," Millie said. "Now come on, let me help you up."

"You best leave me be today."

"You be uncomfortable if you not use the pot. Take my arm." Millie put her arm around Abigail's back and eased her to sitting and onto the chamber pot, then she pulled off the dirty sheets from the bed and put clean ones on before helping Abigail get back under the covers.

"Now this will feel mighty good," Millie said.

Abigail closed her eyes while Millie swabbed her face with a warm, wet cloth.

"Marisita," Abigail said, "tell Mama I don't feel well, and would you brush my hair?"

Millie ran the brush through her hair and counted each stroke to one hundred.

"Marisita?"

"Yes, honey?" Millie said without hesitation.

"Will you tell me a story?"

Slowly, so as not to jostle Abigail too much, Millie eased herself onto the bed and with her arm around her friend's shoulders, held her like one of her own children. "I will tell you a wonderful one," Millie said. "Once upon a time there was a beautiful woman with long blond curls and twinkling blue eyes. She was the most kindest woman in all the county. She was so kind that she took in strangers, people she didn't know at all, and made them her family..."

"Marisita, I love you so much," Abigail said.

Millie was quiet for a moment. "I love you, too, Abigail."

Later when Millie carried in the tray of Abigail's supper and put it on the table by the bed, she told Timothy, who stood at the door, to get the family. With heads down and tears in their eyes, they all came in: Damien, Bertie with her children, Timothy, Daniel, Letty Ann, and Reggie. They could see the truth of her as sure as she had seen when Franklin was passing.

Damien and Millie stood by the side of the bed. The boys, now as tall as their father, were at her feet. Letty Ann threw herself across Abigail's chest.

"Now, Letty Ann, honey, I'm right here." Abigail put her arms around the young woman. "Hand me my box." She put some more papers into it and with Letty Ann's help, closed the lid. "Go ink my pen. Thank you darling. Millie, when I am done please deliver this, will you?"

"I, I will," Millie said barely able to speak.

"Edward?" Abigail asked.

"He went to get the doc," Reggie answered.

"Reggie, come here," Abigail said.

"Ma'am?" His voice was now deep and resonating.

"As an important part of this family, you have to promise me you'll look after the young ones if they need seeing to. Millie and Damien and your parents have their hands full with the ranch. And also keep an eye on the twins when they are here." Abigail tried to smile as she looked into his light blue eyes. "Help Letty Ann with her studies. You know she wants to work with Seamus."

"Yes, ma'am," he smiled through his breaking heart.

"You children go on now. Let me get some rest."

Reggie took Letty Ann's hand and led everyone from the room, Bertie following. They all gazed back at her face as they went.

"Millie? Damien?" Abigail said.

"Right here," they said in unison. Millie took her hand gently and leaned in.

"In case you are wondering," Abigail said quietly, "there's nothing in these papers you've not heard before, and some of it you told me yourself. I thought you wouldn't mind."

"I'm sure it's fine," Millie said as an intense sadness flowed across her face.

"Millie, if you want to, you can read them to Damien before you give them away. Of course, Letty Ann has already read most of them. Ask the boys if they are interested."

"Honey, there is time for all that," she said though Abigail could see she did not believe it. "You rest now."

Abigail could hardly speak, "Thank you for everything." Abigail pulled Millie's hand to her chest, and she reached for Damien. She slipped Bradley's ring from her finger and set it in Millie's hand. "This was given to me by the only man I truly loved. I want you to have it."

"Are you sure you want me to have it?" Millie asked.

"You understand why I've worn it all these years." Damien slipped the diamond ring onto his wife's finger.

Millie held tight to her hand. "You rest now," she said. "I'll come back to help you with supper."

Their faces filled with such tenderness it nearly broke her heart.

*I don't have much time to finish this. Breathing is hard, holding the pen to paper is hard, and I am afraid to go to sleep for fear I'll not wake again. Though there is little left in me, there are more memories I want to jot down before I go.*

*I would like to think in leaving Auburn and Franklin that some smarter part of me knew where I was headed, but I had no plan. If asked now I would have to say I searched for higher ground, a place to get my bearings, somewhere I could feel relaxed and at home, something more permanent that I could count on—not that I had ever had that kind of tranquility in my life nor even knew how to get it. Truth is I just wanted to feel at peace. Even if my body is broken my heart is full. And I have learned you have to let yourself be loved. If you do, then loving in return is so much easier.*

# SIXTY-NINE

## The Brown Ranch, southeast of Sacramento 1875

The late December sun warmed the cold morning air. The rain from the week before had left the roadbed deep with troughs that made the rented carriage dance roughly over the now-dusty road. In the back of their rig was the box of Abigail's writings Millie and Damien had promised to take to Julia Brown. The drive from the train to the house seemed long because of the news they carried of the death of their friend.

"Not one for sitting a long time," Damien said and arched his back uncomfortably. He took out his handkerchief and wiped his brow and a tear from his cheek. "You tell her yet?" Damien asked.

"No. Guess she'll find out soon enough," Millie said and wiped her own tears. "She gonna be right upset when she hears Abigail's gone."

"Mighty sad," Damien agreed solemnly.

"I just can't believe it myself!" Millie exclaimed. "I miss her something terrible."

"Breaks my heart to even think about it," Damien agreed.

Horseflies landed on their arms. "*Them* pests, eh," Millie said annoyed. "Those pests. The Lord must have some purpose for them. Some purpose, I am sure, other than biting into me. I sure wish they'd find somewhere else to spend their time." She slammed her hand onto her arm hard and killed one. "Ha!" she said victoriously.

Ahead they could see the end of this part of the day's journey, Julia and Bernard's homestead. The home was large and welcoming. The white, two-story house had a generous wraparound porch. Two doors opened onto a large balcony above the front door. Planted at the entrance were pink and yellow rose trees filled in with white geraniums. The drive was lined with fruit trees–apple, pear, and apricot.

The twin nine-year-old Brown boys played in the yard while Julia sat on the porch braiding the hair of her five-year-old girl. Damien pulled the buggy to the front door and engaged the brake. He lifted Millie from the carriage while Julia came down the steps to welcome her friends. She took Millie's hands then saw Abigail's diamond ring on Millie's finger, and sank back.

"Yes, ma'am. On Friday, Miss Julia, she wouldn't let us tell you."

"Doc says her heart gave out," Damien said. "Letty Ann was with her when she went."

Damien handed Julia the large persimmon wood box, the one with *A Full Heart* engraved in Spanish on its lid, and Millie gave her the wrapped bundle of Abigail's drawings.

With her arms tightly wrapped around the gifts, Julia was both disquieted and curious. "Won't you stay and have some dinner with us?"

"Thank you, ma'am, but we need to get back to the children," Millie said. "They are pretty upset, 'specially Letty Ann. Sometimes we find her up in the barn loft hiding in the hay bales tears streaming down her cheeks. You know it's not like her to be off by herself. The boys are not much better. Seems like we're all feeling her absence and don't know what to do with the hole she left."

Damien pulled out his pocket watch. "Better be off. Last train to Folsom at three. Got just enough time to get back to the station. Visit us soon, will you Miss Julia?"

"Yes, of course," she said, distracted by the container in her arms.

Julia watched as the buggy disappeared, then called into the house for Maria to take the children.

When Julia opened the lid of that persimmon wood box, on top of the papers was a small gift tied with a pink satin ribbon. She pulled the off ribbon and found a gold locket that held two photographs: one of Abigail as a young woman of about thirty years of age, and the other a man she remembered from Auburn who used to buy her mints. He was kind to her, but his breath always smelled heavily of alcohol.

Instinctively, she latched the locket around her neck. Then she lifted out a page and began to read the first of the many that filled the container:

April 28, 1875

*My Dearest Julia,*
*You must be wondering why I have asked Millie and Damien to bring you my writings. As you read—if you do—your questions may be answered. At least, I hope so.*

*Would it not be wonderful to be able to see our lives as clearly while we are living it as we do when we look back? If I had been more aware I might have made better decisions, not so many mistakes. At least, that's my hope.*

*Regrets? I do have some, of course, and there have been difficult, unexpected, even devastating losses I could have done without, but at the same time they have made me who I am, and so, in the end, I am content. And though it would be easier to gloss over the troubled* times here, I do want to recount what actually transpired, and not what I wish had been.

Some memories burst forth like a horse to the field yearning for freedom. But many recollections, having been locked away in the barn for so long, in their frenzy for acknowledgement have left me filled with sadness. Only now do I see they have almost destroyed the stable where they were hidden.

But I have also been blessed with many joys in my life that uplifted me to the heavens, relationships with people who have helped me along the way, many who have become dear friends, surprises that have made my life worth living. And now this warm and affectionate Hahl Ranch family surrounds me with love. It is something that I never knew I wanted.

I must admit that in a furious battle with myself and at times with those I cared for, I have not always been the easiest person to live with, and any consideration I might have given to this earlier has been put off until now, when I feel less vital. Some of them are gone so I can no longer apologize, but to those still living I express my regrets. But I don't offer judgment because I have come to see that what has happened in my life is neither good nor bad. For through it all, I have learned to be happy.

By the time you finish this, dear Julia, if you do, you will know more about my life and me, and I believe you will be interested if only for consistency in your own history.

Do forgive me, however; with my memory not being as keen as it was I can't attest to the dates being precise or accurate.

All that now said, I begin my story...

After supper, Julia went into the study where a number of finished oil paintings of landscapes and still lives as well as a portrait of Julia in charcoal leaned against the stacks of books. An unfinished canvas stood on the easel next to the chair by the large desk where Julia was reading, the beginning of a portrait of Abigail she had sketched out. She lit the lamps and sat again with the writings.

"Excuse me, *señora*, the children are asleep and I'm ready to go home now," Maria said.

"*Buenos noches*, Maria," Julia said.

"*Buenos noches, señora*." And Maria closed the door. The next morning she found Julia in the library asleep in her chair with the open locket in her hand. "You have been here all night?"

Julia stood to loosen the ache in her back. Outside the sky held a brilliant sun with an occasional cloud, but there was also a slight breeze bringing with it the winter chill. "I still have a few pages left to read," she said, distracted.

"*Si, señora*," Maria said. "Let me know when you want something to eat."

Julia lifted the last stack from the beautiful persimmon wood box:

*Julia, my dear,*

*I have so enjoyed our visits together, getting to know you and learning how you were raised. The times we spent together at the ranch I hold dear to my heart, an opportunity I never thought I'd have.*

*For a little girl who was so precious, so full of life, it was a rough beginning. I like to think the adversity may have made her strong enough to accept this truth with the grace she now has in abundance.*

*The question was to let you live with a lie or reveal what actually happened—and how was I going to tell you? And why? Were you not better off with your version of your life? I have wrestled with this question. But the answer I have come to is this: I believe we feel the rightness when we are being told the truth, and the wrongness of it when we're not. A lie becomes a current that flows through us like lightning down a pole. It jangles us even though we don't know why. But I have come to acknowledge that what is real is more important, no matter how hard it is to understand or to accept.*

*Your father had wanted me to tell you something, and truthfully*

*I have been unable to do so until now. Only as I began to feel my time come to an end did I write most of these memories and resolve, if I had not found the courage to do so to your face, to at least tell you in my pages. I have tried several times over the years to broach the subject, but in the end, like your father, I was afraid to see the disappointment you might feel. Forgive me. Julia, dear, please, take a seat. You will want to read this while sitting.*

*Julia, Franklin Clayborn was your blood father, and I am your blood mother.*

*When I saw you for the first time in front of the fireplace, I would have known you anywhere. It was as if I was seeing myself in a looking glass—only twenty years earlier. You had my eyes, my mouth, my hair—the rest was all Franklin, tall and slim.*

*For a moment I couldn't comprehend what I saw, but then all the rage I felt against Franklin welled into a huge firestorm and landed right on Preston. At that moment, I hated him beyond all words. The baby I thought had died was alive. And Preston had my baby, and he knew it. My insides churned. My mind filled with dust, and I couldn't make out what to think or how to behave. I ran out of the building like a wounded animal ready to strike. Looking for a way out of my feelings, I rode hard and fast across the acres of Hahl Ranch until I could hardly sit any more. Most of the way, I cried, first with tears of rage, then relief, and finally, tears of joy. Years of anguish over the loss of my child let go in an instant. My baby girl was alive.*

*Upon reflection I know Franklin could not have been a good parent or could have possibly given you this rich life, nor could I have done so at the time of your birth. But let me say you have only one father and that is Preston Hahl. And though it's sad for me to say this, Helen Hahl is your real mother. They raised you to become a loving, caring young woman, a tender wife and a devoted mother. You have become just like your parents—good, decent, and kind.*

*Julia, my dear daughter, I hope this account gives you understanding about your family and in time, comfort—well, once the* shock wears off.

You should also know the photograph Franklin had in his book, was taken at the same time as the image your mother and father had in their bedroom. He paid the photographer to shoot one just for him, and he carried it with him all those years.

If there is one more thing I would want you to know, it is that there has never been a day since you were born I have not thought of you, not wondered what you would have looked like, how you would have grown, what you would have loved or disliked. You have been the constant in my life like the rising of the sun.

And from the moment I came to Hahl Ranch, pulled here by fate, my life has been the happiest I can remember. Since the day I saw you it has felt complete.

With all my love,
Abigail
October 25, 1875

One day in Sacramento as Preston and Helen Hahl got into their buggy, a man who had overheard their conversation introduced himself and said he knew of a child due in a month who would need a home. The mother was a prostitute and didn't want the baby. "Helen and I had wanted to have children for years," Preston explained to Abigail, "but we never did. We were overjoyed at the prospect of having a baby so soon." After the child was born, Clayborn sent them a telegram. Eagerly, they went to the Bradley Hotel the next morning. "Mr. Clayborn handed us our baby girl–our Julia. 'Take her. She's yours,' he scoffed. 'The mother will not even notice it's gone.' I am so sorry, Abigail. I didn't know Clayborn would give us a child without the mother's consent. If we had realized she was stolen, we couldn't have taken her. When you stood at our door, we were shocked to see the resemblance." In all earnestness Preston continued, "Abigail, to us Julia was a heaven-sent gift. Now that I know you, I can see where she got her big-heartedness and compassionate nature."

With Helen gone and his time shortened by illness, Preston didn't want Julia to be alone, so he insisted Abigail continue to live on the ranch. "You're her mother. Who else should be here for her when I am gone?" When Preston finished and looked at Abigail with his kind eyes, she didn't have the heart to hate him anymore.

And Millie also saw the resemblance back then. "Julia look just like her mother, and I not mean Helen Hahl." Abigail told her the truth. Millie's mouth gaped open and her fingers flew up to cover it. "I knew it!" she blurted. "Way you both walk, color of her hair, her eyes. Just knew she yours! She know she is? Bet not. You gonna tell her? You gotta tell her, Abigail. Oh, my Lord Jesus, how you gonna do that? What'd Mr. Preston say when you told him you knew? To be a fly on the wall! Lordy–Sweet Jesus, Mother of God, Abigail, how you gonna tell her? How you gonna to do that?"

And Damien felt the same. "Oh, you in a hell of a predicament, Abigail. She at the ranch all the time. I see how you look at her. 'Course Millie did tell me you her mother, but it hit me hard just now with Mr. Preston gone, and seeing Miss Julia so sad and everything. Seem like you might want to tell her. It would be a jolt for sure, finding out you're her mama, but that'd wear off. Abigail, she would wanna know, with you being sick and all. When I see the two of you talking, I can tell she cares about you. Don't suppose she knows why. Sure am glad it not me who have to do such a hard thing," he said, distracted. "You know Mr. Preston did say to me once he hoped you would tell her, so she would have someone after he gone. 'She say it just right,' he say. But he out of his head with fever, and if the Lord asked me for the truth, I don't think he even knew he were talking out loud."

For the first time in hours, Julia put down the papers and

quietly took in what she had read. She could hardly move. Not only had she been sitting in the same position for hours, but she was also struck by what she had read.

During supper, she couldn't think of anything else, so she barely heard the cheerful stories of her children making nut cookies with Maria.

"It sounds like fun," she said, not quite in line with the conversation. When Maria came in with the dessert, Julia said, "I would ask you to save some of these for Mr. Brown, but he'll not be home till the end of the week. Maria, would you put the children to bed tonight? I'm still reading Mrs. Wilcox's story and would like to finish it."

"*Si, señora.*"

Julia took her cup and returned to the library, took a sip of coffee, stretched her back, and read Abigail's will.

*This is the last will and testament of me, Abigail Johnston Wilcox. Today is October 9th, of the year 1874, in Placerville, California. I am of as sound of mind as I have ever been in my life.*

*All of my estate, which includes Hahl Ranch, the wealth of my bank account, my portion of the income from Smathers Emporium in Auburn, and whatever else I own—furniture, jewelry, clothing—will be divided as follows:*

*The ranch in its entirety, including livestock, poultry, the ancient dog, Nanny, and one half of my financial wealth will, upon my death, belong to Damien and Mildred "Millie" Adams Wilcox. It is my hope Millie will continue to teach at the Coloma School at least until her children and those of Edward and Bertie Millar have graduated.*

*The box containing my writings, the gold locket holding the pictures of Franklin Clayborn and me, the citrine, diamond and ruby ring, and the remaining half of my financial wealth shall be given to Julia Hahl Brown, my blood daughter. Millie and Damien are to hand-deliver to Julia the locket, the ring, the box of my papers and a*

*letter to the bank for the remainder of my money. Julia's address can be found in the upper-right-hand drawer of Mr. Hahl's desk.*
*Signed by:*

*Abigail Johnston Wilcox*

*Witnessed by:*

*Harold J. Brockwieller, President, Placerville City Bank, and Ashford T. George, Vice President, Placerville City Bank.*

Underneath the last page in Abigail's container was the small gilded box holding the ruby ring and with it a note: "This belonged to Franklin. He wanted you to have it."

But Julia did not feel the disquiet her parents had feared when she finished reading the account of Abigail's life, but instead she was filled with a pervasive sense of peace. This truth about her parentage had answered so many questions she had about her life and had been afraid to ask. Why, for instance, with both parents short in stature and having dark hair and eyes, was she tall, blue-eyed, and blond? Why had her parents never talked about her birth? And why had Franklin Clayborn taken such an interest in her, going out of his way to greet her each time he saw her in town? And now, knowing the truth she had sensed all along, she understood the kinship she felt with Abigail. Since she had grown to love her, the shock that Abigail was indeed her birth mother, rather than confusing or distressing her, was instead comforting. But now she had many more questions, so she decided to go to the Bradley Hotel to get some answers.

# SEVENTY

Julia didn't know what she was going to say when she met Marguerite, but she knew she wanted to find out as much as she could about Abigail and Franklin, so she took a train from Folsom to Auburn and then retained a buggy.

As the horse clopped up Main Street she began to see the town in a new way, as if through Abigail's eyes. The sights, sounds, and smells were just as she had described them in her pages. The Bradley Hotel's silver and gold sign, though somewhat tarnished, still shone in the sun.

When she stepped into the saloon a tall muscular man in his fifties saw her and asked, "May I help you, miss?"

"You must be Sam?"

"Yes, ma'am. What can I do for you?" Sam was jolted back in time, as this woman had the same face as Abigail when he had met her so many years ago.

"Is Marguerite Atalier available?" Julia asked.

There was a clatter of dishes, pots, and pans in the kitchen and a voice with a French accent yelled, "*Merde*, Cheng! I did not drop it. It was you." Cheng, irritated, answered back in rapid Chinese. "And put that knife down, Cheng. You are going to hurt somebody."

"Let me get her," Sam said.

Julia could hear loud whispers, and then in a more somber tone, "*Mon Dieu.*" The door opened and in walked Marguerite, her dress, face, and flaming red hair covered in egg whites and flour. "Excuse my appearance, Miss-?" Just as Sam had known, Marguerite knew immediately who the woman was. The resemblance to Abigail was uncanny. When she saw Abigail's daughter her heart opened like a flower, as it does when you see an old friend after a long absence.

"Julia, Mrs. Julia Hahl Brown."

"Madame Brown," Marguerite said warmly, "what can I do for you?"

"I wonder if we can go someplace where I can speak with you in private?"

"Of course." Then Marguerite yelled into the kitchen, "Cheng, clean up that mess!"

Cheng yelled back, "No come in kitchen if make mess!" Marguerite rolled her eyes.

"We can go to my suite, if it is all right with you."

"Certainly."

As they walked past the men and ladies and up the staircase, Marguerite gave a wide-eyed glance to Sam. All eyes in the parlor watched as Julia ascended the steps.

"Is that one of Abigail's drawings?" Julia asked of the framed piece above the couch, a portrait of Marguerite.

"It's a good likeness, no?" Marguerite indicated for her to sit. "How may I help you, Madame Brown?"

"You knew Abigail Wilcox," she said. "Abigail—my birth mother—wrote about her life, and of course, you were mentioned many times with great fondness."

"Wrote of me?" Marguerite asked.

"She passed last week." Marguerite felt as if the blood drained from her legs and she sat heavily as the shock hit her deep in the pit of her stomach. "You didn't know?"

"*Non*, I had not heard."

"I am sorry to be the one to tell you. Her heart gave out." Julia looked around at what had been Abigail's rooms, the place where she herself had been born. "Perhaps you were aware–but this is all new to me–that Abigail was my mother. I only found out when I read her notes. Would you tell me about her, your impressions, I mean? And you also knew my birth father, Franklin Clayborn?"

Marguerite settled into her chair for what she knew was going to be a long conversation. She spent the rest of the afternoon with Julia. Some of the young woman's questions were easy to answer, and some were not, but she did her best to help her know more about her parents.

"Julia," Marguerite said as the young woman began to leave, "people are not black or white. Like me, like you, they are good and also not so good. Abigail and Franklin, they were no different."

"My only regret now is that I didn't spend more time with her." Julia took Marguerite's hand in both of hers. "Thank you."

As Julia prompted her horse to go, she decided she would stop at Hahl Ranch before she caught the train home.

# EPILOGUE

As the years went by, both Marguerite and the city of Auburn settled into a more mature age. By 1884 most of the mines had closed down, and the town had grown into a full municipality. It became an important stop on the California Stagecoach route, which connected the Central Pacific Railroad with its transcontinental lines. Travelers from the east coast were now of a different sort, more genteel than the patrons who frequented the Bradley Hotel during the Gold Rush.

Marguerite, with help from Edward and Reggie and Julia's boys, made the Bradley into a legitimate inn, a respite for the weary traveler who might be in need of a hot bath, a bed for the night, and perhaps a dinner of Chen's stew.

## 1940, El Dorado County, California

Old Letty Ann rested her hand on the steady shoulder of her youngest grandson, thirty-five-year-old Levon. The old woman with bowed knees hitched her way to her favorite chair, a bench swing hung from the ceiling of the covered front porch of the ranch house where she had lived for all but the first eight or ten years of her life—she wasn't sure which. He handed her the favored, well-worn blue shawl. She gave him a quick hug before he went back inside. Her three-month-old puppy sniffed the ground, then bounded up the stairs and jumped into Letty Ann's lap. Letty Ann scratched its ears, then set the young dog back onto the floor next to her.

As she did every afternoon at this time, she sat on the porch and gazed over the property "to enjoy the beauty of it all," as her friend Abigail had reminded so her many times.

Yarrow, black-eyed-Susans, and Mexican sage planted around the house dotted the landscape with purple and yellow. Hens dusted themselves under the bushes. Cows and horses grazed in the rolling hills. The vegetable garden, with its abundance of peppers, cucumbers, potatoes, carrots, beets, and more, awaited harvest. An ancient grove of gnarled valley oaks cast shade in the yard, including one with a tire swing, where her great grandchildren played.

She fingered the diamond ring on her hand and pulled the blue shawl across her shoulders. As usual she nodded off but woke from her dream and took a sip of now-cold coffee. Levon poked his head out of the door. "You need anything, Gramma?"

"Maybe a bit of fresh coffee."

Levon came back with a cup and a piece of blackberry pie, and he set them down on the table next to her.

"That smells delicious, son," Letty Ann said. "Levon what day is this?"

"Sunday, the fourth of July, your birthday, Gramma," he said. "Happy birthday."

"You know, before coming to California I never knew when my birthday was." Levon nodded having heard this before. "Miss Abigail decided it was today 'cause she wanted a day to give me a present. She gave us all our special days. Papa's was a month after Christmas 'cause she didn't think it fair to him for it to be on the holiday, but she always said he was a big present to the ranch. Mama had hers on the first day of spring 'cause she made the ranch blossom. Daniel and Timothy had theirs in the fall when the weather was cool, and you could play outside all day without suffering. She put mine on July 4th 'cause she said I was just like a firecracker lighting up the sky." Letty Ann took a bite of pie. "Now, honey, bring me that old box, will you?"

Levon brought out the large persimmon wood box that held all the recollections of a life. Letty Ann opened it for the thousandth time and pulled out several sheets from the top of the stack. As she read, she let her fingers slide across the pages as if she could actually feel her dear Abigail's handwriting each word. Each time she read the papers Letty Ann's mind and body became overwhelmed with a combination of joy and tears, appreciation and feelings of loss. As she grew older, and the memories of yesterday became harder to find, and even the recollections of her early life were, at times, out of reach, rereading the pages written so many years ago opened her life like a movie at a picture show.

She read and reread those pages often to bring to life her family and the woman who had meant so much to her. Each time she noted that while her life had been different from Abigail's, many of the struggles and sorrows were like her own when she was very young.

The old woman took another bite of pie. She pulled out a second sheet, and she ran her fingers along the lines. A gentle smile creased her face as the recollections played across her mind. Before long, however, she fell asleep and again dove into the dream of the life she had lived so many years ago. When she awoke she pulled the shawl up around her neck and stared off past the tops of the trees, her throat tight and her breathing halted. She dabbed her tears and blew her nose into her handkerchief and pulled out more pages. What was coming next was the beginning of the train wreck that changed all their lives. Abigail met Franklin. She always told Abigail she would have sent her father to protect her if they had known her then.

Soon the puppy scratched its neck, then nosed Letty Ann's wrist. "You're a sweet little thing," she said and wiggled the dog's ears remembering the first time she met the old dog Nanny.

She took another bite of the sweet pie and drank what was left of the once again cold coffee. She pulled out another sheaf of papers and told the puppy, "I'll just read this bunch. This is one of my favorite parts. Once I read this bit we'll go in for something to eat, all right?"

She settled back in her porch swing and began to read the entries. The puppy barked at a squirrel, then turned several times and settled down on Letty Ann's feet for the rest of the morning while she read.

Around eleven Levon came out of the door with his fishing pole and a net.

"Come sit with me for a while, son. I'm just beginning where we all come to the ranch. I want you to know about that," she said. Levon had heard the story many times but didn't mind hearing it again.

The young puppy went up the hill to the burying spot for loved ones, to nap under the trees and lean against the cool tombstones.

After a while Letty Ann put the persimmon wood box on the table and closed the lid. Days like this set her heart to warming, and she felt the embrace in her soul of those she loved and those who had loved her. Her beloved Abigail had always encouraged the young girl to swing higher, ask questions, read more, and to trust that she would know what was a right answer.

Her parents, Millie and Damien, had passed long ago, and her husband, Reggie, had died several years before. Her own children lived with her on the property with their spouses and children: three boys—William Seamus, Sean Preston, and Edward Damien—and a daughter, Abigail Ann. Every house on the property was full, and she liked it that way.

One of her six granddaughters came out of the kitchen door and swung the clapper on the bell. Soon a Ford truck pulled into the driveway past the old sign that read:

Coloma Veterinary Clinic

Animals Big & Small

Doctors. Seamus O'Brian & Letty Ann Millar

Letty Ann's sons and their offspring jumped out of the truck and went into the house. From the barn and the closer fields other family members made their way home for supper.

Her youngest great granddaughter came out of the door. "Gamma," the little girl said, "time to eat."

"I am so hungry," Letty Ann said. "Are you hungry, little one?"

"I'm so hungry, too," she said with the slight lisp that comes with lost baby teeth.

The girl took Letty Ann's hand and guided her into the house where all gathered for the evening meal.

"Come on, little Nanny," Letty Ann called to the puppy. "I believe we're having a pot roast. There is sure to be a bone in it for you." Little Nanny wagged her tail so hard she nearly knocked herself over following Letty Ann into the house.

Made in the USA
Middletown, DE
24 August 2024

59064866R10191